Larry put the truck into gear and drove around the curve of the loop.

"What's that?" the giant asked.

"A hopper. Where they load coal, I guess." As they drove under it, something white flashed toward them, a leaping figure, arms waving. Larry hit the brakes; the engine died. He had just time to see that the pale figure was a dummy, a scarecrow with a face, jerking and swinging in front of the windshield. Then the cab shook to an insane roar; the figure was gone behind a tumbling stream of darkness that cascaded past the windshield.

"Oh, God!" said Larry. "We're going to be buried alive . . ."

Berkley books by Damon Knight

THE MAN IN THE TREE
THE WORLD AND THORINN

DAMON KNIGHT
THE
MAN
IN THE
TREE

BERKLEY BOOKS, NEW YORK

THE MAN IN THE TREE

A Berkley Book / published by arrangement with
the author

PRINTING HISTORY
Berkley edition / January 1984

ISBN: 0-425-06006-3

I have taken some liberties with geography in this novel, but Dog River, Oregon, exists, although it is no longer called by that name. There really is such a place as the Lost Forest, and it really is not on most maps.

I wish to acknowledge my debt to the authors of two books not mentioned in the text: *Jesus the Magician*, by Morton Smith (Harper, 1978), and *The Trial and Death of Jesus*, by Haim Cohn (Harper, 1971).

D.K.

To

AMIT and MAGGIE GOSWAMI

The God of our fathers raised up Jesus, whom ye slew and hanged on a tree.

Acts, 5:30

Now I Joseph was walking, and I walked not. And I looked up to the air and saw the air in amazement. And I looked up to the pole of the heaven and saw it standing still, and the fowls of the heaven without motion. And I looked upon the earth and saw a dish set, and workmen lying *by it*, and their hands were in the dish: and they that were chewing chewed not, and they that were lifting *the food* lifted it not, and they that put it to their mouth put it not thereto, but the faces of all of them were looking upward. And behold there were sheep being driven, and they went not forward but stood still; and the shepherd lifted his hand to smite them with his staff, and his hand remained up. And I looked upon the stream of the river and saw the mouths of the kids upon *the water* and they drank not. And of a sudden all things moved onward in their course.

Book of James, or Protevangelium, XVIII:2

Chapter One

When I was young we were giants' captives.
They stripped us, tortured us with facecloths,
Left us to endure alone
The moonwashed branches on the windows
In the long clock-ticking night.
We voyaged deep under that black ocean
Where Earth eats her daughters in silence,
And always returned. By day we had red-jam smiles,
Breadcrumb fingers, corn hair.
In our pockets were stones, gray string, nails
Scavenged as we went. We knew the secret
Undersides of things, the roofs of tables.
Only insects were smaller than ourselves.
We caught locusts and made them spit tobacco,
Poured dust on pismires, puffed ladybirds away.
We dreamed of being smaller still: built pebble fences,
Roads in dirt, peered with one eye
Under green blades. All Eden was
Our afternoon. It was the time before
They taught us time: before we knew.

—Gene Anderson

Before he was born he remembered the darkness and the light. The darkness was the color of old blood, and in it there were drifting shapes that were not stars.

He remembered the doctor's face—he had plump cheeks

1

and a ragged black mustache—and a voice saying: "My gosh, he's a big one, isn't he?"

When he was four, he told his mother some of the things he could remember; later he heard her saying to his father, "What an imagination Gene has." But she was thinking, What a strange child.

By the time he learned to walk, he was already too large for infants' clothing, and his mother had to buy shoes for him at the boys' store. His father, who was worried about money then, said that he had taken up the wrong trade; he should have been a cobbler.

The Andersons lived in a small town called Dog River in northern Oregon. It was the only world Gene knew, and he did not understand then how pure the air and water were, how blue the sky. From their yard he could see two snowcapped mountains, Hood and Adams.

From the time Gene was very young he could glimpse the other worlds that were all around him; in some of these worlds, things were just the same as they were here, and in some they were different. He was not more than two when he found out how to reach with his mind into another world and turn it. He could put a marble on the floor, for instance, and then reach into another world where the marble was in a slightly different place, and bring it into this world: then there would be two marbles. He was four when he first realized that other people could not do this.

One afternoon he was turning somersaults on the lawn with Zelda Owens' little brother Danny, mesmerized by the stiff grass-blades against his forehead, the green sun-warmed smell, and the surprising way the world turned to thump him on the back. Danny was looking for something in the grass, tearing out big clumps with his fingers. He was crying. Gene asked him what the matter was, and he said he had lost his nickel.

"Why don't you make it come back?" Gene asked. Danny did not seem to understand; he kept on beating the lawn with his hands, pulling up grass and dirt. Gene gave him a nickel to make him stop crying, and then Danny said it was his nickel and that Gene had stolen it, and ran into the house to tell his mother.

Later that day, on Zelda's porch, Zelda and Petie Everett were playing "Can you do this?" Zelda could wriggle her ears and cross her eyes; Petie could make a noise like a cork by putting his finger into his mouth and pulling it out again, and he could bend his thumb back until it touched his arm. Gene could not do any of these things, but he said, "Can you do this?"

A beetle was crawling across the warped yellow boards of the porch. Gene knelt and put his finger in front of it to make it change direction. Then he reached into the shadows and found the place where it could just as easily have gone the other way. Gene turned it there, and then there were two beetles. He turned the beetle again, and now there were three, crawling away from each other as fast as they could.

Zelda and Petie were crouching beside him. Petie said, "Aw, that ain't nothing. You had them in your hand."

They argued about this, and Gene lost because he was outnumbered. When he left, Zelda and Petie were shouting, "Liar, liar, your pants on fire!"

One day when Gene was five, after a hard morning rain, he was sailing walnut boats in the gutter. When he tired of this, he brought a bucket full of dirt from the garden and made dams. The mud washed away, but he built the dams up again with twigs and straw, and sent his boats down the stream to watch them tip over the dams and spin in the whirlpools.

A boy he didn't know came down the street carrying a long stick. Before Gene realized what he was doing, he had broken one of the dams. "Don't do that," Gene said, but already the boy was breaking another one.

Gene got up and rushed at him; he was the taller, although the other boy was two years older. The boy jabbed him with his stick and danced away; Gene could not get near enough to hit him. The boy broke the last of the dams and then hit him with the stick again; Gene was crying with anger and pain. At that moment he felt with his mind where the nerves and muscles of the other boy's arm were; he reached in and turned them in a way he had never done before. The stick fell. Gene picked it up and began to beat the other boy, who ran away crying.

That evening the boy's father brought him to Gene's house with his right arm in a sling; he said the boy's arm was paralyzed because Gene had hit him on the shoulder. He was very angry, and shouted at Gene's father. Gene denied everything, but he was frightened, and he reached in again to make the boy's arm well. When the father saw him moving his arm, his face changed, and he took the boy away.

Gene's parents were nearly the same height, but his father was squarely built, dark and muscular, whereas his mother was small-boned and had thick auburn hair, now turning gray. Her skin was very pale and fine, and she had bright blue eyes. Gene was their only child. She told him, weeping, about her two stillborn daughters, and he used to imagine that he would meet them in heaven. His birth had been so difficult, she told him, that she could never have another baby. He felt guilty about this, and resolved to make it up to her by being a good son, but he forgot this whenever he was angry with her.

Gene's father was a carpenter; he had a shop in the garage where Gene often sat and watched him work. Gene loved the aromatic smells of cut pine, glue and shellac, and he liked to watch the clean white shavings curl out under the plane. When he was still very young his father began letting him help with small tasks, carrying boards from the stack, measuring, clamping pieces together to be glued. He let Gene use the hand-saw and play at nailing boards together. One day when he was busy, he said, "Cut this piece eighteen and seven-eighths inches for me, Gene, can you do that?" Feeling proud and honored, the boy measured the board and sawed it, but when he brought it to his father, it was too short; he had made a mistake in the measurement. "Well, that's ruined," his father said, and threw the piece down.

Gene's eyes filled with tears. "I can fix it," he said.

"No, you can't." His father went to the other side of the room for another board.

Gene picked up the rejected piece and laid it on the work-table beside the frame his father was making. He reached into the shadows to a place where he had cut it correctly; it jumped a little and was longer. "Look, Dad," he said, "it's all right."

At first Gene's father would not come; when Gene insisted, he looked at the board impatiently, then stared at it, picked it up, and finally measured it with his steel rule. He knew it was the same board because of the two knots near one end. There was something in his mind that he would not let himself think.

"It's all right, isn't it?" Gene asked. He was afraid, and didn't know why.

"Yes, it is," Gene's father said slowly. He rubbed his eyes with his hands. "I must be getting tired. Gene, you go on out and play."

From these things he learned that his power was somehow dangerous and shameful, and he kept it a secret. For a long time he did not even use it when he was alone, unless he had lost some toy and wanted to bring it back. Once or twice it happened by itself, and that disturbed him.

He often daydreamed that he was a magical changeling, a prince given away in infancy, and that someday his real father would come to take him away to his kingdom, or perhaps would touch Gene on the forehead while he was asleep, conferring on him some power greater than he could imagine.

In the first grade he was a foot taller than any of the other children. The desks were too small for him; he had to sit sideways with his legs in the aisle. On the first day, the teacher gave all the children strips of purple and yellow paper and showed them how to make paper chains, first a purple link, then a yellow one. Gene liked the yellow ones best, and made his chain all of yellow. A girl across the aisle showed it to the teacher and said, "He's doing it wrong."

Later they were coloring in their books; there was a picture of a rabbit; Gene colored its fur blue, as the teacher had told them, but he made the insides of its ears yellow instead of pink. When the teacher came by to look at their work, the same girl said, "Look, he's doing it wrong again. He can't do anything right, can he?"

The teacher said, "That's all right, Dolores; he can do it that way if he wants to," but when she was gone the girl stuck out her tongue. Gene was angry, and turned all her crayons to yellow ones. When she saw them, she called to the teacher that he had taken her crayons. Gene denied it, and the teacher brought her other crayons, but as soon as her back was turned Gene changed them to yellow too. She began to scream, and the teacher moved Gene all the way across the room. From that day on, the other children understood that he was a troublemaker. They began calling him "Big Feet," then just "Feet." They were not brave enough to attack him, because he was so much bigger, but they threw stones at him from behind, and when he chased them they scattered, shouting, "Fee-eet, Fee-eet, can't sit in his sea-eat."

After a few weeks of this he discovered an overgrown corner of the playground where he could lie hidden, and then he spent every recess there, pulling sweet grass stems and sucking the nectar. He daydreamed often of sending himself into another world, but his power was not strong enough for that:

the largest thing he had ever turned from one world into another was the piece of wood for his father, and afterward he had had a headache. Even with smaller things, if he used his power too often, he became weak and dizzy.

After school and on weekends life was better; there was a group of neighborhood children of mixed ages, none of whom were Gene's classmates, and they did not mind his being tall. In the winter they went sledding and had snowball fights, and made snowmen that melted little by little until they were only slumped mounds in their circles of grass. In the long summer evenings they played King of the Hill, Red Light and hide-and-seek. He never forgot the scent of the tall lilacs in the dusk, and the lonesome sound of "All-ee-all-ee-out's in free."

Long after the other children had left it behind, he was still engrossed by the world of small things. There were different sorts of grasses that were good to suck: one kind slipped with a sliding sweetness out of its sheath, and another would only break. There was a weed growing close to the ground that bore tiny grayish-green buttons, and these buttons were also good to eat. He learned to stretch a grass-blade tight between his thumbs pressed together as if in prayer, and then by blowing into the hollow between the first and second joints of his thumbs, to make a shattering squawk. Noises could be made with the bitter milky stems of dandelions, too, and with the stalks of green onions.

He never had a tricycle, because by the time he was old enough he was too big. When he was seven his parents gave him a bicycle, and all that summer he explored the country roads across the river and into the hills.

Often he left his bicycle beside the road and walked up a little way into the woods. When he sat down with the trees all around him he had a curious feeling that they were aware of him as he was of them, or at least that there was some intelligence watching him. This feeling disturbed him, and he never stayed long in the woods, but he kept on going there because he needed solitude.

Even in town, however, there were quiet places where he could be alone. One of them was the long tree-shaded lawn below the library, where he sat for hours reading books of fairy tales. The library had a set of Grimm, with old-fashioned engraved illustrations that were all the more mysterious because they were so dark and badly printed. He avoided stories about giants—they were always monsters, to be outwitted or killed by the hero—but he liked stories about the Little People, their trickiness and magical powers, and he liked the "Brownie" books of Palmer Cox. The verses were labored and dull, but he never tired of the illustrations; each one was full of hundreds of tiny figures, all doing different things, but all together. His daydreams were of secret caverns under the earth, hidden treasures, and a mysterious fellowship.

Because he was growing so fast, his clothes seldom fitted; either his wrists and ankles stuck out and his shirts bound him across the chest, or, if he had new clothes, the sleeves hung over his hands and his pants-legs had to be rolled up. He used this as an excuse not to go to church with his parents, but there were other reasons. The first time he went to Sunday school, the lesson was about David and Goliath, and after that, for a while, he had a new nickname. The hard pews in church made his bottom ache, and he did not understand the purpose of all that varnished wood, the tall organ-pipes, the minister in his pulpit talking on and on, the bad singing.

When he had a nickel and had spent it, he could always reach into another world where it was still in his pocket. If he wanted more, he could multiply the nickel as he had done with the beetle. From the time he found this out, he always had money for candy or anything else he wanted, and he sometimes treated other children to a bottle of pop or a package of gum. Once or twice they asked him for money, saying, "Come on, you're rich," and he foolishly gave it to them.

One day his mother said to him, "Gene, Mrs. Everett says Petie told her you bought him a model airplane. Did you?"

He saw that he was in trouble, although he didn't understand why, and he said, "Petie's a liar. He lies all the time."

"But she says Zelda Owens saw you. And I talked to her mother, and Zelda says you gave her some money, too."

"Only a quarter."

She put her hand on his jaw to make him look at her. "Gene, tell me the truth. Did you give Petie the money to buy that airplane?"

"Aw—yeah."

"But where did you get the money?"

He knew that if he told the truth his father would beat him for lying. He told his mother that he had found a five-dollar bill on the street. She let him go, but he knew she thought he had stolen the money.

That night while his mother was washing the dishes, his

father made him sit down in the living room and gave him a lecture about stealing. Gene insisted on his story about finding money on the street; the guiltier he felt, the more vehement he became. At last he said, "You believe everybody else, but you won't believe me," and ran into his room.

After that he never gave other children money, and whenever he got anything for himself that he could not have bought with his allowance, he smuggled it into the house and hid it.

Gene Anderson never had any of the usual childhood illnesses; once in a while he had a fever, but it passed away overnight. When he was seven his mother took him to the dentist for the first time, and he disliked this so much that from then on he examined his teeth every night, using a little piece of mirror that he had found behind the garage, and when he discovered a cavity, he made it go away. After a while he must have learned how to recognize them without looking; he stopped thinking about cavities, but he never had another.

One Saturday when he was eight, his father took him downtown to Dr. Rodeman's office where he was to have his tonsils out. He was apprehensive about this, but his father told him that it would not hurt, and that he could have an ice cream cone afterward.

Dr. Rodeman made him lie down on his table and put a little gauze mask over his face. Something sweetish and stinging dripped onto the mask; his lungs were full of tiny bright needles. In terror of his life, he reached out and did something without knowing what it was. He heard the doctor say, "That's funny, this can seems to be empty. Just a minute."

Then he understood what he had done, and when the doctor brought another can, he made that one empty, too. Dr. Rodeman took the mask away and stood looking at him with an odd expression. He told Gene's father that they would have to come back next week, but they never did, and he never had his tonsils out.

Gene knew that his parents suspected there was something strange about him, other than his tallness, but they never talked to him about it. He knew that they were worried about his future. Once a visitor stupidly asked him, "And what do you want to be when you grow up?" Gene was almost as tall as he was. "I mean, when you get older."

"I want to be a giant," Gene said, and left the room. His

mother lectured him about politeness afterward, but her eyes were moist.

Because Gene was so tall and strong, his father began to make use of him again, in the afternoons after school and on weekends. He learned to plane a board smooth, to use a miter box, to make and read working drawings. Under supervision, he was allowed to use the bench saw, and his father promised that in a year or two he would teach him to work on the lathe.

Once or twice, during school vacations, Gene's father took him to a house he was building with another carpenter, and it was here that Gene first glimpsed the satisfaction of having imagined something new and then made it real. The things he could make were only copies of other things. He tried imagining things and then looking for them in the shadows, but they were not always there. Occasionally, when he had been given a present he didn't like, he found that he could reach through into another world where his parents had decided on something else. In this way he got a book that was his favorite for a long time: an illustrated copy of *The Little Lame Prince*, by Miss Mulock.

All through school he was too big to sit with his knees under the desk. It did not occur to anybody, and certainly not to him, that they might have brought in a bigger desk from another grade. He sat sideways, cramped into the narrow space between the seat and the desk, with his feet in the aisle. He wore men's shoes with pointed toes until the fourth grade, when the teacher gave him permission to come to school in tennis shoes. "Feet" was still his nickname. Several times the teacher called him that without thinking, and there was a roar of laughter.

In school he wrote at first in large, awkward loops, but when the teacher criticized him for this, he began to write smaller, then smaller still. The teacher complained about that, too, but he kept on until he could get hundreds of words on a page. He began to make carvings out of soft pine, little figures that he kept in walnut shells hinged with adhesive tape.

In the fourth grade there was another boy who was almost as tall as Gene, a lumpish, red-faced creature whose lower lip was always shiny with spit. His name was Paul Cooley; he was twelve years old and had been kept back three times. He was the son of the police chief, a red-faced man who dressed like a sheriff and carried a revolver on his hip. Whenever Paul saw

Gene he called out, "Hey, Feet, you stink," and then laughed, looking around as if he had said something clever. They fought at recess, and Gene beat him; afterward Paul wanted to make friends, but Gene disliked his dullness and his slobbering lip.

One Sunday afternoon Gene was playing alone in the upper story of a half-finished house of his father's, as he often did. The floor was strewn with sawdust and with nails dropped by the carpenters; through the window openings he could see the tops of maple trees. He was pretending that it was his house, and that he was grown and could do anything he liked.

He heard footsteps below, and in a moment a shaggy head appeared over the top of the stairwell: it was Paul's. He hesitated when he saw Gene, then came up. "Hey, Feet, what you doing here?"

"Nothing."

"You want a cigarette?" He pulled a pack of Luckies out of his pocket and offered it.

"No."

"Well, okay." Paul lit a cigarette and tossed the match away, still burning.

"Don't do that," said Gene, and stamped it out. Paul struck another match and dropped it.

"This is my dad's house. You better quit." Gene stepped on the second match, but Paul was already lighting a third. Because Gene did not want to fight him again, he reached with his mind and made the match disappear, then the rest of the pack.

Paul looked stupidly at his empty hand. "What'd you do with my matches?"

"Nothing."

There was a whistle outside, then a low voice: "Hey, Paul?"

He turned his head. "Up here!" Two boys came up the stairs; they were twelve-year-olds, friends of Paul's. One of them, a tall boy wearing a baseball cap, was already smoking. "Who's this?" he said.

"That's Feet, he stinks," said Paul, and laughed vacantly. "He took my matches away and he won't give 'em back."

"Yeah?" The two boys came toward Gene. "Listen, why don't you give him back his matches?"

"I haven't got them."

The two looked at each other. "Grab him!" said one, and they wrestled him to the floor. While they held him, Paul went through his pockets, pulling out a few coins, a wad of string, some baseball cards and a wadded handkerchief. "Guess I'll keep these for my matches," he said, and laughed again.

"Lemme see them cards," said the tall one, and they let Gene up. Paul was backing away, but they tripped him, sat on him, took the cards and money out of his fist. While Gene was putting out their dropped cigarettes, Paul got up and rushed at him. He took Gene off balance and fell with him half out of the window. "You took my matches! You took my matches!" he blubbered. Gene was pinned by his weight across the window frame, one arm under him, his head down.

"Get his pants," somebody said. Hands were fumbling with Gene's belt buckle. He kicked and struggled, but all he accomplished was to force his body farther out the window. He was crying. Blindly he reached and turned, felt Paul's weight slip away from him. He heard a shriek, then a thump below that echoed against the house like a pistol shot.

He grasped the window frame and pulled himself in. Below, Paul lay with his head on a blood-spattered two-by-four.

The other two were gray-faced. "You killed him!" the tall one said. "I'm going to tell my dad!"

Their footsteps rattled down the stairs. Gene followed. They were running down the street toward town; he went the other way. He ran until a pain in his side forced him to stop; then he went on, weeping and groaning, up the hill into the trees. It was about three o'clock on a Sunday afternoon; he was nine years old, and he knew he couldn't go home.

Chapter Two

Dog River, Oregon, named after the stream discovered by Lewis and Clark in 1805, is situated at the confluence of the Dog and the Columbia. The river was originally named Labeasche, after Francis Labiche, one of the expedition's French watermen. (Neither Lewis nor Clark was strong on spelling.) "Labiche" was taken by many to mean "the bitch," but this fact apparently has nothing to do with the name finally selected for the river and the town: it comes, rather, from the experience of some early travelers who were reduced by starvation to eating dogs.

Dog River lies in a fertile valley largely devoted to apples, pears, and strawberries. Most of the valley is flat as a table, but the town itself is hilly; up from the river, the streets rise so steeply that at some intersections there are concrete steps with pipe railings. Behind the County Library, the hill is so abrupt that there is no street at all, only a switchback wooden staircase that rises to the suburban district sixty feet above.

The business section, which is entirely modern, is four blocks long; here will be found the First National Bank, the Odeon Theatre, the courthouse, the Bon Ton department store, the newspaper office, the two drug stores, the Medical Building, Stein's Meat Market, and the Book and Art Shoppe.

The town is not hostile to immigrants, of whom there are many: Mayor Hilbert, for example, was born in Germany, and Desmond Pike, the editor and publisher of the *Dog River Gazette*, is English; but it congratulates itself that its young people are almost uniformly fair-skinned and pleasing in appearance.

12

Morris Stein and his family are the only Jews known to live in town. There is one black family, headed by a man who works as a janitor at the Dog River Hotel near the railroad depot. Out in the valley, much of the most productive orchard land was formerly owned by Japanese immigrants and their descendants, all of whom, however, were taken away to internment camps during the Second World War. The town is staunchly Republican. The state anthem, "Oregon, My Oregon," is sung with fervor in the schools. The high-school football team, known as the Beavers, has a traditional rivalry with the team of Dalles City, twenty miles to the east.

Many of the residents of Dog River came to Oregon during the first quarter of the century from Iowa, Nebraska, and other midwestern states. Among these were Donald R. Anderson, from North Dakota, and Mildred Sonderlund, from Ohio. They met in Springfield, where Anderson was working in a sawmill and Mildred was teaching elementary school. After their marriage in 1939 they moved to Dog River, where Anderson set himself up as a carpenter and builder. Their only child, Gene, was born there in 1944.

Tom Cooley, the son of a Portland bootlegger, was nineteen when he married Ellen McIntyre, the daughter of a Dog River orchardist. Their first child, Paul, was born in 1941; he was an infant when the war broke out. Cooley served in the Marine Corps, reaching the rank of sergeant. After his discharge, he worked for a while as a beer distributor and had a part interest in the Idle Hour Billiard Parlor, along with his cousin Jerry, who had been in the Marines with him. In 1944 he and Jerry sold out their shares in the billiard parlor and bought an apple orchard which had come on the market cheap. (The former owner, a Mr. Takamatsu, was in a relocation camp in Colorado.) Cooley was a silent partner in the orchard operation; he wanted something to keep him busy. In 1947 he became Dog River's chief of police.

Chief Cooley cruised the back roads around Dog River for three days and nights, ranging as far east as Dalles City and as far west as Portland. He drove slowly in his eight-cylinder Buick, watching both sides of the road and peering into every car he passed. Once on Monday morning and twice on Tuesday he saw a man on foot ducking into the underbrush. Cooley leaped out each time with his gun drawn, pursued the man and caught him, but all three times it turned out to be some tramp or migrant laborer with a guilty conscience. At night Cooley sometimes drove with his lights and motor off, coasting down a long hill, looking and listening. Toward dawn he parked the car and slept for a few hours. He stopped five times for gas and food, once for a bottle of blended rye. By Wednesday morning he had put nearly two thousand miles on the Buick.

Cooley was a short, sturdy, red-faced man who carried a .45 in a belt holster and wore a cowboy hat. He was the entire police department of Dog River. Under ordinary circumstances, the job did not call for anything more demanding than hustling an occasional drunk or vagrant into the county jail.

He came down out of the hills into town, red-eyed and unshaven; he slewed into the driveway, scattering chickens, and yanked on the emergency brake. Tess Williams, his wife's sister, met him inside the door. His voice was thick. "How's Ellen?"

"Where have you been, you sawed-off son of a bitch? She's half out of her mind, is how she is."

Cooley started up the stairs. "And Mayor Hilbert's been on the phone *seven times*!" she called after him.

"Tell'm go shit in his hat," said Cooley, and staggered into the bedroom.

Gus Hilbert came around at four that afternoon, when Cooley was up and dressed. Hilbert was a big man, popeyed and balding; he ran the town's one movie theater, in which, until her retirement a few years ago, his wife Ethel had played the Golden Wurlitzer organ.

He found Cooley at the kitchen table eating bacon and eggs. The chief had shaved, and looked a little better, but he still looked like a man who had been on a three-day drunk.

Hilbert dropped his hat on the table and sat down. "Tom, you through making a fool of yourself now?"

Cooley looked at him and said nothing.

"You know by now that kid's gone. Hitched a ride somewhere, he's out of the state."

"By now," said Cooley.

"Even if he wasn't, he's a juvenile. What was you going to do if you found him, beat him up? Shoot him with that damn gun?"

"He killed my boy, Gus."

Hilbert said after a moment, "How's Ellen?"

"Okay. She's asleep upstairs. Doc Phillips gave her something."

"I know what a knock this is for you, Tom, and Ellen too, but you can't take the damn law in your own hands, and I can't let you do it. Now what I want to know is, have you given it up? Because if you haven't, I've got to take your badge."

"Think you're man enough?" Cooley asked, and put down his fork.

"Now, Tom, don't be that way."

"You can have the goddamn badge any time you want it," Cooley said. He got up and threw his plate into the sink. The scared faces of two young children appeared in the doorway and then vanished. "You kids stay the hell out of here!" Cooley shouted.

"Tom, are you coming back to work? That's all I'm asking. There was an armed robbery at the Idle Hour Monday night, I had to call in the sheriff, and there's some vandalism up at the junior high school."

"Yeah, I'm coming back to work. What the hell else can I do?"

"Okay. Get some rest first. God, you look awful."

The following afternoon, just after lunch time, Cooley got out of his car in front of the Andersons' house and stood looking it over. It was a white one-story house with wood siding and a shake roof, behind a picket fence and a big maple tree. Unraked leaves were all over the yard. At the end of the driveway was a garage; through the open doors he could see workbenches and stacks of lumber. He climbed the porch steps, looking at the scratches on the paint, and rang the bell.

After a moment the door opened. "Afternoon, Miz Anderson," Cooley said. "Like to come in and talk to you, if you don't mind." She was pale, and her eyes were pink-rimmed.

"Yes, come in," she said. She led him into the living room. "Mr. Cooley, I want you to know we're terribly sorry about what happened."

"Appreciate that," Cooley said. He put his hat on his knee and took out a dog-eared notebook.

"My husband and I were at your house Tuesday night, but Mrs. Williams told us you were out of town. She said your wife was ill. I hope she's feeling better?"

"Sure. She'll be all right. Now about your boy—haven't heard from him, I suppose?"

"No. Nothing."

"Any idea where he might of gone?"

"No. I've racked my brains."

"Some relative, maybe?"

She shook her head. "We don't have any family in Oregon. I have a sister in Iowa, and Don's brother lives in Utah."

"Mind giving me their addresses?"

After a moment Mrs. Anderson said, "I don't see any point in it. They never met Gene—he doesn't know where they are."

"Might help anyway—you never know."

When she remained silent, Cooley said, "What about the boy—what does he like to do? Any hobbies?"

"He likes to draw. And reading—he likes to read."

"Got a recent photo of him?"

She shook her head slowly. "No."

"Well, an old one, then—whatever you got. You must have some pictures."

"They're put away," she said. "I don't know where they are."

Chief Cooley closed his notebook. "This ain't the right attitude, Miz Anderson," he said. "I'm just trying to do my job."

"I'm sorry," she said.

"Well, thanks a hell of a lot for nothing," Cooley told her, and put on his hat. "I can find my way out."

When Donald Anderson came home that night, she told him about Cooley's visit.

"Why didn't you give him the pictures?" Anderson asked. "What are you afraid of?"

"I don't know. I don't trust that man."

"Well, I don't like him either, but he's trying to find Gene. What can he do to him? He's just a boy—it must of been an accident. The worst that could happen, they'd send him to a home for a year."

Mrs. Anderson closed her eyes. "I hope he's safe," she said. "And I hope Chief Cooley doesn't find him, ever."

On the Sunday after the funeral, Cooley drove past the

Methodist Church and saw Donald Anderson's gray Chevy pickup in the parking lot. He kept on going, drove through the quiet neighborhood where the Andersons lived, and parked in the alley. The air was crisp and cool; threads of blue smoke rose from chimneys toward an overcast sky. There was no sound except for the lonesome barking of a dog up the hill.

Cooley jimmied open a basement window and let himself down into the musty darkness. He found the stairs, climbed them, opened the door into the kitchen. The pendulum clock on the wall was ticking quietly. There was a rich fragrance in the room; he felt the oven door, and it was warm. A gray cat came from somewhere, looked at him with slitted eyes and made a querulous sound.

There were two doors in the back of the kitchen; one led to the narrow screened porch. Cooley opened the other and went in, followed by the cat. This room was obviously newer than the rest of the house; the walls and ceiling were covered with Fir-tex, a gray, pulpy material made from wood fibers. The room was cold, and the air had a lifeless smell. There was a narrow metal bed, some bookshelves, a bureau, a wooden desk, an easy chair, and a floor lamp. A model airplane hung from the ceiling. Games and puzzles were stacked on the bookshelves. The bare floor and the woodwork were painted dark blue.

The cat watched him as he opened desk drawers one by one and sorted through the papers inside. Most of them were drawings in pencil and ink; some were partly ink, partly crayon. There was a clutter of ink bottles, pens, brushes, erasers, rulers; some baseball cards with a rubber band around them; gum wrappers, dice, a stamp album; glue, string, paper clips. He put everything back and closed the drawers.

In the closet he found a gray windbreaker, a yellow slicker and hood, galoshes, a pair of shoes neatly lined up with the laces tied. In the corner there was a tall stack of magazines, mostly *Boy's Life*. Bile rose in Cooley's throat. They had kept the kid's room and all his stuff waiting for him, because they thought he was coming back.

Cooley thought about Paul's room at home. He had cleaned it all out, the baseball bat and mitt, the piles of dirty socks, trading cards, the clothing, the cigarettes hidden in the back of the drawer. He didn't want anything to remind him. He had closed the door on the empty room.

The other two, the girls, were not much good; he had never wanted girls. It was Paul he had counted on, his firstborn, awkward and eager. All that life and energy now was nothing but a lump of meat in a box with dirt shoveled over it.

The cat followed him out, and he shut the door. Beyond the kitchen was the living-dining room—a table with an embroidered cloth, an oil space heater emitting a cheerful warmth, a sofa, chairs. The walls were plaster painted with gray calsomine, powdery to the touch. The first of the three doors opened into a room crowded with a brass bed, a desk, a green metal filing cabinet. The room smelled of stale cigars.

The next was the bathroom. The third was a woman's bedroom, with a flowered quilt on the bed, a dressing table and chiffonier. Cooley went through the drawers, feeling under stacks of stockings, underwear, folded clothing. In the third drawer his fingers struck something hard. He drew out a leather jewel case and a stack of photo albums.

The cat climbed on the bed to watch him. He turned the pages of the first album: snapshots of the Andersons with their arms around each other in front of what looked like a 1928 Ford sedan. Mrs. Anderson's hair was bobbed, and she wore a cloche hat. The Andersons at the beach, with four other people, waving at the camera. Pictures of houses.

The next album was baby pictures, all of the same child, fat-cheeked and bright-eyed, patent-leather shoes on his feet and a knitted cap on his head. Under this there was a stack of matted enlargements, and as soon as he felt that one of them was in a metal frame, Cooley knew. He pulled it out: it was a picture of the kid in his first suit, gawky and shy, probably taken not more than a year or two ago.

Cooley wrapped the picture and the jewel box in a pillowcase, put everything else back where he had found it. On the way home he looked into the jewel box—a few garnet rings and pendants that looked old, some junk necklaces and earrings, a gold two-and-a-half dollar piece. He kept the coin and threw the rest of the jewelry into a ravine. Let them wonder.

Chapter Three

Trees
Reach up in darkness
Fingers tasting water
Secret drinkers

Light
Filters up their trunks
Their itchy toes
Dabble in the sun

—Gene Anderson

Five miles from Dog River, up an old logging road, there was a hunting lodge, formerly the property of Dr. C. B. Landecker, who gave it to the Boy Scouts in 1938. The lodge consisted of a large living room, a primitive kitchen and pantry, and two small bedrooms downstairs; upstairs there was a loft full of camp beds and cots. In the clearing behind the house there were two outbuildings in an advanced state of disrepair, a well, a barbecue pit, a clothesline, and a heap of old lumber, the remains of a third outbuilding, which the Scouts had been using for firewood. There were recent tire-marks in the soft ground when Gene came into the clearing at twilight, but the building was empty and dark. He felt the lock with his fingers, turned it and went in.

Vague shapes of furniture loomed in the darkness; there was a stale smell. Gene felt his way into one of the bedrooms, took two blankets and carried them outside. Under the sagging porch he cleared away a few rocks and tin cans, spread his blankets, and rolled himself up in them for the night.

Out in the deep darkness there were howls, cries of anguish, with long silent intervals between them. Even in his refuge, there were mysterious and alarming sounds—skitterings of tiny legs, crunches, clicks. The apples he had eaten on his way through the orchards were a hard lump in his stomach. He knew that he would lie awake all night and be tired in the morning; in the middle of this thought, he fell asleep.

In the morning, the clearing was empty and silent. Gene went into the house again and looked around. In the kitchen and pantry he found some useful things, a pot and a skillet, a knife, fork, and spoon, a can-opener, a can of pork and beans, a box of matches, a salt-shaker and half a box of crackers. He copied the pot and skillet, for fear they would be missed; the rest of the things he simply took. He rolled everything up in the blankets and tied them together with a clothesline. Then he slipped out of the house and into the trees, following a little stream.

In the hills above the river, the trees stand shoulder to shoulder, more than a hundred feet tall and five hundred years old: Douglas fir, western hemlock, red cedar, Ponderosa pine, Oregon white oak. Some of them were full-grown in 1579, when Sir Francis Drake sailed up the Pacific coast looking for a northwest passage. Where the land is level, the trees stand by themselves in a brown gloom, but on the slopes and in the narrow valleys they are surrounded by an anarchy of underbrush, hazel and mazzard cherry, bracken fern, trailing blackberry.

Before noon Gene Anderson had found the place he wanted, in a thick stand of fir and oak on a hillside so steep that no one would think of climbing it. Halfway up the hill, entirely screened by tall firs, stood a giant oak. Its trunk was more than two feet across, gray and fissured like an elephant's body; the thick branches curved out knobby and strong to support the crown fifty feet overhead.

Gene ate his pork and beans on the hillside, then rolled everything up in the blankets again and hid them under a log. He went back to the Boy Scout camp; the clearing was deserted except for a few sparrows pecking around the kitchen door.

In one of the outbuildings he found a hammer and some nails, a hatchet, a saw, a pick, and a little shovel. He wrapped these in a tarpaulin and carried them back to his hillside. By that time it was late afternoon, and it was dark under the trees.

He ate pork and beans again, spread the tarpaulin under the log and slept there wrapped in his blankets.

The next day he went back to the camp and sorted out pieces of usable lumber from the pile in the clearing. He carried these up to the hillside and went back for more. Exhausted, he slept again under the log.

Early the next morning he climbed to the fork of the old oak, pulled up lumber with the clothesline and began to build his house. He notched the limbs to make the floor level, and braced it underneath with pieces cut from two-by-fours. By nightfall he had the framing up and the floor laid, and he slept there that night, under the tarpaulin, in a cold drizzle of rain.

The house took shape as he had seen it in his mind: eight feet square, eight feet high at one end and seven feet at the other, with a sloping shed roof. He covered the roof with a tarpaulin and nailed it down around the edges. The only opening was a narrow door, hinged at the top with shoe leather. Along one side he made his bed of fir branches; on another wall he put up shelves for his belongings, and on the third wall, the one opposite the door, a wider shelf that could serve as a desk or workbench.

On Monday he went down to the Boy Scout camp again. No one was there, but he saw fresh tire-marks in the road, and that made him uneasy. He determined to get everything he needed in this one trip and not come back again.

Inside, the living room was in some disorder; sofa cushions and scattered newspapers were on the floor. Gene went through into the pantry, found a gunny sack, and began to fill it. He took cans of soup, condensed milk, Spam, beef stew, green beans, corn, and peaches; a tin plate and cup, a candle, and a roll of toilet paper; a flashlight and some batteries, a kerosene lamp, a bar of soap. In one of the closets he found a pair of heavy boots, a sheepskin coat, and a hat with earlaps; they were all too big for him, but he took them anyhow.

The gunny sack was full, and he began on another one. In the tool shed he found a gallon jug, a bucket, a screwdriver and some other tools, a yardstick, a rusty pair of scissors, some brushes and cans of paint. He finished filling up his sack with the books he found over a desk in the living room: a dictionary, a cook book, the *Boy Scout Handbook for Boys*, and four novels in worn cloth bindings. He copied and replaced all the books, because he was afraid their absence would be too conspicuous. He gathered up the newspapers from the floor and put them in too, and an old copy of *The American Boy*. A little kerosene heater and a can of kerosene went into a third sack, along with a pillow from one of the beds.

He now had far more than he could carry in one trip, but it was getting late, and he was afraid of being caught in the house if someone should come back. He carried the gunny sacks, and a folding canvas chair that caught his eye at the last moment, a few hundred yards into the woods and left two of the sacks there while he carried the third sack home. By the time he had come back twice, for the other two sacks and the chair, he was too tired to sort out his belongings. He set up the kerosene stove, filled and lit it, and for the first time had a hot meal in his own house: vegetable soup, Spam, pork and beans, with condensed milk to drink and a chocolate bar for dessert.

Afterward he took the folded newspapers out of the sack and put them in order. One was the *Oregonian*, the other the *Dog River Gazette*. On the first page of the *Gazette* was an article headlined "Missing Boy Sought in Death of Juvenile."

> Police are seeking a 9-year-old Dog River boy for questioning in connection with the death of another boy Sunday. The dead youth is Paul Cooley, 12, son of Chief of Police Tom Cooley.
>
> According to witnesses, young Cooley and Gene Anderson, 9, were playing in the upper story of an unfinished house under construction by the Anderson boy's father, Donald R. Anderson. The two quarreled, and young Anderson pushed the Cooley boy out the window.
>
> The witnesses, two youngsters who were also playing in the house, ran for help. An ambulance from the Memorial Hospital was dispatched at 3:50 P.M., but young Cooley was found dead of a broken neck and internal injuries.
>
> Gene Anderson has not been seen since Sunday afternoon. He is tall for his age and gives the appearance of a boy of 12 or 13. When last seen he was wearing a blue sweater and dark pants.
>
> A reward has been offered for any information as to his whereabouts.

Chief Cooley ran into Frank Buston, the carrier who delivered the mail to town, at the Idle Hour Billiard Parlor where he could usually be found after work. They took their beers to a table in the corner behind the pool tables. Two cowboys from eastern Oregon were playing eight-ball, with loud whoops of triumph or defeat. "Frank," Cooley said, "you know I'm hunting for the boy that killed my kid."

Buston nodded sympathetically. He was a man in his fifties, with gray strands of hair combed sideways over his bald head. "Terrible thing, Tom," he said. "I heard Ellen was all cut up."

"That's right," Cooley said. "Now, Frank, there's a little something you could do for me if you was a mind to."

"What's that, Tom?"

"The Andersons might be getting a letter in a kid's hand-writing, or maybe a postcard."

"From their kid," Buston said, nodding.

"Right. Now, all's I'd want you to do is just let me see that letter before you deliver it."

Buston was shaking his head. "Can't do that, Tom, no. That's against the law. Federal law, Tom, can't do that."

"All right, how's this?" Cooley said. "If they get a letter like that, you just write down the return address. Or, say there isn't any return address, then just tell me the postmark. I'll make it worth your while, Frank, and I'd sure appreciate it."

Buston hunched his shoulders. "Well—guess there's no harm in that. All right, sure."

Cooley had sent out a flyer about Gene Anderson to police departments in seven states. California was his choice; he thought the boy would have hitchhiked down there where it was warm and nobody knew him. Two or three times a month he got a report of some kid picked up for vagrancy, and he would get on the phone and talk to somebody in Modesto or Stockton, but the description never came near matching. Cooley had some friends on the police force in Portland and Seattle, and one in Austin, Texas, and they were keeping an eye out for him. It was not enough.

Cooley sometimes closed his eyes and tried to imagine where the kid was. He was in a pickup truck rolling through the desert; or he was in a flophouse in San Francisco being hustled by a wino. None of these images satisfied him. A nine-year-old kid traveling alone was too conspicuous, even if he was over five feet tall. It didn't make sense that *nobody* had seen him; he must have found a hiding place, or someone to protect him.

Maybe even right around here.

The novels Gene had brought from the Boy Scout camp were *David Copperfield, Treasure Island, The Count of Monte Cristo* and *The Benson Murder Case*, by S. S. Van Dine. He found the murder mystery incomprehensible, but he read it anyhow. The others he read over and over. His favorite parts were David's school days, so much worse than anything he had suffered; Jim Hawkins climbing the mast to get away from the pirate; and Edmond Dantès being thrown into the sea from the Chateau d'If. All these scenes were so vivid to him that he felt he was living them.

There were many words he did not know in these books, but he was satisfied to guess at their meaning. When he did look up a word, as often as not he could not find it. The *Handbook for Boys*, for instance, advised him to talk frankly to his doctor about masturbation. "If it has happened, don't let it scare you into being blue and ill. If it's a habit, break it for your own peace of mind." But "masturbation" was not in the dictionary. And in *The Count of Monte Cristo*, he was puzzled by the scene when mysterious veiled women seemed to come into the room where the two men were eating hasheesh. He looked up "hasheesh," and found that it was something that made you drunk; but that did not explain the women.

He read the *Handbook for Boys* with close attention, especially the parts about knots and woodcraft. With his yardstick as a guide, he made a six-foot rule marked off in quarters of an inch, and by using this he was able to fill in the blanks in the section on "Personal Measurements":

My height is	5 feet 2 inches
Height of my eyes above ground	4 feet 8½ inches
My reach up to tip of outstretched fingers	6 feet 6¾ inches
My reach across, from outstretched fingertips	5 feet 2¼ inches
Span of my hand, from thumb to little finger	0 feet 8¼ inches
Length of my foot	0 feet 11 inches
Length of my step	1 feet 6 inches

One afternoon, lying on his bed after lunch with the door-flap open, he fell into a doze and dreamed, or half-dreamed, that he was floating invisible over the treetops, down the hill to his own street, moving easily and weightlessly to the kitchen window and then through it like a sound too faint to hear. His mother was sitting at the table with one hand on an open cook book and the other holding a red-and-white checked napkin against her chin. He whispered, "Mom, I'm all right." She heard him without knowing it. "It's so hard to bear," she said.

"I can't come back now, but don't worry, I'm okay." She wiped her eyes with the napkin, gave a deep sigh, and put the napkin down. She began to read the cook book.

He went out as he had come in, and found himself drawn unwillingly up the slope to the unfinished house where Paul had died. He expected to see Paul's body still on the ground, but even the bloody two-by-four was gone. Gene's father and his father's helper were sitting on the sill of the doorway with their hands hanging over their thighs. The fine sawdust that clung to the hairs on their hands was pale orange in the sunlight.

"Dad, I'm sorry," Gene said.

"Takes the heart out of a man," said his father. His mouth twitched. He rubbed his face for a moment, then let his hand fall again.

"Sure is tough on you and the missus," said the other man. "Maybe he's safe somewheres."

"I'm safe," Gene said. "It's all right, Dad, I'm okay."

His father took a deep breath and stood up. "Well—this isn't getting the job done." He and the other man turned and walked into the house.

Early one morning in October Gene heard gunshots in the woods, and when they continued through the day he realized that the hunting season had begun. He was afraid of being surprised by a hunter, and he stayed in his house in the daytime except for visits to the latrine.

For the next two weeks, in spite of the rain, he continued to hear occasional gunshots; then they stopped, and since it was now the first week of November, he concluded that the season was over. When he ventured out, he found the woods transformed, all their color gone. Tree-trunks and branches were black with moisture, every leaf dripping; the ground squelched underfoot. Down the middle of the valley, the little stream had expanded into a sluggish, muddy river, widening in places into a pool black with fallen leaves and debris.

He kept up his calendar, marking off each day in pencil before he went to bed. On weekends he stayed in his house or close to the tree. One Thursday in November, he was returning from a walk when he heard voices down the valley. He climbed the slope hastily and worked his way diagonally up to his house. When he looked at the calendar, he realized that it must be Thanksgiving; he had forgotten about that.

He celebrated with a special meal of all his favorite things: Spam, beef stew, kernel corn, and canned peaches for dessert.

On Christmas Day he cut a little spruce sapling, made a wooden base for it, and decorated it with painted fir cones and acorns. For tinsel he used the foil wrappings from chewing gum, cut into narrow strips.

While the wind howled outside and the snow pattered against his walls, he sang "Silent Night," "O Little Town of Bethlehem," "Old Black Joe," "Git Along, Little Dogie," and a tune whose name he did not know, the one his father had taught him that summer when they went camping in the desert:

> I love the flowers, I love the daffodils.
> I love the mountains, I love the rolling hills.
> When all the lights are low, I love the picture show,
> Boomelay, boomelay, boomelay, boom.

Chapter Four

The disappearance of Gene Anderson was a seven days' wonder in Dog City. In six months even the children had forgotten him. Grownups sometimes said to each other, "Wonder what ever happened to that kid?" The reply was usually, "Guess he'll turn up." After a year it became: "Must be dead by now."

The only ones who did not forget were the Andersons and the Cooleys. Ellen Cooley, whose health never had been strong, grew increasingly despondent after the death of her son. She was not able to care for the house; her sister, Mrs. Williams, had a husband and children of her own to worry about. Cooley hired a woman, Agnes Yount, the widow of a railway telegrapher, to come in by the day, take care of the children and prepare meals. A year after the accident, Ellen seemed to be better, but in January she had a minor automobile accident near the Safeway store: her little Ford struck a car driven by Orville Newcome as Newcome was pulling out of the parking lot, damaging his right-front door and crumpling the fender of the Ford. Ellen Cooley got out of the car and walked away, ignoring Newcome's shouts. She was found hours later walking hatless down by the railroad tracks; she did not seem to know where she was or what had happened. Dr. Phillips treated her for a few days, and when there was no improvement, he sent her to the State Hospital in Salem for observation. When it became obvious that she was not coming home, her sister took the two children in.

Cooley let Mrs. Yount go and stayed on in the house by

himself, cooking an occasional meal and washing the dishes
every four or five days.

On a Monday in March, he walked into the *Dog River
Gazette* office after lunchtime. The two printers looked up in-
curiously; one of them was sitting at the linotype keyboard,
the other was feeding the job press in the back. There was a
smell of ink and hot metal. Cooley knocked on the door of the
glass-enclosed office where Desmond Pike sat with his book-
keeper, Miss Knippel. Pike looked up, beckoned him in.
"Yes, Chief? What can we do for you?"

Cooley sat down in the oak chair and put his hat on his
knee. "Like to see your subscription list, Mr. Pike."

"The list? What for, may I ask?" Pike was a tall white-
haired man with an abrupt manner; he did not like Cooley.

"Police business. I have an idea somebody we're looking
for might of took out a subscription under a phony name."

"You don't intend to make any other use of this information?"

"I don't get you."

Pike looked sour. "Show him the card file, would you
please, Miss Knippel."

"It isn't up to date. I'm trying to catch up on the ledgers."
She pulled out a long file drawer and brought it to the desk.
"We file these by expiration, and under each date they're
alphabetical."

Cooley leaned forward, fingered the cards. "How do you
tell which ones are new?"

"Hard to say. Most folks subscribe for a year, but some for
six months, some for two years. Expiration date is what we go
by. That's when the subscription runs out." She pushed a
strand of hair back behind her ear with a pencil.

"You say this isn't up to date. You got some subscriptions
you haven't filed yet?"

Miss Knippel glanced at Pike; he nodded, and she went to
the filing cabinet for a folder. Inside were a few letters, each
with its envelope attached by a paper clip. Cooley looked
through them, got out his notebook and wrote slowly.
"California," he said. "You get many from there?"

"Folks move away, like to keep up with the hometown
paper."

Cooley put the file down and began to turn over the cards at
the back of the box. "Canada," he said. "Wyoming. Utah.

What about back issues? Any call for them?"

"Once in a while."

"You keep a record of those?"

"Depends. If it's just for a back issue, there wouldn't be any record. But suppose somebody orders a subscription and asks for some back issues at the same time, then you could tell by the card—the amount would be different." She came around the desk and looked over his shoulder. "Like here, two fifty, that's just a year's subscription. But if it was two sixty-five, say, that'd mean they got an extra paper."

Cooley went through the cards again and made more notes. "Much obliged," he said finally, and stood up.

"Any time, Chief."

"Might take you up on that," Cooley said.

In the spring of his second year in the woods, Gene explored farther north than he had ever done before. At last he came to open fields, saw houses and a line of trees in the distance. It was a disappointment at first to find that his domain was so small; then he began thinking about those houses on the county road. He knew that the *Dog River Gazette* was published on Fridays and mailed to subscribers, and he wanted a copy so badly that he made up his mind to take a risk.

Early one morning he hid in the brush across the road from a cluster of mailboxes. The mail truck arrived about an hour after noon. When it was gone again, he walked across the road. No one was in sight. He found a copy of the newspaper in the first box he opened, along with some letters and a magazine in a paper wrapper. He copied the newspaper and the magazine as well, put the copies in his jacket and hurried home.

There was nothing in the paper about him, or his parents or Chief Cooley, or in fact about anybody he knew. He was tormented by the thought that there might have been something important to him in the issues he had missed, or indeed that there might be something next week or the week after. He made up his mind that he would go back for another paper next week, but the moment he had decided this he became frightened. He had done it once, but how many times more could he do it without being seen?

That night he dreamed that he had his own mailbox in a tree, where every day letters and packages were delivered.

He woke up very happy, and his disappointment was acute when he realized that the dream was not real. It was so vivid that in his mind he could see the very tree, an oak like his own but much smaller, and the mailbox, nailed to a plank between two branches, with his name on it in red letters. That much was wrong, he knew; it would have to be some other name.

He remembered the cluster of mailboxes on the county road; they were on a long plank supported by three uprights, and there was room on the plank for several more boxes. Why should he not put his there?

Late that afternoon, carrying tools in a gunny sack, he went to the county road again. Each mailbox was nailed at the sides to a plank which in turn was nailed to the crosspieces. Gene pried one up with a screwdriver, plank and all, put it in his gunny sack and carried it home. In his house, by lantern light, he pried out all the nails and copied both the mailbox and the plank. In the mailbox he found two stamped letters; he copied them too. He carried the original mailbox back through the woods and nailed it up again before dawn.

At home again, he painted in red enamel on the side of his mailbox the name he had chosen, "J. Hawkins." He enlarged all the nail holes in the plank so that the nails could be tapped in easily. When the paint was dry, he took the mailbox back to the county road and set it up beside the others. His was on the end, and the name was plainly visible.

It was common knowledge around Dog River that Chief Cooley "had it in for" Don Anderson and his wife. At the annual spaghetti feed at the Grange Hall in April, Cooley sat next to Fred Moss and talked to him in an undertone for half an hour. Later that month, when Anderson went out to sign a contract for some remodeling, Moss informed him that he had changed his mind. The same thing happened with another customer in May.

Mr. Beumeler, the Lutheran minister, preached a sermon on forgiveness on the first Sunday in June, taking as his text Matthew 18:21-35, the story of the unjust servant, ending with the verse: "So likewise shall my heavenly Father do also unto you, if ye from your hearts forgive not every one his brother their trespasses."

As the congregation filed out after the service, Chief Cooley shook the pastor's hand and smiled. "Nice sermon, Reverend," he said.

Early in July, the Andersons put their house up for sale and moved to Chehalis, Washington, where Anderson went to work for a builder named Keegan.

Urged by an instinct he could not explain or suppress, Cooley cruised the back roads on weekends and slow afternoons, visiting hunting lodges and remote farms and filling stations up and down the river. He talked to the rural mail carriers in Dog River, Mosier, Odell, and Dalles City; not much happened out in the country that they did not know.

In August he got a call from Steve Logan, the Route 1 carrier in Dog River. "Say, Tom, you remember you asked me to keep an eye out for anything peculiar out on my route?"

"Sure do."

"Well, this may not be what you want, but there's something really funny out on Dyer Road. Somebody moved in out there, put up a box, name of Hawkins. Been getting mail regular for three-four months."

"What's funny about that, Steve?"

"Why, nobody out there *knows* him. I talked to Clyde McFarland and Bill Funsch and old Miz Gambrell, they all live on that road, and they say they never heard of this Hawkins, and there's no place for him to *be*. Nobody's moved in out there, or built a new house, or a trailer, or nothing."

Cooley put down his cigar carefully. "Tell me whereabouts that is exactly, would you, Steve?" He took down directions on the back of an envelope, nodding. "Uh-huh. Uh-huh. I'll check into that, Steve, many thanks."

Cooley parked his car on the farm road, just below the crest of the rise, looking down on the county road and the cluster of mailboxes. He watched through binoculars when the mail truck came by, stopped briefly and drove on again. The day was clear and still. An hour passed. Cooley got out and went behind the car to take a piss. When he got back in and raised the binoculars, he saw a flicker of movement back in the trees on the other side of the county road. He stopped breathing. There it came again; now a figure was crossing the road. It was the kid, all right. He went straight to the mailbox at the end of the row, took something out, turned, and walked back.

Cooley watched him until he disappeared into the trees.

He knew better than to try to follow the boy's tracks; he would leave footprints of his own and the kid might see them next time. Instead, early the following afternoon, he entered the woods a hundred yards away, climbed a ridge, and followed it back about a quarter of a mile to a basalt outcrop where the trees were thin. He stayed there, drinking coffee laced with rye whisky out of a thermos, until he saw the kid moving through the underbrush. He marked the direction he had come from; when the boy was out of sight, he moved down the ridge another few hundred yards and waited. In ten minutes the boy was back; Cooley watched him out of sight through the trees and then went home.

The next day he took up his station farther away from the road, and the next day farther still, extending his observation points little by little, until on the fourth day he was rewarded: he saw the boy climb the opposite slope and disappear into a thick stand of fir. He watched the ridge-line, visible through the trees, and did not see him emerge.

The next day he was watching when the boy came down from the hillside. As soon as he was out of sight Cooley scrambled down the slope, jumped over the little stream, and climbed the opposite ridge fifty yards away from the point where he had seen the boy appear. Halfway up the hill, he worked back through the trees in the other direction. There it was: a house built of scrap lumber in an old oak tree. In the shadowless light he could see the footholds nailed to the tree-trunk in a zigzag line: they were made of sawed-off pieces of oak branches, most of them with the bark still on; their color and texture was so close to that of the trunk that from a few feet away they would have been unnoticeable.

Cooley drove out to his cousin Jerry's place a few miles outside Odell. Jerry was three years younger than Cooley, a lank, hollow-cheeked man. They talked on the front porch; it was late in the evening, and Jerry's wife was yelling at the kids in the kitchen.

"Here's the way it looks to me," Cooley said. "When he goes out to get his mail, we move in. When he comes back, I'm up in the tree house waiting for him, and you're behind the bushes. That sound all right?"

"Sure, but why not just be there when he comes out and then nail him? Easy as pie."

"Because if anything goes wrong, either he ducks back into the house and we have to go in after him, or else he's out of the tree and off into the damn woods. If you don't want to do it, tell me."

"No, I'm in."

"Got a gun?"

"Sure—same old Police Special."

"I don't mean that. A rifle—what kind?"

"Remington .30-30, sweet little scope. Last year, doe season, I got one right behind the ear at two hundred yards."

"No good. A scope would just get in the way. Wait a minute." Cooley went out to his car and came back with a short-barreled rifle.

"This here is an Enfield carbine, for jungle fighting. War surplus, I got it from a place in Corvallis four years ago. The ammo is .303 British, ten in the clip and one in the chamber. Plink some tin cans with it tomorrow, get used to the feel. Monday morning, I pick you up and we go. That a deal?"

"Okay, Tom."

They parked their cars on the country road, out of sight of the mailboxes, and went into the woods. Jerry had the carbine and his Police Special, "just in case," and Cooley was armed with his usual Colt .45. They followed the ridge down to the observation point Cooley had used before. Shortly after noon they saw the boy come down from the hillside. When he was out of sight, they crossed the valley and climbed the slope to the treehouse. Jerry clucked his tongue admiringly. "Imagine him doing that," he said.

"It's just a damn treehouse, Jerry."

"Sure, but way out here? Pretty slick kid."

Cooley spat. "We've got about an hour before he gets back. Pick yourself a good spot right over there in the brush and just take it easy. No smoking, he might see it or smell it. Soon as he starts to climb the tree, you get a bead on him, but don't pull the trigger unless he starts down again. Chances are you won't have to do a thing."

"You sure you want to do it this way? I mean, he's just a kid."

"Jerry, that's the *reason*. Suppose I haul him in, what will the law do? They'll put him in the juvenile detention house for a year, maybe, and then he's walking around, and my kid is dead."

Jerry nodded. "Guess I'd feel the same way."

Cooley climbed the footholds, eased the door up and looked in. He saw wooden shelves, a canvas camp chair, a bucket. When he eased himself inside and let the door swing shut behind him, it was black dark. He turned on his flashlight. From the walls, painted figures looked back at him. They were angular, outlined in black paint and filled in with blue, red, and yellow; they looked more like Indian designs than what a kid would draw.

Shirts and pants were piled on the shelves, cans of food, tools. There was a shelf of books, including catalogues from Sears and Montgomery Ward. Cooley looked at the titles. *Grimm's Fairy Tales. Wild Life of the Pacific Northwest. Camping and Woodcraft.*

On the broad shelf behind the camp chair there was a kerosene lamp, a half-finished wood carving, a stack of papers. Cooley picked up the top sheet and looked at it in the beam of the flashlight. It was an airletter with a foreign stamp, addressed to "J. Hawkins, Route 1, Dog City, Oregon, U.S.A." He turned it over. "Dear Pen Pal! I am well, how are you? Here in Lucerne the weather is fine. Soon I will to go on my vacation trip in Austria."

Cooley put the letter down. He moved the camp chair to the side of the room, took out his revolver and pushed the safety off, turned off the flashlight and sat down to wait.

Jerry was sitting behind a cluster of vine maple stems with his back against a tree and the Enfield in his lap. His butt was cold, and there was a rock or a root under him whichever way he shifted. He looked at his wristwatch; he had been here almost an hour.

Brush crackled a few yards away, and when he looked up he saw the kid climbing the tree with some kind of parcel in his hand. Jerry rolled over to one knee and stood up, but a twig cracked under his foot and the kid looked around. He was just hanging there, one leg and one arm up, looking down over his shoulder with a frightened expression. Jerry had to make up his mind in a hurry, because in another second it might be too late. He got the bead in the notch of the peep-sight, centered on the kid's back just under the shoulderblade, squeezed the trigger. He saw the kid go over, arms and legs flying, and heard him hit with a solid thump at the base of the tree. He scrambled over there. The kid was lying on his back, blood all over the front of his shirt, but his eyes were open and focused; he was alive. Hell! said Jerry to himself, but there was no other way on God's earth now, and he aimed the rifle again. A piercing pain struck him in the chest, and he felt himself floating away light as a leaf on a dark wind.

Chapter Five

Cooley heard the shot, swore, and butted his way out of the tree house. He saw the kid at the base of the tree, but had only a glance to spare him, because Jerry was lying on the slope a few yards away, spread-eagled on the ground, jerking and twitching like a rag doll on a string. Cooley got down the tree as fast as he could and knelt beside him. Jerry's eyes were rolled back in their sockets; his skin was turning blue. The jerking of his limbs stopped with a final shudder. His face turned darker until it was indigo blue, the color of ink, color of venous blood. His pants-leg was wet, and there was a fecal smell. Cooley had seen dead men before, and knew better, but he unbuttoned Jerry's shirt and put his hand on his chest.

After a minute he stood up and looked at the kid. Blood was pulsing out through the wet spot on his shirt and there was more of it spattered over the brush behind him. His eyes were closed, mouth open. His skin was yellowish-white. Not dead yet, but soon.

"Jesus *Christ!*" said Cooley, and hit the tree with his fist. He sat down and put his head in his hands; warm tears were leaking out of his eyes. What the hell was he going to do now, leave both bodies there and just walk away? Pretend he didn't know a thing about it? That would be too much of a coincidence. What a hell of a time for a heart attack. They might not find the bodies here for years, maybe never, but he couldn't count on that. Then there was Steve Logan, the mailman—would he keep his mouth shut?

He took a deep breath and stood up. He leaned over and got

his revolver from the ground where he had dropped it, put it away in the holster. He knelt beside Jerry's body again, buttoned up his shirt. He reached into Jerry's jacket, found the Police Special, flicked the safety off, and stood up. Supporting his wrist with his other hand, he aimed straight down at Jerry's chest and pulled the trigger. The body jumped once more. Cooley turned away, hiccuping. When he could see straight again, he went to the boy's body and dipped up some blood on his finger. He smeared the blood carefully on the ragged little hole in Jerry's shirt and on the chest underneath. He wiped his finger on the dirt and leaves at the base of the tree, then put the safety back on the revolver and wiped it all over with the tail of his shirt. Holding the gun by the barrel, he put it carefully into the boy's left hand, then his right, closing the index finger over the trigger, thumb on the frame. He wiped the barrel again, nudged the safety off, and dropped the gun beside the boy. Blood was still welling from the kid's chest, but more slowly.

Cooley walked out of the woods, got into his car and drove to the nearest farmhouse to telephone. The Memorial Hospital sent an ambulance and four men with stretchers. When they got to the tree house a little after two, Jerry's body was still there but the kid's wasn't: there was nothing under the tree but a roll of magazines tied up with string, and a splatter of blood in the brush. One of the men knelt over Jerry's body. "He's dead."

"Well, leave him there for the sheriff. Help me find the other one, would you?"

The four of them and Cooley hunted up and down the slope, but they didn't find a thing, not even a drop of blood on a leaf to show which way the kid had gone.

Cooley went back to the farmhouse again to telephone. Old Mrs. Gambrell, who owned the place, was quite excited; Cooley had to put one hand over his ear because she kept saying in a loud voice, "Oh, dear! Oh, dear!" He called the sheriff's office and was told that they had already been notified by the hospital and the sheriff was on his way out. Cooley hung up and called the state police. He described the missing boy and said, "I need some road blocks, west and east of Dog River and south on route thirty-five." The duty officer said he would see what he could do.

Cooley, fretting, went back to the county road and waited until Sheriff Beach turned up. Beach was a tall pale-eyed man in his early fifties, running a little to fat. He nodded to Cooley when he got out of his car. "Is it Jerry?" he asked. "How'd it happen?"

"Kid was living in a tree house in the woods. We staked it out—he shot Jerry. Jerry shot him, too, but he got away."

"Uh-huh. How'd you know the kid was there?"

"Got a tip from Steve Logan."

"Uh-huh," said Beach. When they got to the tree house, Beach gave it one curious glance and then hunkered down beside Jerry's body. He looked at the bullet wound. "Shot in the heart."

"That's right."

"And where were you?"

"Up in the tree house, waiting for the kid."

" 'Bout what time was that?"

"Little after one."

"Uh-huh. So you heard the shot, come down and the kid was gone?"

"No, he was laying there too, shot, and I thought he was dead. But when I come back from phoning, he was gone."

Beach took several photographs of the body, then turned. The revolver lay beside the splatter of blood in the bushes: a short-barreled Smith & Wesson, blued steel, with a brown grip. It was an old gun; the bluing was partly worn off around the cylinder. "And that's where the kid was?" said Beach. "Jerry shoots him, he falls right there, drops his gun. Now, where's Jerry's gun?"

Cooley looked around. "I never thought," he said. "Jesus, this is an awful thing."

They found the rifle suspended muzzle down in a stand of young vine maple two yards away. "Looks like he must have throwed his arms up when he got hit," Beach said. He photographed the rifle without touching it, then took several more pictures of the revolver where it lay.

"Let's see if I've got this straight," he said. "Jerry's here, hiding in the brush." He stood beside the sprawled body. "Kid comes up over there—you be the kid, Tom."

Reluctantly, Cooley walked over and stood beside the dropped revolver. "Good," said Beach. "Kid hears Jerry, I guess, Jerry stands up and the kid shoots him." He crouched a little, holding an imaginary rifle aimed at Cooley. "That's about the way it had to be, wouldn't you say?"

"Right," Cooley said uncomfortably.

"Hits Jerry right here," said Beach, touching his own chest. "Jerry's gun goes off, shoots the kid, they both fall down." He picked up his camera, took a picture of Cooley. "Kid was hit where?"

"Right about here," Cooley said, indicating a spot high on his chest.

"You know, Tom, it's funny. Man is shot in the heart, throws up his arms, heaves that rifle six feet away, and still shoots the kid right in the chest."

"Way I look at it, must have been the other way around," Cooley said. "The kid pulled a gun, Jerry seen he was about to shoot and got him first. Then the kid's gun went off. Just dumb luck."

"Could be," Beach said. He glanced up at the tree house. "What's up there?"

"Kid's junk. Listen, Wayne, if you can spare me, I sure would like to get back and see what the troopers are doing about those road blocks."

"Hang on a minute," Beach said. He climbed the tree, swung the door up and disappeared inside. When he came out again five minutes later, he was holding a bulging gunny sack. He saw the clothesline knotted to the limb beside the door, pulled it up, tied the gunny sack to it, and lowered it to the ground.

He climbed down again, holding an empty gunny sack in one hand. He picked up the revolver by the end of the barrel, looked it over curiously, then dropped it into the sack. Next he went to the rifle in the bushes, wrapped the sack around it and picked it up. "Guess that's all for now," he said. "Tom, if you wouldn't mind—" He gestured toward the full sack. Cooley untied it in silence and hoisted it over his shoulder. They climbed down the slope.

"I'll have to send somebody back for the rest of the stuff," Beach said. After a moment he added, "You tell Jerry's wife?"

"Hell!" said Cooley, stopping short. "No, I never. I'll do it, first thing."

When they got to Beach's car, the sheriff unlocked the trunk and Cooley dumped the gunny sack in it. Beach laid the other sack with the two guns carefully in the back seat.

"I'll go on up to Miz Gambrell's and make a couple of calls," Cooley said. "Check with you later, Wayne."

"No, now," said Beach, putting a hand on his arm, "we're not half through yet, Tom. You follow me down to my office —you can make your calls from there."

"Meanwhile that kid's getting away. Won't it keep till tomorrow?"

"That's for me to say."

Cooley stared at him for a moment, then turned and got into his car. They drove to the parking lot behind the court-house in Dog River; Cooley helped Beach carry the sacks of evidence inside. A young deputy was sitting behind the desk smoking a cigarette. He nodded to Cooley. "Tom."

"Hello, Stan."

"Call Eileen and see if she can get over here right away," said Beach. "Tell her I need her for an hour or so." He cleared some books off a table and dumped the contents of the gunny sacks on it: books, a stack of papers, games in boxes, tools, some painted wood carvings, pencils and pens. Beach pushed the two guns to one side and began separating the other things with one finger.

"She'll be right over," the deputy said.

"Good." Beach motioned Cooley to a seat. "Make yourself comfortable, Tom. You wanted to call Jerry's wife?"

"Was going to call the troopers, too, but maybe that'd come better from you."

"Maybe so. Stan, get me the State Police."

The deputy dialed and brought the phone over.

"Beach, in Dog River. Let me talk to Mullen." Beach tapped a cigarette out of a pack of Camels and lit it. "Hello, Hal? Tom Cooley call you about some road blocks awhile ago? Yeah? Hell, I don't know—till tomorrow night, I guess. I know it. Well, it's a homicide. Yeah, all right." He hung up. "They'll get the road blocks up in about an hour."

Cooley's hands clenched into fists. "They haven't got off their butts *yet*?" he said. "That kid could be halfway to California by now."

"Probably not. Shot, lost some blood—we'll probably find him in the woods tomorrow. Want this?" He shoved the telephone across the table.

"Yeah, I guess so." Cooley dialed Jerry's number. An un-familiar voice answered.

"This is Tom Cooley—is Alma there?"

"Just a minute." A pause. "If it's about Jerry, she knows it already, and she don't want to talk to you right now." The line went dead.

"I should of called her before," Cooley said, rubbing his hand across his face. "Somebody at the hospital must have told her. That makes me feel like hell."

"It's a tough business," Beach said. "Stan, call Thomas Funeral, ask them to get out there and collect the body, will you? See if they can get one of the ambulance guys from the hospital to show them the way. And then call Doc Swanson about the autopsy."

The door opened; a dark-haired young woman came in. "Eileen, you know Tom Cooley?" She nodded, her eyes bright and curious. "Let's go in the back. Eileen, bring your book."

In the back office, Beach sat down behind the desk, Cooley to his right, the secretary on the other side. "Now let's start from the beginning," Beach said. "Just tell it your own way, Tom."

Cooley began, "About a week ago, Thursday I believe it was, Steve Logan called me and told me there was something funny going on out on route one. . . ." Beach sat back, smoking and listening. He asked an occasional question. When Cooley was finished, the sheriff took him back over it again. About six o'clock, he sent the deputy out for sandwiches. Shortly after seven, Beach said, "All right, Eileen, type that up—just the statement, three copies. Then you can go home." She left with her book, and in a moment they heard the clatter of her typewriter.

"Now, Tom, there's one or two things about this that don't add up to me. One is the gun—where did he get it?"

"Must of stole it somewhere."

"Maybe. Another thing is, here's the kid coming back to his tree house. He doesn't know there's anybody there, but he's got the gun in his hand? Or else he can pull it out quick enough to get the drop on Jerry? That doesn't make sense. Wait a minute." He held up his hand, pressed down the third finger. "Next thing is, the kid shoots him in the heart while Jerry's aiming a rifle at him. Doesn't hit the gun, or Jerry's arm, or even his sleeve. Pretty amazing." Beach sat back and folded his arms. "But the main thing is, here's two Dog River police officers pursuing a felon out in the county, in my jurisdiction,

Tom. What I ask myself is, why did you and Jerry go out there without a word to me? The answer I get I don't like."

"You accusing me of something, Wayne?"

"No, because if I did how would I prove it? Jerry's dead, the kid's gone, and you're a liar."

Cooley stood up. "Well, at least we know where we stand."

"That's right."

Cooley stopped in at the Idle Hour for a shot and a glass of beer and then drove out to Jerry's place. He found Alma in the kitchen with a woman he didn't know, who gave him a hostile glance and left the room.

"Alma, I'm sorry as hell about this."

"You didn't even call me for *four hours*. I had to find out from strangers."

"I know, and I'm sorry. I got so tied up—"

"For all I know, you killed him yourself. I wouldn't put it past you."

"That's a shitty thing to say, Alma."

"Shitty thing to do, too. I know one thing, if he hadn't of gone with you, he'd be alive this minute."

Volunteers searched the woods for four days. The State Police manned road blocks on the highways until Tuesday night, stopping every car, but the boy was gone.

Beach spent a few hours tramping through the woods on Tuesday. He couldn't rid himself of the idea that Cooley and Jerry Munk had killed the boy and got rid of his body somehow, and that Cooley had then shot Jerry to keep him quiet. He found himself looking for traces of a recent excavation, even though he knew that was unlikely; to dig in these woods you would need not only a pick and shovel but an ax to cut through the roots and a crowbar to hoist out stones, and when you were done, if you buried anything, it wouldn't be easy to hide the dirt. He knew there was some essential thing he didn't know; he knew he was guessing wrong, but he didn't know how wrong.

The FBI office in Portland put together a complete set of Gene Anderson's fingerprints except for the left little finger, and these prints were duly entered in their files together with a photograph of the boy furnished by Chief Cooley.

Beach went out to talk to Alma Munk when she had had a

day or two to pull herself together. He asked her where Jerry's revolver was, and she said she didn't know. Beach sent the serial number of the gun to the manufacturer, and eventually learned that it had been sold in 1939 to a sporting goods store in Laramie. Beach knew there was no point in trying to trace it through the store's records; the gun had probably had three or four owners since then.

The *Gazette* ran an unprecedented two-column front page story about the "Tree House Murder"; reporters from the Portland and Salem papers came out, and there was even a photographer from *Time*, but his pictures never appeared in the magazine. Souvenir hunters climbed the tree and pulled off boards to take home. A psychic in Corvallis claimed to have seen in a vision that Gene Anderson was living in a mountain cabin, "in a Western state, near running water."

John and Mildred Anderson drove down from Chehalis as soon as they heard. They talked to Sheriff Beach, and he showed them the books, games, and papers he had taken from the tree house. There were letters from correspondents in Switzerland, France, and Italy. "How did he ever get to writing all those people?" Donald Anderson asked.

"Pen pals. They advertise in magazines for kids. I've written letters to all those addresses, asking them to let us know if they hear from Gene, but I'd guess he's too smart for that." There was also a letter to his parents, never mailed.

"He was afraid to let us know where he was because Tom Cooley might find out and kill him," Mildred said. "Is that what happened? Do you think he's dead?"

Beach shook his head. "No telling. If he's alive, maybe he'll turn up."

"Can't you *find* him?—can't the police—?"

"Mrs. Anderson, I know how you feel, but there's thousands of missing kids every year. Runaways, mostly; they don't want to be found, and there's just too many of them. If he happens to get picked up and fingerprinted, then they'll identify him."

Beach would not give them their boy's belongings, but he allowed Mrs. Anderson to copy down the names and addresses of his correspondents, and when she got home she wrote them urgent letters. Eventually she got three replies; the writers all said that they would certainly let her know if Gene wrote to them again. After that there was nothing.

• • •

The coroner's jury met in late November; they listened to Cooley's account of the incident, and Sheriff Beach's report, and they heard Dr. Swanson testify that the victim's injuries were consistent with death caused by a .38 revolver bullet, fired at short range, and passing through the left ventricle of the heart. The jury brought in a verdict of murder by a person or persons unknown.

Cooley went up to the district attorney's office afterward. "What the hell do they mean, persons unknown, it was the damn kid!"

The district attorney, Quentin Hoagland, gave him a cold look over the tops of his gold-rimmed glasses. "Mr. Cooley, that was a responsible verdict in my opinion, and I'm a little surprised in fact, because this is a one-horse county. I'll tell you this, too, there are things about your testimony that I personally find hard to believe. I'm issuing a warrant for Gene Anderson as a material witness, in case you're interested. But there's something about this case that smells, and I don't mind telling you that if I had a little more evidence I'd be putting out two warrants, not one."

Early in March of the following year word came back to Dog River that Mr. and Mrs. Donald Anderson had died in a house fire of undetermined origin in Chehalis, Washington. It had happened on a weekend when Chief Cooley had been away on one of his trips, and the rumor went around that the fire had been set by an arsonist.

Chief Cooley noticed during the following weeks that some people were avoiding him on the street; even old friends, when he sat down beside them at the Idle Hour or the Elk Tavern on route thirty-five, sometimes sat in embarrassed silence for a while and then got up to play a game of pinball or make a phone call.

Cooley was not surprised when Mayor Hilbert came to see him one Friday evening. "Hello, Gus. Come on in. You can throw those magazines off the chair."

Hilbert sat down. "Good Christ, Tom, this place is a damn pigsty."

"That what you came about?"

"No, Tom. It's about the Anderson business."

"Goddamn it, Gus, are you going to bring that up again? I

was in Sacramento—I showed you the motel receipt.''

"I know it, Tom, but people talk anyway. And, you know, there's some bad feeling about what happened to Jerry. Well, maybe they're right or maybe they're wrong, but people are telling me things like that shouldn't happen in Dog River. You know what I'm telling you, Tom.''

"Sure. You're not going to renew my contract.''

"That's it. I'm sorry, Tom, that's the way it has to be.''

"All right. Got anybody else in mind?''

Hilbert shifted uneasily in the chair. "Nothing definite. Walt Barrett has an uncle, a police sergeant in Portland, he's retiring next month—he might be innarested.''

"Contract isn't up till September, Gus.''

"I know that. Nobody's rushing you, Tom.''

"Want a beer?''

"No, thanks—well, all right.''

Cooley brought two bottles from the refrigerator and a glass for Hilbert. "Down the hatch,'' he said. "You know, Gus, I want to make this easy on you if I can.''

Hilbert wiped the foam off his upper lip. "You do?''

"Sure, I do. Let's make a deal. Suppose I resign, whenever you say—May first or whatever. I'll show the new guy the ropes, break him in and so forth. I been thinking of moving on, anyhow.''

Hilbert looked thoughtful. "You said a deal, Tom?''

"All I want is two months' salary and a letter of recommendation. A good letter, Gus. And if anybody asks you for a reference, I want you to tell them I resigned to look for a better job, and I'm the best damn chief of police you ever saw.''

"That letter you can have, no problem. About the two months, I'll have to talk to the town council.''

"You do that. And, Gus—''

"Yeah?''

"You tell them if I don't get it, I'm going to be the meanest son of a bitch north of Mexico.''

Cooley sold his house, auctioned off the furniture, and put everything he had left into the trunk and back seat of the Buick. He closed his account at the bank, took a few hundred dollars in travelers' checks and cash, and got a cashier's check for the rest.

It was his belief now that the kid was alive, and he was still convinced that he had gone south. The only thing he had to go on, besides a hunch, was something Mrs. Anderson had said: "He likes to draw." Cooley got into the Buick early one morning in May and headed for Los Angeles. If he drew a blank there, it was his intention to work north again—San Francisco, then up to Salem, then Portland, but he didn't think the kid would have stopped that close to home. He wouldn't feel safe until he was as far away as he could get without leaving the country. Los Angeles: that was where he'd find him.

Chapter Six

In his dreams, the boy was coming up out of deep water, fighting to reach the surface. When he got there, he felt the hard ground under him and a pain in his chest as if he had been clubbed with a baseball bat. It was worse when he tried to roll over, and when he finally managed to sit up, a pink froth dripped from his chin and spattered the legs of his pants. The pain now was a hard thin spear that went through him slantwise, starting under one arm and coming out over the shoulderblade on the other side.

He got to his feet, swayed, and saw the man lying half hidden by a clump of vine maple. He walked toward the man, not able to stop himself until he was standing right above him. The man's face was blue.

After the dream, he would sit hugging his knees and remembering. The first thing he really remembered was being in the forest, all alone, leaning against a tree and feeling under his shirt to find out what was the matter. Low on one side there was a dimpled tender place, a little soft bulge in his skin, and under that his rib was sore, but even that pain was going away. He looked at his shirt and saw that there was a great smear of dried blood down the side of it; there were spatters on his pants, too.

Then he was sitting in a car, hurtling down a dark road, and the driver, beside him, kept looking at the blood on his shirt. They were out on the desert someplace; he didn't know where he was. The driver, a pale old man with a white mustache, pulled up at a crossroads and said, "This here's as far as I can take you."

He felt thick-witted and sleepy. "I have to get out?"

"Yeah, get out. I can't take you no farther."

The door slammed behind him; he saw the red taillights receding. He turned and started walking up the other road, a gravel road between tall cut banks, dim under the early stars. After a long time he came to a forest of black trees growing in sand. It was dark now, and beginning to rain; he went into the forest and lay down under a tree.

Early in the morning he woke up and heard a voice talking to him from the sky. He couldn't understand what the voice said, but it scared him.

His pain was gone. Even the funny tender place on his side was gone, but he was very hungry and thirsty.

It was strange to be out in the world, where people could see him; it made him feel itchy and ashamed somehow, like the kind of dreams when you walk into class and discover that you are in your underwear. And he still couldn't remember what had happened in the woods, but he knew he couldn't go back there.

It was nearly noon before he reached a traveled road again and got a ride heading south. In a place called Lakeview he found a pay phone in a grocery store and tried to call home. "That number has been disconnected," the operator said.

"Uh—could you tell me if they have another number?"

"What is the name of the party you are calling?"

"Mr. and Mrs. Donald Anderson."

"One moment. I have a listing for a D. W. Anderson."

"No, that isn't it. Donald R. Anderson, six oh four Columbia Street?"

"I have no listing for an Anderson at that address."

"Thank you," he said numbly, and hung up.

He had had nothing to eat all day but candy bars and two hot dogs, bought at a roadside stand early in the afternoon. He went into a railroad diner, sat in a booth, and had roast beef with gravy and mashed potatoes, two glasses of milk and a piece of apple pie with vanilla ice cream; he marveled that anything could taste so good.

There were only a few coins in his pockets, and the largest was a quarter. Sitting in the back of the booth, out of sight of the counterman and the waitress, he duplicated the quarter, making stacks and then copying the stacks, until he had eight dollars' worth. At the counter he said, "Could you give me some bills for these, please?"

"Sure—I can always use the change." The woman counted out a five and three ones, subtracted the amount of his check, and handed him the rest.

Then it was getting dark, and he was sleepy. He went into a motel and asked for a room. "Traveling alone?" the clerk said.

"Yes."

"That'll be five-fifty, in advance."

He paid and took the key. His room was not very nice, but it had a bathtub with a shower and soap and towels. He covered himself with soapsuds, washed his hair, rinsed off and did it all over again for sheer pleasure.

In the morning he went into a store and bought two shirts and a little canvas bag which he thought would make him look more respectable. He changed his shirt in the back room, put the others in his bag, and got on the road again.

Los Angeles now was his destination, but his first sight of the Golden Gate Bridge—that astonishing construction, soaring light as air across the blue water—so filled him with wonder that he stopped in San Francisco and never thought of going on again. He liked the hilly streets, and the cable cars, and the crowds of cheerful people.

He stayed in a cheap hotel for two nights, and might have stayed there longer, but on one of his walks he passed a sign in a window: "Furnished Apt. For Rent." He went in and asked about it: it was two rooms and a kitchenette, with a linoleum floor and maple furniture; the rent was fifty-five dollars a month.

He remembered that his Uncle Bruce lived in Provo, Utah; that had stuck in his mind because of the funny name. He got the number from the operator and called on a Saturday afternoon.

"Hello?" A woman's voice.

"Hello, is this—Does Bruce Anderson live there?"

"Yes, he does, but he's not home right now. Can I help you?"

"Well, this is Gene Anderson, I'm his nephew—"

"Why, Gene! It's real nice to hear from you. How's your mom and dad?"

"That's what I was wondering. You haven't heard from them?"

"Why, *no*. Is there anything the matter?"

"Well, it's just that—I was away from home, and they kind of moved, and I don't know where they are."

"Well, I never heard of such a thing! My heavens! Where are you now, Gene?"

"I'm, uh, in Texas. Could you—"

"Well, you tell me your address and phone number, Gene, and when your uncle gets home I'll ask him—You know, it's funny, your dad was never much for writing, but we always used to get a Christmas card. And I said to Bruce last year, no, it was *two* years ago Christmas, I said, no card from your brother this year, I wonder if they're all right. Now let me get a pencil."

"I can't—I haven't got an address to give you, because I'm just passing through, kind of, but I wondered, could you tell me my aunt Cora's number? In Davenport, Iowa? I don't even know what her name is—I mean her husband's name."

"Well, her husband's name is Johnson, or, wait a minute, is it Jackson? Something like that, but Gene, what do you *mean* you're just passing through? Who are you staying with? You tell me where to reach you, because I know Bruce will want—"

"I have to go now," said Gene, and hung up.

In a curious way, he was relieved. For the first time in his life he was free to do whatever he liked, go where he pleased, buy anything he wanted. It seemed to him that he had died and been reborn, back there in the darkness under the tree. Both his old lives were gone, the one at home with his parents and the one in the tree house, and he felt no regret, only a sense of gratitude and liberation.

He changed his dollar bills at the bank for fives and tens, spent them, took change, got more fives and tens. He bought books, paints and brushes, stretched canvases, an easel. He went to the movies every night; his favorite films were those with Glenn Ford and John Wayne, but he watched everything with uncritical appreciation, even Ma and Pa Kettle.

Television was a marvel to him; there had been no such thing in Dog River two years ago. He bought a set for two hundred dollars; it had a round picture tube on which the faces of actors bloomed in furry lines of blue-white.

He ate prodigiously and with a pleasure that went beyond the simple satisfaction of hunger: satiny scrambled eggs, toast covered with jam or marmalade, rubbery cheese that broke in conchoidal fractures when he pulled it apart, soda crackers with their mineral incrustations, each one a pure glittering crystal. Every day for lunch and dinner he had roast beef or ham, mashed potatoes hollowed by the chef's ladle and filled with gravy, pale translucent slices of tomato on a bed of lettuce, and for dessert a piece of cream pie, banana or chocolate, that seemed to coat him inside with luxury.

His experiments in painting on canvas were not turning out well. No one had told him about using a medium; he was putting the paint on as it came from the tube, and his paintings seemed thick and lifeless.

On a side street, tucked in between two grimy office buildings, one day he found an art school: it was called the Porgorny Institute of Fine Arts, and a sign in the window said, "Register for Fall Classes." He opened the double doors and found himself in a wide hall. The office was on the right. "Fill out this application," said the mousy-blonde woman behind the counter. Gene wrote down "Stephen Miller," and his address. Under "Age" he put "15," and under "Education" he wrote "High school."

"Now you've checked four classes," said the woman, "and there's only three periods a day, so we'll have to work out a schedule for you. The best thing would be to take *two* of these classes every day, and then, the third period, you would go back and forth between the other two."

"I don't understand," Gene said.

"Well, for *instance*, suppose you want to take Figure Drawing and Oil Painting every day. That's your first two periods. Then, you could take Sculpture on Tuesdays, Thursdays, and Saturdays—"

A large, heavy woman came in from the hall carrying a sheaf of papers. She had an imposing bosom under a purple blouse, and a black ribbon hung from her eyeglasses; her dark hair, streaked with gray, was piled on her head in a haphazard fashion. "What is it?" she asked in a deep voice. "What is the matter?"

"This young man is applying for classes—"

"So." She looked him over. "You are how old?"

Her accent was so strange that he could hardly understand her. "Fifteen," he said.

"Perhaps." She was thinking. No pimples. Tall, but not more than twelve. "And you think you can become artist?"

"I like to draw," Gene said.

"He likes to draw. So many like to draw. But why not? It is better than murdering people in the streets." She turned to the woman behind the counter. "Well, then, Miss Olney, what is problem?"

"It's just his schedule, Madame Porgorny—he wants to take four classes—"

"Work it out! Work it out! Do not bother me with these details." Madame Porgorny swept around the counter and into the inner office, where, presently, they could hear her shouting on the telephone.

"Does she teach any of the classes?" Gene asked.

"Only China Painting, Wednesday and Saturday evenings. Did you want to—?"

"Oh, no," Gene said hastily. He paid the application fee and got his schedule. "When do the classes start?"

"September fourth."

The Porgorny Institute was not like any other school he had known. Down behind the reception room and office was a row of large studios whose individual smells were at first strange, then loved and familiar: smells of oil and turpentine, charcoal dust, plaster dust.

Madame Porgorny's booming voice could be heard at intervals all day long in the corridors. She seemed to live in a state of constant exasperation; Gene heard her shouting at the instructors, at Miss Olney the receptionist, at electricians and plumbers.

In the figure-drawing class the model was a dark-haired young man with broad shoulders and narrow hips; he wore a thing like a black jockstrap, but much skimpier—the side part was only a narrow ribbon. He never spoke; between posing sessions he smoked in the little courtyard, and when he was through for the day he left, sometimes with a woman student.

In this class the students were given hard black crayons and large sheets of paper torn off a roll. They were instructed to hold the crayon like a knife and use the arm and wrist in drawing, but Gene could not do this; he sharpened his crayon to a fine point, held it like a pencil, and made careful, minute drawings that occupied only a small part of the sheet. He drew the head, then the shoulders and chest, the arms and hands, then the hips, thighs, calves, and feet. His drawings were careful and accurate in outline, but there was always something wrong with them; they were off balance, or out of proportion, and he tore them up.

When he looked at the other students' work, he could see that they were doing something entirely different. They seemed not to care about accuracy of detail; their drawings were large, cloudy sketches of bodies in the same posture as the model's but otherwise having no resemblance to it, and they were all different: some fat and shapeless, some angular and thin.

The instructor, an auburn-haired young woman called Miss Williams, pointed out that everybody tended to draw bodies like their own: wide, muscular people drew wide, muscular bodies, and so on. Gene held up one of his tiny sketches, and she laughed. "Well, Stephen is an exception to everything," she said.

With the other students he felt the continual embarrassment of being the wrong age; he was sure they all knew he was too young to be there, and he sensed in them the unspoken conspiracy of being grown up. When they spoke to him kindly, he felt they were being condescending, and when they ignored him he felt excluded. The very shapes of their bodies, their hairiness, their smells (unsuccessfully disguised by perfume) proclaimed them a different kind of humanity; the hints they gave of their pleasures outside the classroom were alien to him; they laughed at different things, and with a different laughter. He felt himself an intruder, in constant danger of being found out.

He took the ceramics class and tried to throw pots on the wheel, but he could never center the lump of clay properly, and his pots came out lopsided; they wobbled on the wheel, and no matter what he did he could never make them straight. He liked them anyhow because of their magical transformation in the kiln ("the kill," Miss Jacoby called it): from dried, leathery clay the color of lead they had turned pale and hard as stone, scritching under his fingernails. The glazes were equally magical: you painted them on like pale mud, and when they came out they were clear, brilliant orange or blue or purple. He experimented with his most ambitious piece, a tall vase that was only a little lopsided: he painted it first with green glaze, then with blue. When he saw it after the weekend firing, it was covered with luminous streaks of blue melting into peacock green, and all the other students admired it. "You took a chance, but it worked," said Miss Jacoby.

In Mr. Berthelot's class he learned the mysteries of armatures and plaster casting. The hollow shape inside the mold was tantalizingly strange; it was recognizable—there was the arm, here the head—and yet absolutely unfamiliar. When they lubricated the mold and poured plaster into it, then chipped the mold away, the result was again a magical transformation: the clay model had been turned first into a mere vacancy, an absence, and then into hard, chalky plaster. In a way it seemed to him that the change was for the worse: the clay model, now destroyed, had been alive, and the plaster cast was dead.

The school did not teach wood carving. "Old Lady says it's too dangerous," Mr. Berthelot told him. "Some student cuts his finger off, the insurance wouldn't cover it. I don't know too much about it myself, tell you the truth, and the students we got here, they just want to play with clay."

In an art store he saw a beautiful set of wood carving tools with wooden handles all alike, shaped to fit the palm. He bought them, and some blocks of hardwood, and took them home. He bungled his first attempts, but then he got the hang of the tools, how the mallet drove the sweet cutting edge through the surface of the wood, curling off a precise shaving. He smoothed his sculptures with a broad blade, then with sandpaper, until the wood was as round and slick as stone, but later he began to like the texture of the worked surface, the trace of the tools, as if patient worms had gone around and around the wood eating it away to leave a beautiful shape.

Mr. Velton, the painting instructor, sent him out with a sketchbook, and when he came back with simple drawings of tombstones in the cemetery, sent him away again. It was clear enough to Gene what Mr. Velton wanted: he wanted landscapes crowded with trees, stones, houses, a sky full of clouds; but when Gene looked at landscapes he saw only a meaningless jumble. At last, in despair, he sketched a pile of junk on a vacant lot: barrel hoops, old tires, tin cans. Velton looked at this with pleased surprise, and pointed out various dynamic relationships of which Gene had been unaware.

In his frustration he dropped the oil painting class and signed up for Madame Porgorny's china painting class on Wednesday and Saturday evenings. The other students, gray-haired women in smocks, were already painting on dishes, but Madame Porgorny gave him glazed tiles to practice on: first to learn the strokes, and then to draw simple patterns of stems and leaves. There was something wrong with her hands; the knuckles and fingers were swollen, and she could not straighten them entirely, but it never seemed to interfere with her painting.

When she came to Gene's table, she said, "No, it is not good. See here, the lines are broken, that is ugly. In nature are no broken lines. Every line must be one line, not three." She took his brush from him and fitted it into a leather strap she was wearing on her hand, so that the brush stood out beyond her swollen knuckles. She took a blank tile, dipped the brush, and drew in one motion a long delicate curve that became a curled leaf; then another. "Do you see now?"

"Yes, but why are you doing it with that?"

She looked at him. "Sometimes my fingers will not hold the brush," she said. "It does not matter. Painting is with the wrist, so, not with the fingers. Now make for me a yellow flower like this one." She showed him a design in the book.

He dipped a brush in yellow and painstakingly drew each of the five petals; he mixed a little white with the yellow and tipped each petal, then a little orange and darkened their stems. Madame Porgorny came back while he was finishing.

"No, again it is wrong. Look here." She sat beside him in a cloud of perfume. She took his brush, fitted it into the strap of her hand, dipped up paint, and with one stroke made a perfect petal, then another, and another, until there were five. "Now do you see?"

"I'll never do that," Gene said.

"You can learn if you wish, but why should you? This is not what you want. Tell me, why did you take this class?"

"It was the figure drawing. I can't do it big the way Miss Williams wants me to."

"And so you thought you would do china painting because it is small? But you see it is the same. Big, small, it does not matter, you must learn to use wrist, not fingers. Do you understand?"

"Yes."

"Figure drawing you must have, if you want to be artist. I will speak to Miss Williams."

"Let's try something different," Miss Williams said to him the next day. She took the paper off his easel and handed him another sheet. It was torn off a roll like the other, but it was white and faintly glossy. When he had pinned it up, she gave him a cup of black paint and a soft round brush.

Almost from the first, he discovered a new freedom with the brush and paint. He was not tempted to use the brush like a pen; he could stand away from the easel and let the brush move by itself. His drawings were no longer cramped and tight; they were not so accurately detailed, either, but he liked them better because there was a sense of volume in them. When he was interested in something, the hands, for instance, he allowed himself to make them bigger, out of proportion, and yet they seemed right. "Now *that's* a lot better," said Miss Williams, and he was filled with a gratitude and love that choked him.

Every other month he measured himself against the wall with a book, not the way most people do, balancing the book on the top of the head, but in the proper way, using the book as a carpenter's square pressed firmly against the head and the wall. He marked his height each time, and dated the marks. Each one was a little more than three-eighths of an inch higher than the last; he was growing at the rate of two and a half inches a year.

He was sprouting hair in unexpected places, and he discovered that he had to wash oftener than before, especially his armpits, or he would smell. One morning when he lay naked on his bed after a shower, his penis stiffened, rose, and began twitching in a slow rhythm. He watched this phenomenon with interest until it stopped. The third or fourth time it happened, a few weeks later, he touched his penis curiously, feeling how the thin skin slid up and down as if it were not attached at all. After a few moments, to his utter astonishment, his penis stiffened convulsively and a spurt of milky fluid came out. The pleasure he felt at the same moment was so intense that he knew instinctively it must be wrong.

He bought a book about sex and discovered that masturbation, or "self-abuse," would weaken your system or even drive you insane; but he kept on doing it anyhow.

One afternoon Madame Porgorny stopped him in the hall. "You are thin," she said critically, holding him at arm's length. "You do not eat enough. Come to my house for dinner, tomorrow at eight o'clock." She took a pad from the pocket of her smock, scrawled an address.

Gene was alarmed by this invitation but dared not refuse. After school the next day he washed and put on clean clothes. The address she had given him was an apartment house on Nob Hill. By the time he got there he was already very hungry; ordinarily he would have eaten dinner an hour ago. In the lobby he found her name ornately lettered on a card, with another name under it:

Mme. Evgenia Porgorny
Mlle. Vasilisa Tershchova

Above, the door was opened by a heavy gray-haired woman in an apron; her face was very wide, her eyes narrow and shrewd. She smiled when she saw him. "Come in." Her accent was even thicker than Madame Porgorny's.

She urged him through a narrow hall cluttered with dark furniture into a living room where Madame Porgorny sat in a blue dress, her hair done up tidily for once. "Ah, Stephen," she said. "Sit down. This is Vasilisa, she does not speak English very well."

"No English," the woman agreed, with a broad smile. "Welcome. Sit down."

"I'm glad to know you," Gene said.

"Welcome," she repeated. "Good." She patted him once on the shoulder, then turned and left the room.

"You are hungry?" Madame Porgorny demanded.

"Yes, a little."

"Good. Dinner will be very soon. Do you like our apartment?"

Gene looked around him politely. All the furniture was heavy, dark, and old; there were many pictures in gold frames, lamps with tasseled shades, china figurines. "It's very nice. Have you lived here long?"

"Sixteen years. We came from Paris in nineteen thirty-nine.

Now any longer you could not find such an apartment." She picked up a fluted glass and drank the last few drops of something pale as water, then called through the doorway. The other woman's voice answered.

"Come," said Madame Porgorny, "now you will see how Russians eat." She led him into a dining room where a table was set for three. Vasilisa came in carrying a soup tureen; when she lifted the domed cover, fragrant steam came out. She ladled the soup into their bowls; it was dark red, almost the color of blood, with things floating in it.

"What kind of soup is this?" Gene asked. "It's very good," he added, although it tasted like beets.

"It is *borshch*, made from beets and other things." She exchanged a few rapid words with Vasilisa. "This kind is from the Ukraine. It is with vegetables and *kolbasa*—that is the sausage. I myself know nothing about it," she added. "My mother would never let me enter the kitchen, but Vasilisa knows all. Everything."

The other woman beamed. "You like?"

"It's very good." And, in fact, he thought he was getting used to it.

Vasilisa took away the bowls and brought in a huge pastry, then three other dishes. The pastry turned out to be filled with salmon and mushrooms; it was meltingly delicious. With it they ate little carrot patties covered with a pale sauce; golden poppy-seed rolls; and some green vegetable cooked so thoroughly that it was like a pudding. Gene had a tall glass of milk, but the other two drank wine. For dessert they had triangular pastries filled with fruit and nuts.

"Now we will have coffee in the living room," Madame Porgorny announced. Gene's coffee was in a cup, but Madame Porgorny had hers in a glass. "So, did you have enough to eat?" she asked him. Gene smiled; he was stuffed so full that he felt he could barely move. "Good. You are still growing; you must eat, eat, to grow strong. Come into the light." She led him to a little table and sat down opposite him.

"You are a very strange young man," she said, and took his arm. "See here, not a blemish. For everyone is something, a mole, freckle, but for you, nothing. Show me your teeth." Feeling like a fool, Gene opened his mouth wide. "So," she said, peering in. "Perfect. Even if I looked at you all over, I believe I would find nothing. Don't worry, I am not going to do it. Sit down.''

She took a worn deck of cards out of the drawer in the table and began to shuffle them in her swollen fingers. The cards had designs Gene had never seen before: men and women in antique costumes, castles, lions, flowers.

"Have you ever had your fortune told? No?" She spread the cards, picked out one and laid it by itself on the table. "This is you." It was a young man in tights with a feather in his cap. She shuffled the cards again, handed them to him. "Cut. No, with your left hand, toward me, in three piles.''

She took the cards back, dealt one on top of the other. "This is what covers you.'' Another, crosswise, on top of the first two. "This, what crosses you." She dealt four more in a cross-shape around the center. "This is behind you—your past. This below, this above, this ahead of you.''

She dealt four more cards in a vertical row to the right of the center. "Here are three major trumps. That is very unusual in reading for a young person. Their cards are always wishy-washy, not this, not that. For you, the cards are not wishy-washy. Also, here are many swords, covering you, crossing you, behind you. You have left a home where you were safe and protected, is that not so?''

"Yes," said Gene. His throat was dry. He stared with fascination at the cards, the woman's face, her swollen fingers.

"There was a struggle with an older man. It is not over yet. Ahead of you—the Sun. That is wealth; you will be very rich. Do you think that will make you happy?''

"Yes." Gene smiled.

"No, it will not. Now here again, this is you—the Hermit. Wealth will not be enough for you, you will also seek wisdom. The next card is your life now: you are satisfied, but you will not be for long. Next, this is what you wish for yourself. It is very little. You will discover that you want more. And this is your future—the third major trump. It is Justice.''

"I don't understand what that means.''

"Later you will." She gathered the cards, tapped them straight, put them back into the deck.

"Could you read the cards again, Madame Porgorny? About the older man you said was against me?''

"Yes, if you wish, and then no more. It is not good to read them too often." This time she found the knight of swords and put it down, then shuffled and dealt as before. He recognized two of the cards besides the first one—the young man with the feather in his cap, and the man with the row of cups.

"He wants to settle something that is unfinished. It has to do with you—here is your card, do you see? He cannot settle it because of money—either he has not enough or you have too much. Here he is beginning to plan something, and here"—she tapped the lowest card—"this is the Moon, the card of deception. That is how he will do it. Here before him is the Fool, he will not succeed." She studied the row of four cards on the right. "This is the man himself, he has suffered a terrible loss. He is strong, he has everything on his side. Here is his wish, it is for dominion, for mastery. And—this I do not understand—he will achieve wholeness."

Chapter Seven

Cooley was disappointed in Los Angeles; he spent a week there, going to art schools and asking questions, but found no trace of the boy. He drove north to San Francisco, checked into a hotel. The next morning, he got a city map at the desk, then went to a phone booth and tore out the page of the directory that listed "Schools—Private." Seventeen of the listings seemed to have something to do with art. In his room, he called them one by one, found out their hours, and divided them into districts with the aid of the map.

That afternoon he visited the Academy of Fine and Useful Arts, the Adams Free Expression Art School, the Beacon Hill Art Centre, and the Co-op Art School. His procedure was always the same. He told the registrar, "My name is Andrew McDonnel, the painter—maybe you've seen my work? Well, it don't matter. Now I'm looking for a particlar kind of model, very particlar—the model agencies, they don't have what I want."

"What kind of a model, Mr. McDonnel?"

"Has to be a young boy, not more than, say, fifteen or sixteen, but he has to be tall. Now I thought maybe one of your students wouldn't mind earning a little extra money—?"

Then the registrar would open her record book and frown, and say something like, "No, we don't have anybody that young, I'm afraid. Here's a girl, but she's seventeen." And Cooley would thank her and say good-bye.

On the second day, at the Devonshire Gallery and Art School, the woman at the desk told him they had a student,

61

Bob Young, who was sixteen, and she thought he was tall, although she really couldn't remember. Cooley asked when he could see the boy.

"Well, he's down here for Oil Painting on Thursday evenings at eight o'clock—that's tomorrow. You could come and talk to him then."

Cooley said, "That's funny. I used to know a Young. Wonder if it's the same one. Does he live on Lincoln Way, by any chance?"

"No, Eleventh Avenue—four twenty-five Eleventh."

Cooley looked up Youngs in the telephone book, and there was one at that address. The kid couldn't have been here long enough to get in the phone book, but there was just a chance that he had got himself adopted by somebody, or maybe he was living with a family and using their name at school.

He was across the street having his shoes shined at a quarter to eight the next day. He watched the students go in, first one, then three together, then a bunch. About half were college-age kids, the other half middle-aged women. There was one younger boy—tall, sallow, black-haired. Cooley crossed the school off his list.

On Saturday, at the second place he tried, the woman said, "Why, yes, we do have a boy that age. Let's see, he's fifteen. Stephen Miller, and he is quite tall."

"Funny, I have an old friend named Miller—wonder if it's the same one. Does he live on Lincoln Way?"

"What is it?" asked a loud voice behind him. He turned; it was a tall woman with an imposing bust and a black ribbon for her glasses; she was staring at him as if he were a burglar. "We don't give out addresses of our students," she said in a strong accent. "Why are you asking such questions?"

Cooley started his set speech all over again, but she interrupted him. "McDonnel? I have never heard of you. Go away, or I will call the police." Her voice carried very well; as he left, Cooley could hear her saying, "Miss Olney, we must be on our guard against perverts of all descriptions, *constantly* on our guard."

He got into the Buick and thought it over. The kid would lie about his age, naturally, and fifteen would be about the most he could get away with. The first class was at one; he had found out that much on the phone, and it was a quarter after twelve now. He lit a cigar and settled himself to wait.

After about ten minutes a cab pulled up in front of the

school; the driver went inside. In a moment he was back with a woman, the same one—the dragon who had caught him at the desk. She had her coat on, and a funny hat perched on top of her hair. Cooley's first thought was that he was in luck—he could go in and talk to the registrar again and maybe find out something. Then he thought: where is she going, half an hour before school starts?

"There you are, ma'am," the driver said.

Madame Porgorny peered out. "This? You are sure?" It was a corner house, two stories, painted blue, with a porch and a fanlight.

"Twenty-one eighteen," the driver said. "Right there over the door."

Madame Porgorny paid him and walked up the porch steps. Through the glass pane of the door she could see a little foyer and four mailboxes. She stepped inside and read the cards. One of them, in careful ballpoint lettering, said "Stephen Miller, 2A."

She climbed the stairs and knocked. The door opened; the boy stood there with his shirt half buttoned. "Madame Porgorny," he said. He looked startled.

"Let me come in, please."

He said awkwardly, "Oh, sure," and stood aside. "I was just getting ready to come to school. Is something the matter?" Books and magazines were everywhere, on the couch, two of the three chairs, on the floor.

She turned to face him. "Stephen, the man you spoke of, the one who wants to do you harm, is he a short man, strong, with a red face?"

The boy had gone pale. "Did you see him?"

"He was at the school, looking for you."

"Oh." He sat down.

"Now you must tell me, Stephen, what does that man want?"

"I think he wants to kill me," the boy muttered.

"The police, would they protect you from him?"

"No. He—he is the police." He looked at her. "I did something bad, Madame Porgorny, but I didn't mean to."

"And your parents?"

"They couldn't help me."

"So. Well, then," she said, "I will ask you no more questions, but you must go away. And you must not go to art school any more, because that is how he found you." She opened her purse. "Do you have money?"

"Yes."

"Take this anyway, you may need more." She held out fifty dollars. When he shook his head, she pressed the money into his hand. "Do not be foolish."

"Well—I'll send it back to you."

"No, you must not. You must not tell me where you are going, and you must not write to me, or to anyone. Do you understand?"

"Yes."

She looked at him: so tall, but so terribly young. She wanted to hold him for a moment, kiss him on the forehead, but she knew how much he would hate that, and then she would have to wipe off the lipstick. "Good-bye then, Stephen. Be very careful."

"Good-bye, Madame Porgorny."

She went down the stairs more slowly than she had gone up. How could it happen that a child so young should be hunted like a criminal? And what would happen to him now, without friends, alone?

As she turned away from the house she saw a big car parked across the street, and in it a red-faced man. Her heart trembled, and she stopped, afraid to look again. In God's name, what was she to do? If she went back into the house he would know, and if she kept walking— She opened her purse blindly, fumbled in it to gain time, and the ghost of a plan came to her. She closed the purse, turned back with her mouth set angrily. She did not look across the street. He must believe I have left something behind, she told herself. Let him believe it.

She entered the house, climbed the stairs, knocked at the door again. "Stephen, it is I, Madame Porgorny."

He opened the door, looking startled. He had a shopping bag in his hand. "What's the matter?"

"Let me come in. Close the door. Stephen, he is here—that man. He is waiting downstairs in a car. My poor boy, it is my fault. He must have followed me. I led him to you. My God, let us think. Is there a back way from the house?"

"Yes, but—it comes out the side. Would he see me there?"

She thought a moment. "Yes. He is sitting where he can see down both streets. I must lead him away, but how is it possible?"

"I don't know." Something new had come into the boy's

expression; his mouth was firmer, his eyes narrowed. It was a look she did not like to see.

"Wait, Stephen," she said, "there must be a way. My brain is dead. Think, think!" She rubbed her eyes. "Tell me, is there a place where you could hide, not here, but in this house?"

"There's a closet under the stairs."

"Good. Now listen to me. You must hide there, and when you hear us going up the stairs, you must go out quietly and then run as fast as you can. Do you understand?"

"Yes." His expression had softened; he took both her hands. "Madame Porgorny—"

"I know, my poor boy, I know." She let him hold her hands, even though it hurt her swollen fingers. After a moment they did not hurt quite so much. "Thank you for doing this for me," he said.

"It is nothing. And now it is really good-bye. Remember all I have told you."

"Good-bye, Madame Porgorny. I'll remember."

In her mind she rehearsed her part as she went down the stairs. Something terrible has happened, she told herself, I am *bouleversée*, hysterical, but I must not overplay it, he must be convinced.

She opened the front door and stepped out, looking wildly around. "Help!" she cried. She looked again, saw the man in the car as if for the first time, and ran toward him. He was opening the door.

"You!" she said. "Why are you here? What do you want? Never mind, you must help me. The boy is ill—he fell down, he is not breathing."

"Did he faint or what?" the red-faced man asked, following her.

"I do not know. It was like a seizure—suddenly he fell down, and his face so white!" She was toiling up the stairs.

"Which door is it?"

"There. That one."

The red-faced man tried the knob, then knocked and listened. "He may be dying!" cried Madame Porgorny.

"Who locked the door, for Christ sake?"

"I must have done it, when I ran out. My God, what a horrible thing!"

"Hell," said the red-faced man. He stepped back, raised his foot, kicked the door below the lock. A panel splintered. He kicked it again and again until a jagged piece fell into the room. He reached inside, grunting, and opened the door.

She watched him as he went through the cluttered rooms. "He's not here," he said, coming back to her. His face had turned a darker red, and his lips were moist. For a moment she thought he might strike her.

"Stephen, where are you?" she cried, running out into the hall. "Ah, my heart!" She clutched herself, stumbled, and managed to fall at the head of the stairs, sprawled across the way.

"Hell!" said the red-faced man, stepping over her gingerly. She made it as difficult for him as she could; he almost fell, but recovered himself and went running down the stairs. When she got to the street, she heard the tires of his big car squealing as it turned the corner.

Madame Porgorny hailed a cab on the avenue and went back to the school. The plumber was there, making his usual mess, and the janitor was not to be found; the clay for the ceramics class had not come; there was a bill from the electrician that she had already paid. She had enough to keep her busy all day, and it was not until evening, when she was sitting down to dinner, that she realized the swelling in her fingers was entirely gone and that there was no pain.

Chapter Eight

Later Gene Anderson remembered two things about his trip across the country: the Grand Canyon, and a carnival in Columbus, Ohio. The carnival was a sort of traveling amusement park, set up in a vacant lot near the railroad station. He rode the Ferris wheel and the loop-the-loop, ate hot dogs, corn on the cob, and pink cotton candy. Then the cries of a sideshow barker drew him, and he went in.

First they saw the Lizard Man. He was about thirty, partly bald, with expressionless eyes. When he took off his red robe, they saw that his body was covered with shiny scales that looked like a snake's molted skin. "His mother was frightened by a boa constrictor before he was born, ladies and gentlemen. Scientists said it couldn't happen, but here he is, before your very eyes, ladies and gentlemen, one of the Eight Wonders of the World, the Lizard Man, condemned to go through life with the skin of a reptile."

Next was the Fat Lady, and after her the Human Pincushion, who put long needles through his cheeks and tongue, then lay down on a bed of nails with a fifty-pound weight on his chest.

After him was the Bearded Lady, who was bearded all over her face (not just on one half, as in the painting outside). Then came the giant. He sat in a thronelike chair on a little platform, a pale man in a business suit, with wispy dark hair and spectacles. His shoes were like anybody else's, black leather, a little scuffed around the toes, but they were twice as big as any shoes Gene had ever seen before. He took off the gold ring on his finger and the barker showed them that two of his own fingers would fit into it. As he was buying a brass copy of this ring for fifty cents, Gene saw the giant looking at him with a curious expression: he smiled faintly, then closed his eyes and turned his head away.

Out in the midway, Gene was stopped by a man who wore tan denims, with riding boots and a baseball cap. "Hey, kid, how old are you?"

"Twelve," said Gene before he thought.

"Yeah?" The man looked him over. "Well, if you grow another two feet, come and see me." He handed Gene a card and walked away.

Then he was in New York, and it was like coming home to a paradise he had only dreamed of. There were miles of shops, bookstores, galleries; even San Francisco was nothing to this. He rented an apartment in Chelsea. For weeks he saw a different movie every day. He bought books, art supplies, a record player, a television set; he bought Oriental rugs of incredible shimmering colors.

At first it did not bother him that he had no friends or even acquaintances in New York; he liked the feeling of anonymity, invisibility. As long as the golden summer lasted, the city was cheerful; in the autumn it turned melancholy. The first snowfall exhilarated him, but its brilliant whiteness turned overnight to brown freezing slush.

He bought galoshes, a hat, gloves, an overcoat, and a muffler. The overcoat was an absurd garment that could not be closed at the neck, and the muffler did not keep out the bitter wind. Darkness flowed down the streets, and the raw-nosed people walked bending against it, holding their lapels together at the neck. Indoors, in restaurants and theaters, the yellow light made people look feverish. This was not winter as he had known it; it was a nordic underworld.

In a bookstore he found a copy of Sigmund Freud's *Totem and Taboo*, and his world was turned around. He discovered that religion was the delusion of people afraid to face the fact that they must die. The universe became a vast indifference, not a screen with God's baleful eye peering through it. When he saw people coming out of a church, he looked at them with amused contempt.

In December he saw an ad for a private detective agency in a newspaper: "Confidential, reasonable rates." He wrote to them, paid the deposit they required, and six weeks later received a letter on their stationery.

Dear Sir:

Our operative went to Dog River, Oregon on January 13, 1958 as per your request and consulted the current telephone directory for the names Cooley, Tom or Thomas, Anderson, Donald R. and Anderson, Mildred. No listings were found for these names; however, listings were found for Cooley, Ernest, Anderson, B. Walter, Anderson, Billy, Anderson, D. W., Andersen, Sylvia, and Andersen, Olaf.

Consulting previous telephone directories at the public library, no listings were found for Cooley, Tom or Thomas, or Anderson, Donald R. later than the year 1955.

The operative then proceeded to the Dog River Post Office and inquired as to Donald R. Anderson. The postmaster informed him that said Donald R. Anderson and wife Mildred moved to Chehalis, Washington in 1955. The operative also inquired as to the present whereabouts of Thomas Cooley, and was informed that said Cooley left the state in 1957 and his whereabouts were unknown.

The operative then contacted the pastor of the Riverside Church, Rev. Floyd Metcalfe Williams, who stated that Mr. and Mrs. Donald R. Anderson were members of his congregation from 1940–1955, when they moved to Chehalis, Washington, and further stated that he believed said Mr. and Mrs. Anderson lost their lives in a fire in 1956. The operative then proceeded to Chehalis, Washington and confirmed . . .

Gene put the letter down. There were two more paragraphs: ". . . house fire of undetermined origin . . . bill for services enclosed . . . your esteemed favor . . ."

He remembered, as if it were something he had read in a book, the house in Dog River and the yard around it, the smells of crushed grass and earth, the cracked sidewalk, his father's tired face, his mother setting the table. He remembered himself in that house, the wrong size, the wrong age, and yet it was not himself, it was a boy who did not exist anymore, who had died and been reborn outside the tree house in the woods. All those bright pictures belonged to another life; they were gone now; it didn't matter.

That night he dreamed about his parents, but it was not a

true dream like the one he had had in the tree house; his mother and father were in some dark place and they were trying to talk to him, to tell him something, but when their lips moved there was no sound.

He had other dreams in which Paul Cooley was alive, although he was dead at the same time, in the way that opposites often existed together in dreams; Paul was confronting him with his bulging eyes and slobbery lip, saying, "You pushed me out the window!" And Gene was trying to explain that he really hadn't, or hadn't meant to, and all the time he knew he was lying. Then sometimes he woke up, and sometimes he drifted down from the window and touched Paul's body with his hands; and then Paul was alive, and he rose and walked away. And for some reason, these were the most terrible dreams of all.

One day, in a gallery on Fifth Avenue, he saw an astonishing thing—a quasi-human figure made up of blocky forms that seemed to be melting from crystals of metal into metal flesh. The face was a mask, the limbs bulged like an insect's. It was dark bronze, about fourteen inches high. It stood in a dancer's posture, speaking of power under intense control. The card on the pedestal said, "Hierophant, Manuel Avila."

"How much is that?" he asked.

The attendant, a bony young man whose suit and tie were gray, gave him an appraising glance. "That," he said, "is three thousand dollars."

"Three *thousand*?" Gene looked at the figure again. After a moment he said, "I'll take it."

The young man's eyebrows went up. "Very well, sir, will you step this way?"

At the little desk in the back he produced a sales slip and began to fill it in. "Do you have some identification, Mr. Davis?"

"Not with me, no, but I'd like to leave you a deposit now and I'll bring you a certified check later."

"That will be perfectly fine."

"I'd like to meet Mr. Avila sometime. Does he live here in town?"

"Yes, sir. He's in the phone book, actually, but let me write it down for you."

Chapter Nine

"Hello." A deep, impatient voice.

"Can I speak to Mr. Avila, please?"

"This is Avila."

"Mr. Avila, my name is John Davis. I bought your *Hierophant* at the Otis Gallery yesterday."

"Oh, yeah. I heard about that."

"I was wondering, could I come and see your studio? Maybe look at some of your other work?"

"Sure, why not. You know where it is? Come down about five o'clock. Listen, the bell doesn't work. Walk up the stairs, fourth floor. What's your name again?"

"John Davis."

"Okay. See you then."

The address was in a row of dingy, seemingly abandoned commercial buildings on the Lower East Side. The plate-glass window beside the entrance was lettered, "BELLER RESTAURANT SUPPLY," but the interior was dark and empty, and there were cobwebs on the windows.

Gene climbed three flights of uncarpeted echoing stairs and found himself on a landing with a single door painted dark green. A card on the door was neatly lettered, "AVILA." He rang the bell.

"Come in!" called a distant voice.

Gene opened the door and found himself looking down the length of an enormous room, in the middle of which three people sat near an oil heater with a stovepipe that rose, supported by guy wires, through the ceiling high above. Dust motes swam in the gray light from the window wall. "Mr. Davis?" called the voice. The men's faces were in shadow; he could not see which one had spoken.

"Yes."

One of the men stood up and beckoned. "Come in, sit down." Gene walked toward them, trying not to trip over the electrical wires that lay haphazardly on the bare floor. The man who had spoken was stocky, powerfully built, with a seamed brown face. "I'm Avila," he said, putting out his hand. "Sit here. Put your coat on the floor, wherever you want. This is Darío Hernandez"—a young man who put down his guitar to rise and shake Gene's hand; he was as brown as Avila, handsome and bright-eyed. "And this is Gus Vilsmas— Vilis—how the hell you say it?"

"Vlismas," said the third man. He was paler than the others, middle-aged and plump, with a gold tooth that flashed when he smiled. "Glad to know you."

Gene sat in a wooden rocker that creaked under his weight. The others were staring at him. "You're tall, but you're only a kid," said Avila abruptly. "You want some wine? Maybe you're not old enough to drink it."

"No, that's all right," Gene said, flushing. "I just wanted —Could I look around your studio?"

"Sure." Avila stood up. "Come on, I give you the grand tour."

Under the windows there were big bins for clay, sacks of plaster spilling their white dust on the floor, and a cluttered bench that ran half the length of the room.

"I never saw any place as big as this before," Gene said.

"It's a loft," Avila told him. His voice was deep and resonant. "Before, they use them for manufacturing—some places you can still see where the machines were."

Farther down the room there was a large wooden platform on wheels; between it and the windows stood three modeling stands, one of them draped in moist cloth. "Is this something you're working on?" Gene asked.

"Sure. You like to see it?" Avila lifted the bottom of the cloth and carefully pulled it free of the damp clay. Gene saw a blocky figure, contorted, half kneeling. Parts of the surface were lumps of clay carelessly mashed together; other parts showed the marks of tools. "Not finished yet," said Avila, and draped the cloth over it again.

The end of the room was a warren of head-high racks on which stood plaster casts, plaster of paris molds, some of them three or four feet tall, and armatures made of wood, pipe, and wire.

The two men in the middle of the room looked up as they passed going the other way, then resumed their low-voiced conversation. This end of the room evidently was Avila's living quarters. There was a kitchen area with a hot plate and a coffee pot, some cabinets, a sink and a clawfooted bathtub. Under the windows, a small area had been partitioned off with plywood painted bright yellow; through the doorway Gene could see a bed with a red-and-white coverlet. "I had a guest room," Avila said, "but I tore it down. Some bum was always sleeping in there, or some guy making out with his girl. You want coffee?"

Avila poured from the coffee pot into a blue ceramic mug. They joined the others and sat down.

"So, Mr. Davis," said Vlismas, "you are an art collector? Your parents must be rich."

"They died in a plane crash. I have a trust fund."

"Oh, too bad. So you spend your money on art?"

"Sometimes."

Avila was sitting in an upholstered chair with a glass of wine in his hand, one leg draped over the arm of the chair. He looked at Gene steadily. "Is that all you do?" he asked.

"No—I want to be an artist. A sculptor like you, Mr. Avila. I was wondering, do you think—would it be possible for you to take me as a student? I could pay you whatever—"

"So, you could pay," Avila said. "Mr. Davis, I am not a teacher. There are plenty of good schools where you could study."

"I can't go there," said Gene with embarrassment. "I have a kind of problem, with places where there are a lot of people."

Avila looked at him in silence for a moment. "Where have you studied already?"

"At the Porgorny Institute, in San Francisco."

"Porgorny? I know her!" said Avila. "Ten years ago I met her there. How is she?"

"All right, I guess. I haven't talked to her since I left. Mr. Avila, I brought some sketches—" He picked up his coat from the floor, drew out a sketchbook.

"Let me see." Avila took the book and began to turn the pages. Presently he showed one page to Hernandez, who leaned over to look at it but said nothing. Avila leafed through the rest of the book and handed it back. *"¿Que piensas?"* he said to Hernandez.

The young man shrugged. *"No sé."*

"One thing I like," said Avila after a moment. "Some of these drawings, I think you are seeing solid forms when you make them. That is not so common. What have you done in sculpture?"

"Some clay. Piece molds. A few wood carvings."

"I tell you what. We try it for a month. You come here every day, whatever time you want, but not before nine o'clock and not after five, and you work here at least four hours every day. You pay me one hundred dollars for the month. If I ask you to do something, you do it. After the first month, if I like it, if you like it, we continue. If not—goodbye. All right?"

"Yes, that's wonderful. When can I start—tomorrow?"

"Sure, tomorrow."

When he came the next day, precisely at nine o'clock, Avila gave him a modeling stand at the far end of the room near the windows, showed him the clay bins, the shelves of armatures, the racks of tools. Gene chose a wooden armature and began to build up a simple bust, the head of a bald old man. The piece went slowly, because it was hard to keep from watching Avila at work. He moved like a dancer, weight on the balls of his feet, forward and backward in a hypnotic rhythm—adding clay with one hand, cutting it away again with a metal tool in the other; and as he worked, the clay figure evolved through a sequence of organic changes, all different and all beautiful.

When the phone rang Avila would answer it briefly; if it rang too often he would take the receiver off the hook. At noon he brought out bread and cheese, sliced yellow onions, hot peppers, milk for Gene and wine for himself. While he ate, he looked at what Gene had been doing, but made no comment.

In late afternoon people began dropping in, and when Gene got up to go at five, Avila said, "Stick around. After while we all go out to dinner."

Avila's friends and hangers-on were numerous: there was a

cigar-smoking half-Korean silversmith and his father, a white-bearded painter and calligrapher; a plump, short-haired woman ceramicist who was interested in kundalini yoga; several jazz musicians, a poet, a man who owned a sandal shop. The most frequent visitor was Darío Hernandez, who was from Uruguay. He was an expert in building large armatures and in scaling up figures; Avila had no work for him now, but gave him small sums of money when he asked for it. Darío had a girl-friend, Peggy Wood, a ripe young woman with a sullen mouth and a mane of dark-blond hair; they were married or living together, Gene was not sure which. Often in the evening they came together to the loft, but other times Darío came alone, and when Gene left he was still there.

Peggy Wood's clothing surrounded her like a loose cocoon: she wore heavy sweaters and skirts within which her body moved with slow grace. In her silences there was something that was all the heavier for being unspoken. Sometimes Gene glanced up and found her looking at him with an expression that made him uneasy.

It was not clear what Gus Vlismas' principal occupation was. He had various things for sale, which he carried around in his pockets: sometimes gold rings and pendants, sometimes small Japanese carvings in wood or ivory. He was a silent partner in various business enterprises. He knew where to buy almost anything at a discount; he could fix traffic tickets.

One evening he unfolded a little packet of white paper and showed Gene the heap of tiny stones it contained. "You should buy diamonds," he said. "Diamonds are the world's best investment. They always go up, never down."

"I don't like diamonds."

"You don't *like* diamonds?" The gold tooth showed in an incredulous smile. "What do you like?"

"Opals. Star sapphires, things like that. I like some of the semiprecious stones—agates, jasper."

"Do you know, my young friend, how much a flawless one-carat diamond is worth today?"

"I don't care how much it's worth."

One morning Gene saw an envelope on the table; it had a foreign stamp, and was addressed to "Sr. Manuel Avila O." "What's the *O* for?" he asked.

"O-eenz," said Avila, and spelled it: "O, apostrophe, h, i, g, i, n, s. That is my name, Manuel Avila O-eenz, but if I use it here, they call me Mister O'*Higg*ins." Avila's father, he said, had emigrated to Colombia from Mexico; his mother belonged to an old Colombian family, descended from Irish settlers. "On my father's side, too, there is Irish blood. So I am maybe one-quarter Spanish, one-half *indio*, one-quarter Irish. Here they call me a mick-spick."

He had studied at the National University in Bogotá, and later in Mexico City, where he had known Orozco and Rivera. He had also worked as a stone-cutter in Yucatán for a sculptor named Obregón. He had lived in many places; he talked with nostalgia of Rome, London, Paris.

"If you liked it there so much, why did you come to New York?"

He shrugged. "The money is here, and besides, I like New York because it is crazy. Other places crazy too, but not like this. Everything is sex, the toothpaste is sex, but there is no sex, only frustration. To me is like a big machine making energy that goes in the air. I am here now seven years, and still I get excited when I walk on the street."

Avila and Darío spoke together sometimes in English, more often in rapid soft Spanish. After a while Gene began to pick up the sense of what they were saying. Darío, who had a streak of malice, never used Gene's name when he was talking to Avila: he called him *el pollito*, "the little chicken."

One afternoon when he heard Darío use this phrase, Gene turned from his modeling and said, *"No soy pollito."*

The two looked at him in astonishment. Avila said, *"Así, ¿hablas español?"*

"Un poco."

"Bueno." Avila turned to Darío and said something Gene did not quite catch, and they both laughed; but there was a glint of anger in Darío's eye when he looked at Gene. After that he began to use other nicknames: *polla*, which was like *pollito*, only more insulting because it was feminine; *maricón*, which Gene understood to be more insulting still, although he could not make out what it meant even after he had looked it up in Avila's Spanish-English dictionary. When Darío spoke to Gene directly, he was polite, even friendly, but always with an edge of mockery in his voice.

Presently Avila began correcting Gene's grammar when he spoke Spanish. Gene read the books Avila gave him, and discovered in himself an appetite for words. He began to realize that a language was not just a set of arbitrary symbols but a way of looking at the world; there were things that could be said in Spanish very easily and simply that could be said in English only with difficulty, or not at all; and it was the same the other way around. It took six words in Spanish to say "flush the toilet," but there was a single word that meant "to dig around the roots of vines."

When Gene's clay figure was done, Avila came over and looked at it, turned the stand to see the other side, turned it back. The head was simple and stylized; Gene had made it a bald old man in order to emphasize the domed shape of the skull, and also to avoid the problems of hair. He had built up the head with bits of clay, then smoothed them with his fingers until all the curves flowed into one another: the arched nose, the cheekbones, the brow.

Avila said, "This your idea of an old man? Jesus Christ!" He dug his strong fingers into the clay, pulled it off in great lumps, threw it back in the bin. "Take your sketchbook, go over to Washington Square, for God's sake, draw some old men."

Gene dutifully went out with the sketchbook, came back with many drawings, and started afresh. When the second piece was done, Avila said, "Better? A little, maybe." He threw the clay in the bin.

Gradually he came to understand what Avila meant by art: it was a flowering of form that could only come about by working and reworking the material until the original shape had been transformed through many deaths and rebirths into something that had never existed before and could not have come into being except by this torment. A sculpture by Avila was a multidimensional object, shimmering with self-references, containing in itself the vanished forms of previous conceptions, and at the same time it was integral, itself and nothing more, as self-explanatory as a flower or a shell.

One morning he found Avila at his bench playing with some little brass shims, tilting them against each other to make tent-shapes, stacking others on top until they fell down. His eyes were vacant; he did not seem to be watching what his fingers were doing.

Later Gene saw him cutting the shims with a pair of tin-snips, making narrow rectangles of various sizes. After lunch he began cementing the pieces together to make curving shapes like staircases, or like fanned-out playing cards. At the end of the day he had assembled these into a standing hawk-headed figure, a bird-man or man-bird whose arms seemed in the process of turning into wings, or the wings into arms. The next day he took it apart and started over.

"That was beautiful," Gene said. "Why didn't you keep it?"

"Not what I want," Avila grunted. He spent the next two days building up another figure, larger and more complex than the other, and took it apart. The third version occupied him for a week. It had horns now, ending in little brass balls, and it stood in a half-crouching position as if prepared for flight.

The next day, while Gene watched in fascination, he made a two-piece rubber mold around the figure, then a plaster shell to cover the mold. When the plaster was dry, he took the shell and the mold apart, carefully inspected them, and put them back together. He melted beeswax in a pot, upended the mold in its shell, supporting it in a bucket of sand, and poured the hot wax in. After a few moments he poured it out again, leaving a thin coating on the inside of the mold. When he took the mold apart, he had a hollow wax image of the figure, but the tips of the horns were missing.

"No good," he said. "I worry about that." He broke up the wax, dropped it back into the pot and melted it again. This time, before he put the mold together, he brushed hot wax into the pieces that would make the horns. The wax image came out complete and perfect. Then for two days he worked with the wax, smoothing irregularities, sharpening edges with a knife, adding bits here and there.

"Couldn't you work in wax to begin with?" Gene asked.

"Sure, but the wax has to be hollow or there will be too much bronze, too heavy. Watch what I do now." He dipped his fingers into the cooling wax-pot, formed the soft wax into little balls, rolled them into cylinders. He carefully attached these to the figure to make vents and pipes. Two narrow ones went from the head to the tips of the horns. "If I don't do this," he explained, "the same thing will happen with the bronze. Better to make your mistakes in wax."

The pipes were to carry the molten bronze to various parts of the figure, and the vents were to allow air to escape.

"Otherwise you get bubbles. The first time I cast in bronze, there was a big bubble right in the belly. And a big pain in my belly, too. If you make a mistake, it's your fault, not the foundry, and you pay them just the same."

Avila made him build a clay figurine, then copy it in wood. The wood carving was a botch, because he had tried to follow the shape of the clay too faithfully. Avila smiled when he saw it. "Now you have learned something."

Another time Avila had him construct a wooden armature of soft pine, into which he had to drive curving rows of little brads until the armature bristled with them like the body of St. Sebastian. The heads of the brads, Avila explained, had to represent the surface of the clay figure he was to make; he would be allowed to cover them with a sixteenth of an inch of clay, no more; and for three days Gene turned the armature around and around while he stared at it, trying to visualize the clay volume which did not yet exist. Again and again he tapped some of the brads a fraction of an inch deeper, pulled others out and started over. When at last he added the clay, the figure was stiff, mechanical; he tore it apart himself, without waiting for Avila to do it, and threw the clay back in the bin. But from this, too, he learned something.

Chapter Ten

Corrupt and abrading, I desire your smoothness
You cool to my hot, tender to my rough
You integral, one curve, I channeled and weathered.
How can you know yourself if not through me?
Let me pay tribute under your skin
Before worm, rot and canker topple us both
Into the luxury of silence

—Gene Anderson

One evening in October there were six of them sitting around the oil stove—Avila, Gene, Darío and Peggy, Gus Vlismas and a girl he had brought; her name was Lillian. They were all bored and restless; rain was tapping the windows out of an ink-blue sky.

"Let's play *los cadáveres exquisitos*," said Darío, stubbing out his cigarette. *"¿Quieren?"*

"Oh, not that again," said Peggy without looking up. She was tearing a cigarette apart with her fingernails, dropping the shreds of tobacco into an ashtray and smoothing out the paper.

Darío turned on her. "Just because I say do it, you say no."

"God," she muttered. "Do it, then."

"I don't know what it is," Lillian said. "How do you play?"

"It's a game." Darío went to a cabinet, brought sketchpads

and handed them out. "Like this, you fold the paper in three parts, then in the top part you draw a head, any kind of head. You don't show anybody. Then you fold it over so nobody can see it, but you leave the neck showing, okay? Then the next person, he draws the body and folds it over, and the last one draws the legs."

Silence fell as they worked on their drawings. Gene drew the head of a snail with eyes on stalks, and put a top hat on it. He folded it, passed it to Avila. After a moment Lillian handed him her folded paper. Presently everyone was done with the heads except Darío.

"What are you doing, making a masterpiece?" Gus demanded. "Finish it already."

"Wait, be patient," Darío said. He was grinning with amusement.

Gene drew a bird's body with outspread wings; he folded it, leaving four short lines to show where the legs began, and passed it on.

Lillian handed over another folded paper; Gene drew two hairy legs with enormous feet. "Everybody finish?" Darío asked. "Come on, Peg."

"Just a *minute*. I'd be done now if you hadn't taken so long."

When they unfolded the pictures, it was easy to see who had done each part. Avila's drawings were bold, sketchy, and powerful, Darío's fussily detailed, Lillian's bland. The head Darío had drawn was a satiric portrait of Gene, with childish lips, eyes like a doll's. Under it Gus Vlismas had made a female torso with enormous dark-nippled breasts, and Peggy had given it chicken feet. Darío laughed until tears stood in his eyes. "Perfect!" he said. "Now whoever made the head has to give it a title."

They passed the papers around again. Under the snail head Gene had drawn was a seal's body wearing an old-fashioned collar and tie, and under that two barber-pole legs. He titled it "A Little More Off the Top."

Darío had entitled his portrait of Gene *El pollito sin huevos*, "little chicken without balls." Gene wanted to crumple it and throw it on the floor, but instead he passed it to Avila. Their eyes met; Avila shook his head slightly.

Darío leaned back and began talking to Gene about his work. "You always make figures of men, never women," he said. "Why is that? They don't have women models in life classes where you go?"

"No, they didn't."

"Maybe because they think it would make a scandal, if they let you see a naked woman."

"It's better to begin with the male body," Avila said. "If the man is well made, you see all the muscles very easily. In a woman they are covered up."

"That's true, Manolo, but still, how can a man be an artist who has never seen a woman?" He turned to Gene. "You should do a female nude in clay. Don't you think so, Gus?"

"Sure."

"What's wrong with right now?" Darío said, swinging around to Gene again. "Peggy here will pose for you—right, Peggy?"

She glanced up at him with a faint smile. After a moment she put out her cigarette. "Why not," she said.

"There, you see? How about it, kid, let's see how good you are."

"I'd have to make some sketches," Gene said. "I haven't got an armature."

"Armature?" cried Darío. He swung up out of his chair, crossed to the shelf, came back with a wire armature in his hand. "Here you are, just the thing, all ready." He set the armature down on a modeling stand. It was the skeletal framework of a human figure, standing with pelvis thrust out, hands on hips. Darío turned on the overhead lights, then crossed to the bin, came back with a lump of clay the size of a baseball, slapped it down on the base of the armature. "Clay and everything," he said. "See how easy we make it for you? Come on, Peggy."

"He doesn't need me for the first part," she said, still looking down at the ashtray.

Gene looked at Avila, who would not meet his eyes. "You do what you want," he said. "I'm going to bed." He got up and went around the bedroom partition.

"Okay, kid, let's go, we're waiting," said Darío.

Gene got up unwillingly and approached the modeling stand. He picked up the ball of clay, tore off a lump, pressed it into the wires where the figure's torso would be.

The others sat quietly and watched him while he built up the torso, the arms, legs, head. Once he heard Darío and Gus muttering together, then the sound of suppressed laughter.

The figure was roughed out, a crude sketch in clay.

"All set, Peggy?"

When he turned, she was standing up with a glass of wine in her hand. She drank the wine in one long swallow, set the tumbler down, and took off her sweater. She unbuttoned her blouse, pulled it down over her arms, laid it on top of the sweater. She unfastened her skirt and stepped out of it. The others were watching her silently. She reached behind her, unfastened her brassiere and removed it, then her panties. She sat down a moment to take off her shoes, then stepped up onto the dais and assumed the model's position, legs apart, pelvis forward, hands on her hips. Her heavy breasts rose and fell with her breathing; her hips swayed a little, almost imperceptibly, from side to side.

Always before, in life classes, there had been something entirely impersonal in the silence between the model and the students. This was not like that. Peggy's breasts, her pelvis, thrust themselves toward him with an insinuating provocation; as she swayed, the muscles of her thighs tensed and relaxed, tensed and relaxed.

Gene pulled off lumps of clay, began pressing them onto the figure to round out the thighs, hips, breasts. "Who's timing this?" Peggy asked after a moment.

"I am," Darío said. "You want to do half an hour?"

"Okay."

The others were muttering together; Gene could not make out the words, but he knew what they were saying. *Bet you ten bucks he comes in his pants.*

He concentrated on the work he was doing, the clay in his fingers. Gradually it got better. "Would you move your left foot a little?" he said.

"Which way?"

"Out. Yes, like that." He worked on the legs, trying to get the figure balanced properly, weight a little more on one leg than the other. The figure's breasts were too big; he pared them down with a wire tool, built them up again. "Turn around," he said.

Peggy turned her soft buttocks to him, took the pose again. "Like this?"

"Left foot out a little more. Little more forward. Okay."

The room was still. He blocked in the buttocks, built up the round muscles of the thighs.

"Time?" said Peggy after a while.

"Thirty-four minutes. Sorry, Peggy, I forgot to look."

She got down from the dais. "Hand me a robe, somebody." Gus got her a flannel dressing gown; she belted it on and came over to look at the figure. "Not bad," she said after a moment. "Am I as skinny as that?"

"I'd rather build it up than take it off," Gene said. Her scent was in his nostrils. "Anyhow, that's enough for one session."

"Ah, come on," said Darío loudly. "You're not tired, are you, Peg? The evening is early."

"I can do another half hour. Give me a cigarette first." She sat down on the edge of the dais, smoked a cigarette, and drank a glass of wine. Darío and Gus were arguing about something in low voices.

She stubbed the cigarette out, took off the robe again and stepped up on the dais. "Which way now?"

"Sidewise." He glanced at his watch. "Give me your left profile."

He worked on the figure, adding clay and taking it away, trying to get the cant of the torso right. "Elbow a little forward." Standing under the lights with her body in profile, she was no more now than a model; he could not see her eyes, but her expression had changed.

"Time," said Darío.

Peggy stretched, picked up her robe, and came down off the dais.

Darío and Gus were muttering together. "Listen," said Darío, "we're going down to Tony's and get a table. Come on down when you get dressed."

"Okay."

When they were gone, there was a deep silence in the loft. Gene became intensely aware of the darkness around the lights, the emptiness. Peggy was putting her underwear on. Gene sat on a high stool and watched her, unable to look away. She buttoned her blouse, stepped into her skirt and adjusted it, pulled her sweater over her head. She rummaged in her bag a moment, found a comb and pulled it through her hair. When she was done, she put the comb back, picked up a compact and lipstick. Staring intently into the little mirror, she carefully drew the shape of her upper lip. She closed the lipstick, dropped it and the compact into her open bag. She moved toward him, rubbing her lips together, then separating them with a smack.

"That's really not bad," she said, looking at the figure. She was standing so close to him that her hip touched his thigh; he could smell the scent of her lipstick. She turned to face him; now her expression had changed again. There was a faint smile on her lips, and her eyes were narrowed. "You don't like girls?" she asked.

"I like girls."

"Do you?" She moved still closer, and her hand came up between his legs. Gene tried to squirm away, but he was trapped by the stool and her body. "Don't—" he said. "Let me—" He put up his hand; she brushed it aside. She was standing so close now that her thighs were pressed against his, while her hand, between them, went on stroking him through the cloth. Gene realized suddenly that he could not hold back any longer, and then it was too late: he felt a painful contraction and a spurt of wetness.

She kept her hand there a moment longer, then patted him and moved away. Through a haze of tears, he saw her pick up her purse. When she was almost at the door, he said, "Why did you do that?"

She turned and looked at him across the loft. "I don't know," she said. "Sweet dreams." The door closed behind her.

Gene looked at the clay figure. He took it in both hands, squeezed the clay, ripped it off the armature and threw it in the bin. When he turned, Avila was standing there, his face mournful.

"John, I am so sorry," he said. "It is my fault, I should have prevented it."

Gene's muscles were twitching; a sob came up into his throat like a fist. "She—she—"

"I know." The older man's arm came warmly around him. "It was Darío, he does it to hurt me, and Peggy—maybe to hurt him, who knows? Come on." He led Gene to the sink at the end of the room. "Take your pants off." He ran water on a washrag, squeezed it, gently mopped away the stickiness on Gene's leg, then dried him with a towel. When Gene reached for his trousers, Avila said, "Leave them, they'll be dry in the morning. Come on." They were in the bedroom. "Now the shirt, I'm going to rub your back. Go ahead, take it off. Now lie down on your belly."

In a moment the mattress sagged with Avila's weight. "This is just some oil," his voice said. There was a shock of coolness between Gene's shoulders; then Avila's strong hands were kneading the muscles of his neck and shoulders, loosening and relaxing them, molding them as if his body were sculpture. The tension ebbed; Gene began to feel a delicious comfort and drowsiness.

The hands worked down his body, the arms, back, buttocks, legs, turning his flesh into butter. Half asleep, he felt his shoes and socks being pulled off, heard Avila say, "Now the other side."

He rolled over with an effort. Avila, straddling him again, began to knead his chest, his biceps, then his sides, belly, groin. When the first kiss came, it seemed natural and unsurprising.

Afterward Avila pulled the sheet over them and lay against his back in a warm embrace. "Now you can sleep," he said. "It's okay, *grandulón*. Sleep."

Chapter Eleven

Three days later, when he came into the loft early in the morning, Avila and Darío were sitting beside the stove and he heard their voices, low and serious. They did not look up as he came in. And as he stood watching them, Darío said in the same low voice, *"Me cago en tu lástima,"* I shit on your pity. He got up then and started toward the door; he looked through Gene as if he were not there, and as he passed, Gene saw that his eyes were blind with tears.

Later Avila said, "Don't worry about it. It is very bad, but there is nothing to be done."

After that Darío did not come any more; Avila said he had gone back to Uruguay. Peggy turned up once, with another man, at a party in the loft; Avila spoke to her briefly, and she left with her escort.

When the cold weather came, Avila and Gene moved their work space closer to the oil stove in the middle of the loft. It was never quite warm enough even there; the high ceiling drew the heat away, and cold drafts came from every side of the room. Often in the morning the big windows were frosted over, glittering in the sunshine like sheets of ice. There were fewer visitors now, and they worked in a quiet contentment, hardly speaking all day long.

On weekends, if the weather was clear, they took the bus uptown. They went to the Museum of Modern Art to see Tchelitchew's *Hide and Seek* and Calder's delicate mobiles, to the Guggenheim for Kandinsky. They toured the galleries together, and Avila made skeptical noises. There were no living sculptors he liked, and very few painters.

They looked at Greek and Roman sculpture in the Metropolitan, and Avila said, "Here is where most of the crap comes from. They paint their statues, bright colors, but when we dig them up the paint is gone, so for two thousand years we think sculpture has to be white. They make their sculptures to look *alive*, that's why they are so realistic in form, every proportion, every muscle, and what do we do? We make them look dead."

He had nothing but contempt for action painting and minimalist art. "A big mistake," he said. "In eighteen forty, they try to see if they can do without hard lines, invisible brush strokes and all that classical crap, so then everybody says, 'Oh, let's see what else we can do without.' First they do without perspective, then natural forms, then they do without drawing, and now if you get some house paint and paint a canvas gray, they call it art. Pretty soon the only thing left to do is leave the canvas blank."

In the evenings sometimes they went to the ballet with friends, or the theater, or to a movie. Avila was fond of the films of Chaplin and Buster Keaton that turned up occasionally at the Museum of Modern Art, or at the Apollo uptown; he could seldom be persuaded to go to a modern film. He liked everything that was choreographed, economical, and certain in movement; he detested the work of actors who were stars because they were handsome. "What you see makes what you are," he said. "Watch crap long enough, you are crap."

Sometimes when they had been to the Metropolitan Museum, or to a movie uptown, or to the Cloisters, they went back to Gene's apartment because it was closer than the loft. Avila's *Hierophant* was on the bookcase, and Gene saw him looking at it whenever he entered the room. One day he said, "Don't you ever wish you could keep things instead of selling them?"

Avila shrugged. "Sure, I wish. If I was a rich man, maybe I keep everything, like Picasso. Or if I was a bird I would fly."

"I could give you back this one," said Gene.

"No. You bought it, it is yours. Let's talk about something else."

Gene thought about it for a long time. Next week, when they entered the apartment, there were two *Hierophant*s on the coffee table. Avila stopped when he saw them. He looked at Gene, then at the two bronzes. "What is this?" he said. He walked forward, picked up one of the statues and examined it minutely, then the other.

"It's for you, a present," said Gene.

There was something haggard in Avila's expression. "But how did you do it?"

"I had it copied."

"Copied, what do you mean? A mold, then another casting in bronze? No." He turned the two statues on the coffee table. "The patina is the same. Here, these are the marks of my tools. And here, the same. No casting could do this. Don't tell me, I know."

With a sense that he had made a catastrophic blunder, Gene said, "It's my uncle, he has a special process—I don't know how it works."

"I want to meet your uncle. What is his name, where does he live?"

"He's my uncle Walter. He lives out on Long Island, but he doesn't see anybody except me. He's real old and kind of eccentric."

"Now, more than ever I want to meet this uncle. Tell me his address, I write him a letter."

"No, I can't, Manolo; I promised."

Avila looked at him a moment. "You are lying, aren't you."

Gene did not reply.

"There is no uncle. And the money you have—There is no trust fund either, and no parents dying in a plane crash. True? Is this how you get money, by copying things and selling them? How many copies of this have you made?"

"Only one, Manolo. Honest."

"Now you are crying. When a man cries, maybe he is telling the truth." Avila put his hand on Gene's arm a moment and withdrew it. "Show me how you make these copies."

Gene rubbed his eyes with the heels of his hands. "Do you want another copy of this?"

"No. I was worried there were others, that's why I was angry. If there is supposed to be one and there are three, four, then *I* am a liar. Make something else. Here."

He picked up a little brass bell. "Take this, we go to where you make them."

"I can do it here." Gene put his hand over the bell, reached and turned; when he withdrew his hand, there were two bells side by side.

Avila looked at them incredulously, picked them up, weighed them in his hands. He stared at Gene. "This is a trick?"

"No."

Avila put the bells down on the table. "How do you do it?"

"I don't know. I can't explain."

"And it is real—not a trick."

"Yes."

After a moment Avila said, in Spanish, "By the Virgin and all the saints, I have seen many things, but never this. I am sorry that I have seen it, because I am a man who does not believe in magic or in supernatural things." He picked up one of the bells and set it down. "Listen to what I tell you. I know you did this for affection, to please me. I would show my gratitude and keep the *Hierophant*. But I can't; it is a known piece, someone would see that there are two. You must destroy the one you made."

"Yes, Manolo."

"And promise that we will never talk about this again."

Avila had a record player and a large collection of records, most of them classical. Listening with him in the evening, Gene learned to love Satie, Pachelbel, Vivaldi. He bought these records for himself. Once when they were in his apartment, Avila looked them over and said, "These are all the same as mine. Why do you copy my taste? Buy other records, find out what you like yourself." He tried, but it was no good; the only things he could love were the ones he had heard with Avila.

In 1961, when they had been together for a year, Avila allowed him for the first time to cast one of his pieces in bronze. It was nothing like Avila's work; it was a standing figure made up of the shifting planes and curves that obsessed him then; when it was patinaed and polished, the light gleamed like water in the subtle intersections.

Gene wanted to offer it to a gallery, but this Avila would not permit. "You are thinking that you can sell it, if anybody wants to buy, and also retain it for yourself. Even if you say you will not, maybe you will change your mind later. You know what I am speaking of. I said we would never talk about it, but now it is necessary. This power that you have, if you use it to make money, to live, that is nothing to me. But anyone can see that this is a bronze made by the lost wax process, that it is the only one, there are no others. If you make a copy, you cheat the man who buys it. Even if he never knows, that does not matter. Make serigraphs if you want, or etchings, if you want to sell your work; then there is no dishonesty. An artist must not be a criminal."

At first Avila had made a joke of the difference in their height. Once he had said, "Why do you sit down when I talk to you?"

"I don't want to look down at you."

"But if you are not taller than I am, how can you look down at me?"

After a year or so, these jokes stopped. Gene had been a foot taller than Avila when they first met. By 1962 the difference was nearly a foot and a half. Avila, who was taller than most men, was so much shorter than Gene that they looked absurd together.

Year by year, the world and everyone in it was growing smaller around him. Ordinary chairs and tables were not big enough; plates, knives, and forks were like a doll's tea set in his hands. He was better proportioned now, and at a distance he could appear of normal height; he had learned to slump when he sat down, and to keep his hands in his lap as much as possible to avoid calling attention to their size. But it was impossible to walk on the street or in any public place without making people stare. They called, "Hey, Shorty!" or "How's the air up there?" and he had to pretend that he did not mind.

He could no longer travel on buses or subways; he had to jackknife himself into a taxi, and then he took up the whole back seat; Avila rode with the driver. In 1963, when he was not quite twenty, he was seven feet seven inches tall.

That was the year when Avila got a commission for a monumental work to be erected in a shopping plaza in Atlanta; he flew there several times for conferences with the architect and the committee. If it were not for these commissions, Gene realized, Avila would not be able to survive. Even though he had an international reputation and his prices were high, he could not make a living by doing small pieces because he worked so slowly and with such care.

On his return from one of these trips, Avila looked more tired than Gene had ever seen him. At lunch he complained of a pain in the chest, but it passed away quickly. Two days later, when they were eating breakfast together, Avila suddenly put down his coffee cup and bent over, grunting with pain. His face had taken on a grayish hue, and beads of sweat stood out on his forehead. Gene took him in his arms. "Manolo, what is it?"

"Can't breathe," Avila croaked.

Gene felt for his pulse; it was fluttery and weak. He helped Avila out of the chair, carried him into the bedroom and put two pillows under his head. Avila was curled up in agony; his breath wheezed in his throat.

Gene ran to the telephone and called an ambulance. When he got back, Avila's color was worse and he did not seem to hear when Gene spoke to him.

Gene realized with cold clarity that there might not be time for the ambulance. He put his hand on Avila's chest and felt for the heartbeat. It was rapid and irregular. He closed his eyes and felt deeper. He could feel where something was the matter with the heart: the blood was going in the wrong place. He tried desperately to understand. There was a valve, opening and shutting, but it was working out of rhythm, and the blood was not moving through one side. He reached in and felt the nerves. For a moment Avila's heartbeat steadied; then it stopped. He was not breathing. Gene threw himself across the body, willing with all his soul, Make him well! Make him well! But Avila's heart did not beat and he did not breathe. By the time the ambulance came, it was much too late.

Afterward what he felt was not grief but emptiness. There seemed to be no reason to do anything in particular. It was not worth the trouble to go anywhere; there was no one he wanted to see.

In his wallet, preserved all these years, he found the card the carnival man had given him: Ducklin & Ripley Attractions, Ron E. Ducklin, Owner, and a box number in Orlando, Florida. On New Year's Day, 1964, he sent a telegram: CAN YOU USE GIANT?

Chapter Twelve

What does it profit us to preserve these bones,
Pretending that the dead will rise some day
Clotted with earth, like monsters in a movie,
Knowing that underneath the stone
The slow centuries leach them one by one away?

Why should it disturb us that a loved one's eye
Tomorrow may become a coney's foot and join the dance?
Let the molecules go, dispersing into earth and silence:
Let them turn again to wrist and elbow, hip and thigh,
Trying the old game again, taking another chance.

—Gene Anderson

He found Ducklin in a house trailer fitted out as an office, parked among other trailers and semis on a muddy lot outside Orlando. The carnival owner was a little older and fatter; he still wore his baseball cap, pushed back over his balding head. He shook hands and then sat down behind his desk, staring up at Gene. "How tall are you?" he asked.

"Seven feet eight, about."

Ducklin squinted at him and rubbed his cheek with his hand. "Well, we can hype that up a little. Maybe put lifts on you. Now, our season starts March twenty-eight. What I'd like you to do, if you could get down here say about the twenty-sixth, then Mike Wilcox, he's the sideshow agent, he could start showing you the ropes. One thing I can tell you now, you'll need a gold ring that fits easy enough so you can take it on and off and show it to the marks. Just a plain ring, like a wedding ring. Get it made by a jeweler. Then you sell 'em brass copies. Mike might have a box of them brass rings around somewhere to get you started. You buy them by the gross, cost you about eight cents apiece, and you sell 'em for seventy-five cents. Then there's photographs—eight-by-ten glossies—you can get them made before you come down. You ought to have about two thousand to start. You sell them, too, autographed, for a buck a shot. Now about transportation, you probably noticed, we travel by truck. How did you come down here?''

"I flew to Orlando and took a cab.''

"Uh-huh. Well, you'll need a trailer or something to live in. Tim Emerson, that was our last giant, he had a converted moving van—he died in fifty-eight. His widow probably still has it; I'll get Mike to find out and let you know. Now, let's see.'' He opened a drawer of the desk and pawed through it with grunts of exasperation. "Can't find a damn—Oh, here. Now this is our standard contract for performers.'' He took out a ballpoint pen, scribbled briefly, and handed the pages over. "You can fill in your name and address up there, and then just sign at the bottom.''

"I don't have a permanent address; I thought I'd look around for something down here.''

"Well, put down the old one, then, just so we have a mailing address. Then when you get settled, let us know.''

Under "Salary,'' Ducklin had written in an amount that seemed very low, but Gene signed the contract without comment. Ducklin put the pages away in his desk.

"Well, that's about it, then,'' he said, and held out his hand. "Glad to have you with us, John, and we'll see you, say, around the end of March.''

He rented an A-frame cabin on Lake Brantley, north of Orlando, and spent the rest of the winter there alone. He had some of his things shipped down from New York; there was not room for much. The A-frame was jerry-built, and the window wall in front dripped cold air like a slow invisible waterfall.

At the end of January Ducklin sent him a telegram advising him that Mrs. Emerson still had the converted van and was willing to sell. She lived in Augusta, Georgia. Gene telephoned and arranged to meet her.

The dead giant's house was a tall white Victorian building. It needed a coat of paint, and some of the gingerbread was missing. An orange cat rubbed itself against his legs as he rang the bell.

Mrs. Emerson was a pale, auburn-haired woman with discolored pouches under her eyes. He could not judge her height, but she seemed to be a little taller than most women. "You must be Mr. Davis," she said. "Come in."

They sat in the high-ceilinged living room, on faded plush chairs covered with antimacassars. "I understand you're with the Ducklin show now," she said, with a faint smile.

"Yes. I'm sorry about your husband, Mrs. Emerson."

"It's all right. It was hard on me at first, he was only forty-seven. We were talking about him retiring after the next season. It's a pretty poor life he had, on the road all the time, but what can you do?"

"Yes, I see."

"About the van, it's out in back, up on blocks. It's no good to me. It had an engine overhaul just before Tim died. It might need some more work, I don't know." She named a price.

The van was in the barn behind the house. There were pigeon droppings on the cab, and a starred hole in the windshield. The trailer had one door in the side, and no windows. Because of the dropped frame, there was a center section almost twelve feet high; in the front and rear, over the wheels, Gene found that he had about a foot of headroom. The floor and the steps were carpeted in greasy-looking green shag. The bed was set crosswise in the front, next to a discouraged brown loveseat. The dinette table and two chairs were in the center section; one of the chairs was giant-sized. In the rear were the gas range, aluminum sink, refrigerator, toilet, and shower.

He gave her a check for a thousand dollars more than she had asked for. She took it, but her expression told him that she thought he was crazy. She gave him the address of the firm in Augusta where the van had been converted; he went there and talked to a salesman in the shop. "Well, sir, I'd say you want the engine and transmission checked over, and then new plugs, tires, fan belt. The body, now, that ought to be all right."

Gene told him about the hole in the windshield; the salesman made a note. "Yes, sir, we'll take care of that for you, and we'll look at the plumbing and wiring. About the inside, did you want some new carpeting? Maybe furniture? Might be a little wore-out by now."

Gene agreed to everything: new custom furniture, appliances, cabinets, and fixtures. The salesman's cheerfulness increased with each item until his round, honest face shone with pleasure. At last he retired to his office and came back with a long written estimate. Gene wrote him a check. The salesman was actually rubbing his hands; Gene had read about this in books but had never seen it. "Well, Mr. Davis, we'll have her all ready for you by the first of March, and I promise you won't know the old van."

The van was ready on March tenth. Gene hired a driver to take him to Lake Brantley, then another, on the twenty-seventh, to drive him to the carnival winter quarters.

The carnival lot, muddier than ever, was crowded with trucks, semitrailers, and equipment of all kinds. Workmen were busy around a half-assembled Ferris wheel. Two men walked by carrying a long plank between them. Gene put his head out the window. "Can you show us where to park?"

One of the men said, "Hell, I don't know. Over there, I guess."

"My name is John Davis. Will you tell Mr. Ducklin I'm here?"

"Okay."

Gene paid off the driver, sat in the trailer and waited. After half an hour someone put his head in at the open door. It was a young man in a leather jacket; he had sleek brown hair and a friendly, humorous face.

"Hello, Mr. Davis? My name's Mike Wilcox, I'm the talker for the sideshow."

"Come in. The place is a mess."

Wilcox climbed into the trailer and cast an appraising glance around. "Your first time with the carnival?"

"Yes."

"Well, the main thing is not to carry anything you don't absolutely need. It's amazing what you can do without. You'll get the hang of it, though. Are you nervous?"

"A little."

"Not to worry. Being a sideshow attraction is the easiest thing there is in a carnival. You don't have to do anything, you just are, sort of like the Grand Canyon. 'Freak' is the word they use here, but it's not a putdown, you know, a freak is a member of the upper class, because not everybody can be one. You won't worry about that, will you?''

"No."

"Good. Now you've got your rings all right, have you, and your photographs?''

"Yes, they're in those cartons over there. Are you English?''

"Yes, Birmingham, how did you know?''

"Have you been with the carnival long?''

"Three seasons. I like it, I really do. Ducklin's a dear man, and they're all good people here.''

"Would you like a beer, or some coffee?''

"Thanks, I can't stay. I did just want to talk to you for a moment and give you an idea what you're in for. We've got five attractions in the string joint at present, not counting myself—the Fat Lady, the Lizard Man, the Two-Headed Calf, the Sword Swallower, and you. The Sword Swallower has a routine of course, and that's easy on me; I just have to introduce her and she does her act. Now in your case, all you've got to do is sit there, and stand up when I ask you to, and I'll do the usual sort of spiel. What name do you want to use?''

"It doesn't matter. John Davis is all right.''

"No, Davis won't do. Too short. How about, let's see, how about Callaghan? John Callaghan. No, doesn't have the right flow somehow. Pettibone would be good, but for a midget, not a giant.''

"They used to call me Shorty in New York,'' Gene said.

"That's okay in fun, but not for the carnival. Let's see, John Wallingford. John Waterman. I want the three syllables. John Corrigan, too Irish. John Kimberley, Kimberley, I think that's got it. Sounds massive and dignified. What do you say?''

"All right with me.''

"Okay, that's settled. Now you can't do an accent, I suppose, so we'll have to make you American.''

"I thought I didn't have to talk?''

"People will be coming up to buy the rings, and the photos; you'll have to say a few words now and then, and you don't want to sound like a fake. So, let's see, suppose we make you from someplace like Wyoming. The wide-open spaces. Um, yes, I can work this up. Son of a rancher, and so on. Of course, if you have anything else in mind—"

"No, that's all right."

"Now, there's one thing you ought to know. In the carnival, nobody ever asks you who you really are or where you come from."

"I'm sorry."

"No, not a complaint. I don't mind a bit myself, and plenty of people will tell you their life histories if you let them, but it's one of the rules that you don't ask. Actually it's one of the things I like about the carnival. Sort of like not having to show your passport."

"Yes, I see."

Wilcox gave him a keen look. "You're a bit down, aren't you?"

"A little, maybe. I'll get over it."

"Of course you will. Now I've got to move on, but if all goes well we'll have a run-through this afternoon, over in that direction, probably about three o'clock. Oh, one more thing— you'll be needing a driver, and I think I've got one for you, a young man who works on the loop-the-loop. I'll send him round and you can make whatever arrangement you like with him." With a smile and a wave, he was gone.

At three o'clock he found Wilcox and a little group of people standing in a comparatively dry corner of the field. Behind them was a row of chairs, one of which was already occupied by a woman of astounding size; sitting down, she looked as broad as she was tall. Her small head, perched on top of this overflowing mound of flesh, looked as if it belonged to someone else. Her face was soft and sweet. The chair she sat in was a massive wooden construction, much heavier than Gene's, which had been set up at the end of the row; the rest were folding aluminum chairs with plastic webbed seats.

Wilcox saw him and waved him over. "Just in time," he said cheerfully. "Big John, I'd like you to meet the rest of our little troupe. This is Irma LeFever, our fire eater and sword swallower." Irma was a tall young woman, slender and blonde in a T-shirt and blue jeans; she smiled and took Gene's hand for a moment. "Welcome to the show," she said.

"This is Ed Parlow, the Lizard Man." A gray-faced, scholarly-looking man of about forty, dressed in a gray silk robe, nodded, but kept his hands in his pockets. "And this is Betty Ann Forster, our Fat Lady." She smiled and nodded.

"Now what we'll do," said Wilcox, "is just run through for timing. Irma and I will do the bally, but we can skip that. The order will be Irma, then me with some clever card tricks and feats of prestidigitation, then the Fat Lady, the Lizard Man, the Two-Headed Calf, and finally our new giant, Big John Kimberley. What I'd like you to do is just to take your places while I'm doing the act that comes ahead of you. Before and after you can stand here and watch if you like—John, this may be your last chance to see the others perform."

Gene was not sure why this should be so, but he said nothing. Irma, the sword swallower, walked over to the end of the row and stood waiting.

Wilcox cleared his throat. "Now, ladies and gentlemen," he said, "the act you are about to witness is one of the most amazing, the most incredible, in the history of entertainment. I introduce to you Irma LeFever, the only woman fire eater and sword swallower in the world?"

Irma bowed, then pretended to pick up something in both hands. She held these invisible objects up for inspection, then put one of them down and raised the other. Leaning backward until her face was turned to the sky, she raised her hand and slowly brought the invisible thing she was holding nearer to her face. Gene, watching curiously, suddenly realized that the invisible thing was a metal rod with a ball of rags at the end. The ball of rags was blazing, and now she was lowering it to her open mouth. She closed her lips over it, then opened them and withdrew it. She bowed, then picked up something else invisible and appeared to drink. Now she raised the rod again and blew her breath over the end of it while Wilcox stepped out of the way. The illusion had become so vivid that Gene could see the blast of flame as she sprayed some inflammable liquid over the end of the torch.

She bowed again, set the torch down, and picked up something else, equally invisible. "Now, ladies and gentlemen, you are about to see an act of death-defying courage and skill. This sword is twenty-seven inches long, ladies and gentlemen; it is razor sharp and made of the finest Toledo steel. The slightest miscalculation, and Mademoiselle LeFever will die an agonizing death."

Irma, with a bored expression, leaned backward again,

opened her mouth wide, and appeared to lower something into
it very carefully and slowly. Now Gene could see the bright
sword, which she was holding by the blade; it slipped down
into her throat little by little until at last the hilt touched her
mouth. Then she drew it out with a flourish, took another
bow. Gene applauded; she gave him an ironic glance.

"And now, ladies and gentlemen, if you will be kind enough
to follow me into the next room—" Wilcox moved a few feet
down the row, turned, and faced them. "I suppose you know
how hard money is to come by these days, but if you happen
to know a little magic, it's very easy." He removed a coin
from his ear, dropped it into a cup which had appeared in his
other hand. Next he took coins from his nose, his other ear,
and dropped them into the cup. He reached forward and got
another one, apparently from an invisible member of the
audience. Wilcox seemed to be enjoying himself, and he was
very good.

When he had filled the cup with coins, he dropped them,
cup and all, into his pocket and began to produce fans of cards
out of nowhere. Gene applauded again when he was through.

Wilcox bowed. "Thank you, ladies and gentlemen, thank
you. Now because you have been so very kind, in order to
show my appreciation, I am about to make a special offer, for
this day only, it will not be repeated, ladies and gentlemen: I
am going to offer you the secrets of three astounding tricks
with cards, each one of which will mystify your friends; they
require no training, a child can perform them, and I am offer-
ing them to you not for twenty dollars, not for ten, not for
five, no, ladies and gentlemen, not even for one dollar, but all
three tricks for the insignificant sum of fifty cents, a half a
dollar. Step right up, if you please—who will be first? You,
sir? There you are, thank you. And you, madame?" He pretended to sell several other packets of card tricks, then led his
audience through an invisible curtain to the Fat Lady.

"Now, ladies and gentlemen, it is unbelievable but true, the
woman you see before you weighs the astounding total of six
hundred and thirty-five pounds, enough solid human flesh to
make four large men and have enough left over for a small
boy. Betty Ann was born thirty-five years ago in a remote
hamlet of Queensland, Australia. She was a normal infant,
ladies and gentlemen, but when she was five years old she
weighed eighty-five pounds, and she has continued to grow in

weight and girth every year to this day, until, as you see her before you, she is the largest human being ever to live on earth, a model—what do I want to say? Oh, damn. —A miracle of nature, ladies and gentlemen, before your very eyes.''

He moved on to the chair in which the Lizard Man had taken his position quietly.

"Now, ladies and gentlemen, for your edification and amazement, I present the one and only Lizard Man. Ladies and gentlemen, it is unbelievable but true. Born in the dark bayou country of Louisiana, his mother was attacked by alligators in the swamp and lingered for two months between life and death. She recovered from her horrible ordeal, but when her child was born—you see the result before you.''

The Lizard Man removed his robe; he was wearing white boxing shorts. His arms, legs, and chest were covered with gray, peeling scales. Between the patches of scales, his skin was red and chafed.

"Was that okay, Ed?'' Wilcox asked.

"Last year you said, 'Born in the mysterious swamps of Louisiana.' I thought that was better.''

"Right. The mysterious swamps of Louisiana, thanks for reminding me.''

The next space was empty except for a wooden table. Wilcox gestured at it. "And now, ladies and gentlemen, a true freak of nature, one of the mysteries of the age, the Two-Headed Calf. As you can plainly see, the calf has two complete heads, two noses, four eyes, four ears—''

"Is it an invisible calf?'' Gene said to Irma, who was standing near him.

She looked up and smiled with amusement. "It's pickled, in a glass tank. No use bringing it out for the run-through.''

"Oh.''

He saw Wilcox looking at him, and realized that it was his turn next. He walked to his chair and sat down.

"And now, ladies and gentlemen, for your amazement and delight I proudly present Big John Kimberley, nine feet three and one-half inches tall, the tallest man who ever lived. Stand up, if you will, Big John, and let them see you. Isn't that amazing, ladies and gentlemen? Big John was born on a cattle ranch in the wide-open spaces of Wyoming in nineteen forty-four; he is twenty years of age, ladies and gentlemen, and he is still growing! Every article of his clothing has to be specially made for him. His shoes are hand-made in London, England; they are fourteen and one-half inches long. There is enough cloth in his coat and trousers to make suits for three men of normal size. The ring which you see on his finger contains four ounces of fourteen-carat gold, and it is one and three-quarters inches across. If you will, Big John, let me borrow your ring for a moment—I'll be careful of it."

He held up the ring, showed that it would fit over two of his fingers. "Now, ladies and gentlemen, Big John has made replicas of this unique and valuable ring for distribution to the public as souvenirs. These rings are hand-crafted of genuine gold-filled metal, each and every one is an exact duplicate of the ring you see before you, and Big John has consented to sell a limited quantity of these unique and valuable rings for the amazing price of only seventy-five cents each! Take them home, show them to your family and friends, they won't believe you unless they see it with their own eyes. And for an additional proof, ladies and gentlemen, you may purchase for just a dollar one of these large autographed photographs of Big John. Get them now, because this offer may never be repeated! That concludes our performance, ladies and gentlemen, and I hope we have entertained and surprised you. If you can't believe your eyes, if you want to see it again, the next performance will begin in five minutes."

Wilcox looked at his watch and remarked, "Just on eighteen minutes—that's a bit long, but we'll trim it down. Thanks, all."

The performers began to disperse; Gene saw Irma walking away hand in hand with a slender young man in dungarees. A stout little man had come up with a wheelchair, so large that Gene thought it must have been custom made; with the help of two workmen, he got the Fat Lady into the wheelchair and began pushing her toward the line of trailers. After a moment Gene found himself alone with Wilcox.

"I suppose you know you've added a couple of feet to my height," he said.

"Yes, that's all right. The marks don't know the difference, and nobody's going to measure you. There's never been a giant whose size wasn't exaggerated—beginning with Goliath, probably."

"Or the Nephilim."

"Oh, sorry, who were they?"

" 'The sons of God saw the daughters of men that they were fair.' Genesis. The Nephilim were the children born of those unions—'There were giants in the earth in those days.' They had a lot of other names too—Anakim, Emmim, Zamzum-mim. The Israelites found them in Canaan, and they said, 'We were as grasshoppers in their sight.' "

"Yes, I see. I'm not very strong on the Bible, I'm afraid—never got past the begats. But about the nine feet and so on—it's harmless deception, or beneficial really, because the marks pay to see a tall man, and the taller they think he is, the more they get for their money. We're all in the illusion business here. Well, I'm off—tomorrow's the first of May."

"The first of May?"

"That's what they call opening day, heaven knows why. If anybody asks you, 'Are you first of May?' that's what they mean—are you new to the show? You'll catch on. See you tomorrow."

The driver Wilcox had promised appeared later that afternoon; he was a pleasant, shy young man named Larry Scanlon, who seemed to think it was a privilege to drive for a giant. The carnival caravan put itself together late that evening, with what seemed an enormous amount of confusion; it was after one o'clock when Larry told him they were ready to roll.

"Does the carnival always travel at night?" Gene asked.

"Sure, because, you know, you got to tear down one place and set up the next day somewheres else. And besides there's less traffic at night and the staties don't hassle you so much. You might as well go on and go to bed, Mr. Kimberley. I see there's a intercom here in the cab—is it working?"

"I suppose so."

"Let's try her out."

Gene went into the trailer and turned on the intercom over his bed. There was a hiss, then a crackling voice: "Mr. Kimberley, can you hear me?"

"Yes."

"Well, okay, then we're all set. If you want to talk to me, like if you wake up or anything, or there's any problem, give me a holler. Otherwise, why, just get your sleep. Good night, Mr. Kimberley."

Chapter Thirteen

In the morning when he opened the door, he found the carnival already set up. The rides were clustered near the entrance—the sky ride, the Ferris wheel, the merry-go-round, loop-the-loop and the rest. Beyond them, booths selling food and soft drinks were in a line down the middle, and around the sides of the lot were the games of skill and the sideshow. Gene had picked up a little carny jargon; he knew that anybody who sold food or drink was a "butcher," and that the purple and orange drinks that the carnival people made in big tubs were called "flookum."

The freak tent was called "the string joint," because its compartments were arranged in a row or "string." Behind it, campers and trailers were parked, leaving an enclosed space, "the back yard"; the freaks were allowed to use it between performances, but only the Lizard Man did so; the Fat Lady, who was too heavy to move without great effort, sat in her special chair in the freak tent all day long, and Gene Anderson stayed in his trailer.

They showed three days in Orlando, then packed up and moved overnight to Leesburg. All day the carnival went on, out there beyond the walls of the tent; he could hear the canned music bracketing the lot from loudspeakers on poles, and the distant chime of the merry-go-round, and he could hear Wilcox's voice as he gathered a tip, but he could only imagine the crowds, the young men and girls in short-sleeved shirts, the mothers carrying children, the old people in their Sunday clothes.

At night after the show closed he sometimes wandered around the lot, watching as the concessionaires shut up their stands—the dart throw with its limp array of balloons on a board punctured by a thousand misses; the string pull, the penny toss, the steeplechase. The ground was covered with a sad litter, candy wrappers, ticket stubs, paper cups, the detritus of pleasure. He often saw Irma LeFever at the candy-apple stand, where she worked between shows with the sad-faced young man who appeared to be her husband. She spoke to him when he passed, but the other concessionaires were too busy to talk.

In the mornings it was another kind of loneliness: the early sun lit up the wooden and canvas stalls with a pathetic promise; the lot was clean and empty. Everyone was busy then too, the ride attendants taking canvas covers off the cars, butchers filling their popcorn machines, mixing flookum, breaking out cartons of foot-long dogs.

It was an unspoken rule in the carnival that the freaks did not appear on the midway or in town. The fire eater could come and go as she pleased, and so could Wilcox, but if the real freaks had appeared in public, they would have been giving away what they had for sale. They could not eat in local restaurants, or even go to the drugstore for a tube of toothpaste; others performed such errands for them. Their view was always the same: the canvas walls of the tents, the rear ends of trailers, the tattered grass.

The first performance of the sideshow was at one o'clock; after that, as long as the talker could keep gathering a tip, they appeared every twenty minutes until dinner time. By the second week, Gene no longer had to look at his watch; he knew when it was time to leave the trailer, sit for a moment in his outsize canvas chair behind the string joint, and then enter through the back wall and sit on his throne as Wilcox finished his spiel about the preserved calf embryo. He worked only five minutes in every twenty throughout the day, and during those five minutes he learned to carry in his mind the argument of the book he had been reading, to look at the customers—"the marks"—and not see them.

The carnival moved north up the Atlantic coast, then west into Georgia and South Carolina, a week here, three days there. Sometimes they traveled as much as a hundred miles between stops, sometimes only thirty or forty.

One evening after the last performance, Wilcox came up to him at the door of his trailer. "Like to talk to you a moment, John."

"Okay. Come in."

"No, I'll stay here, thanks. It's just this. You've been with the show almost a month, and I'm practically the only one you talk to. You don't even eat with the others. Why is that?"

"Not feeling very social."

"If you don't mind my saying so, you're like a guy running off to join the Foreign Legion because his girl's thrown him over. You came here because you thought it was going to be awful, and now all you can think about is how awful it is. When you look at the others, you're thinking, 'Ugh, they're freaks.'"

"I'm a freak too," Gene said. He was trembling, and he could feel his face growing warm.

"Yes, you are, but we're using the word in two different senses. In a sideshow a freak is a member of the aristocracy, something most people can never be. But when you say 'freak,' you mean not human. Well, they are human, and so are you. Now, if you'll excuse me, I'm going to get drunk." He turned and walked away.

Gene closed the door and sat down with his hands between his knees, staring at nothing. After a few minutes he went to the refrigerator and got out the ham and vegetables he had been thawing for his dinner, but one look was enough; he knew the food would choke him. Shame and anger came in waves. He wanted to hit Wilcox; he wanted to walk out of the trailer and never come back; he didn't know what he wanted.

Over the line of tents the white lights of the Ferris wheel were revolving under a few early stars. The air was cool. Gene walked across the yard to Wilcox's little trailer and knocked on the door.

"Yes?"

"Mike, it's John."

After a moment the door opened; Wilcox stood there, looking a little flushed.

"You were right," Gene said. "Thanks."

Wilcox smiled. "You know, that's the most marvelous— oh, damn. Come in and have a drink."

"I'll just sit here in the doorway for a minute, if it's all right."

"Of course—I wasn't thinking. Half a mo." He disappeared and came back with a tumbler of whiskey in each hand. "You're my first giant, actually—Tim Emerson was before my time. It must be a nuisance, doorways and taxis and so on."

"It wasn't so bad until this year. Then I had some other problems, and I began to think, if it's hard now, what will I do when I'm eight feet tall, or nine? I might as well get used to it."

"Yes, I see. I feel much the same way, if it's any help. There isn't a lot of give in the world, most places, for anybody who's a bit different. I mean they don't seem to make allowances. My God, the people on the street where I lived with my mother in Birmingham, you wouldn't believe it, they lived in identical houses and wore the same clothes, carried the same umbrellas and went to work at the same time every morning, I mean, you couldn't even tell the wives and children apart. I used to think of changing the house numbers; I thought the husbands coming home would go into the wrong houses and say, 'Hullo, Mum, what's for tea?' and nobody would notice. I had dreams about the factory where they made people all alike."

"You said you lived with your mother—was your father dead?"

"Yes, he jumped off a bridge when I was nine—bit of a jolt all round." He held up the bottle. "Have another drop of this."

"What is it, Scotch?"

"Yes. Not the best, I'm afraid, but it does the trick. Look, what I meant to say before—I know it must be hard to get used to. Being on exhibition like a man from Borneo or something, but, you know, these people here are the ones who couldn't stand the conformity. Really when you come to think of it, it's fantastic luck that we've got any place to go to. I can imagine a world where there's nothing *but* those semidetached houses all in a row. That gives me the shudders."

"I understand what you're saying." Gene stood up. "I'm going on back, I've got some thinking to do."

"God bless," said Wilcox.

The next day, instead of going back to his trailer after the first performance, Gene sat down with a book in the back yard. The Lizard Man, who was also reading, glanced over and nodded. After a while they fell into conversation. The book the Lizard Man was reading was called *Genetics and the Races of Man*; he offered to lend it to Gene when he was through.

In the following week he accepted an invitation to a dinner party in the Fat Lady's trailer. Logan Forster, her husband, a beaming little man with a black mustache, cooked spaghetti in a huge pot and served it with a garlicky sauce. Irma and her husband were there, and Wilcox and the Lizard Man, and Ducklin in his baseball cap. Most of them sat on cushions on the floor; Betty Ann was in her wheelchair, and Logan insisted that Gene take the loveseat. The Forsters were from Australia, and Betty Ann, it turned out, had an astonishing repertoire of bawdy songs, performed in an innocent little-girl voice.

Afterward Irma's quiet husband volunteered to help Logan with the cleanup; Irma sat beside Gene on the loveseat and they began talking about sword-swallowing.

"How did you ever learn to do it?" Gene asked.

"The Human Pincushion taught me—Jim Simons. That was three seasons ago. He was with the show till last year, then he went to Texas. I just wanted to learn, and he taught me. The only hard part is, you have to learn to keep from gagging when the sword goes past your glottis, right here, where you swallow. That took me two months, but then the rest was easy. You just bend your head back to make a straight line with your mouth and your throat, and then drop the sword down easy, a little bit at a time, until you feel it touch the bottom of your stomach. That's the part I don't like." She studied him for a moment. "I suppose you've heard about giants and sword-swallowers," she said, "but don't take it too seriously."

"Giants and sword-swallowers?" Gene replied. "No, what do you mean?"

"You really don't know? Well, that's okay too. Maybe we'd better keep it that way."

Gene discovered that Ed Parlow, the Lizard Man, liked to play Scrabble; they played two or three times a week, behind the freak tent while they waited to go on, with an alarm clock to remind them if they got too absorbed in the game.

Parlow seemed extraordinarily well read, although from a casual remark he had made Gene gathered that he had had no schooling beyond the sixth grade. One evening in Gene's trailer, they were talking about a book Parlow had lent him,

The Lore and Language of Schoolchildren, by Iona and Peter Opie.

"It may be that kids that age haven't had time to develop a super-ego," Parlow said, "but I think the main thing is that they haven't got the formal power structure that grownups have. They have to sort themselves out somehow, and they do it through force partly, and partly through mockery—if they make you cry, they win."

"I was too big for the seats in school," Gene said. "I had to sit with my feet in the aisle, and they called me Feet."

"They called me Fish-skin," said Parlow apologetically. "One day two kids caught me going home from school and whitewashed me."

"Whitewashed you?"

"That's right, there was a can of whitewash in somebody's basement—they took me down there, pulled my shirt off and painted me. My mother was crying when she washed it off. It was irritating stuff—my skin was pretty raw for a week or so. My father was furious—he went to the kids' parents and the principal. It didn't do any good, of course. Kids have an instinct about anybody who's visibly different. It may be a Darwinian trait, to weed out anybody who's too far from the norm."

"There's no cure for this?"

Parlow shook his head. "No. I had all kinds of doctors when I was a kid. You see, it's genetic, or at least—they call it 'heredofamilial,' which I take to mean they think it's genetic but they can't prove it. It runs in families, anyway. My father had it on his elbows and knees. As Ambrose Bierce said, the best thing is not to be born."

After a moment he reached across the table and touched Gene's arm lightly. "I didn't mean that the way it sounded," he said with a smile. "If I had the chance to go back and say, 'No, I don't want to be born,' I wouldn't. There are so many people worse off than I am. Brain-damaged kids, just living vegetables—that's awful. I've got all my faculties, such as they are; I can read, I can think. I'm alive, I can move around, I don't have a whole lot of pain. And you can't say this isn't a cushy job."

"What would you have done if things had been different?"

"I've thought about that. I would have gone to college, of course, and probably I would have majored in philosophy. And I suppose by now I'd be teaching philosophy somewhere.

Well, as a matter of fact, a friend of mine is a philosophy professor in Asheville—I see him every year or so when we come through there. He hasn't got tenure, and he's got a wife and three kids, and a house—you know, keeping up with the Joneses. I don't think he respects his students, he doesn't really enjoy what he's doing, and at the same time he's terribly afraid of losing his job.

"I think about him, and his class schedules and meetings and so on. He wears these tweed jackets with patches on the elbows, and he smokes a pipe, but how much time does he have to think about philosophy? I think I've read more than he has. It's funny to say that, but it's true. I always take a carton of books with me, and from October to March I have nothing to do but read. Would I change places with him? I don't know."

One morning in early May, someone rapped on the trailer door. Gene opened it; there stood Irma, dressed in a terrycloth robe.

"Hi there," she said. "Listen, is your plumbing okay?"

"Plumbing? Yes, why?"

"Well, my shower's on the fritz. Would you mind?"

"Mind?"

"If I took a shower."

"Oh. No, of course not—come on in."

She brushed past him with a whiff of fragrance, something flowery, but too faint to identify. "Don't get too near me," she said over her shoulder, "I probably stink like a goat."

"No, you smell good."

She gave him a smile and turned to inspect the trailer. "Hey, this is nice. You had it all done over inside, didn't you?"

"Yes, pretty much."

She glanced up at the unmade bed, then mounted the two steps to the rear section. "Oh, the shower's new, too!" she said as she opened the door. "Oh, this is terrific." She took a yellow plastic cap out of the pocket of her robe.

"Here's a towel," Gene said.

"Keep it for me. Here." She slipped out of her robe, handed it to him and walked with a flash of pale buttocks into the shower stall. The door closed; after a moment the pump started and he heard the water hissing on the metal floor.

Gene put the towel and the terry-cloth robe on the counter. He took off his own dressing gown. His throat was dry; he could feel his heart beating. He opened the shower door and stepped in.

Irma glanced at him with one eye; the other was covered by soapsuds. "Well, hello," she said.

Gene took the soap from her and began to lather her smooth back. Presently he put the soap down and rubbed the lather with his hands over her breasts and belly. She leaned her head back against his breastbone. Her hip came against him, but he twisted away.

"What's the matter?" she asked, and looked down. "Oh. My gosh, he's a big one, isn't he?" She turned around in his arms. "Now I'll do you."

Her hands were gentle. When they were both rinsed, she turned off the water, opened the door, stepped out, and picked up the towel. As soon as he came through the doorway, she began to dry him. Gene reached over her head to the cabinet, got another towel. Their efforts interfered with each other, and she began to laugh. He followed her down the steps and up again to the front of the trailer.

"Do you know why I like you?" she asked between kisses. They were in bed together; she was curled up against him, and his hand was on her breasts. "Because you make me feel small."

"You are small."

"No, I'm *enormous*, I'm five nine and a half. If I wear heels, I'm almost six feet tall. But you make me feel petite. You're so big." Her finger traveled slowly down the length of his erect penis. "Too big for my lady Jane."

"Your what?"

"Didn't you ever read *Lady Chatterley's Lover*? That's what she called her thing. I think it's nicer than 'cunt' or 'muff.' And this is your John Thomas, and *he* must be ten inches long."

Gene tried to get closer to her, but she held him away. "Get up a minute, honey. Please. Just for a minute, all right?"

Angry and confused, he got out of bed. "Stay there," Irma said. She squirmed around on her back until her head hung over the edge. "Now I'm going to show you about sword-swallowers and giants, honey. Come on. Don't worry, it's all right. Come on."

Chapter Fourteen

Armed with his letter of recommendation from the mayor of Dog River, Tom Cooley went to Amherst, Massachusetts, and got a job on the police force. He chose the east because he was convinced the kid had gone that way. A deer might double back to avoid pursuit, but not a kid. He wouldn't go in the same direction twice, and he wouldn't go back to places where he had almost been trapped. He would go east.

Cooley had no illusions about his chances of finding him there. Young as he was, the kid would be smart enough to know that Cooley had tracked him down in San Francisco by going to art schools, and he wouldn't be caught that way again. Cooley had another idea, and he was willing to wait.

It was funny how the thing had grown on him. In the beginning it had just been a thing about evening the score, like when somebody cheats you at cards and takes your money, you don't let them get away with that, you get even and more than even. Only later had he begun to realize that Gene Anderson was really the devil. What kind of a kid could kill his son, throw him out a window, and then live in the woods all by himself for two years, and grow up to be a giant? That wasn't natural; it wasn't even human.

Cooley liked Amherst well enough, and he found some congenial friends, including an ex-Marine named Jacobs whose hobby was incendiary and explosive devices. In 1957 he married a widow who had a half-interest in a bar and grill, and moved into her house on Third Street. After six months they began to quarrel frequently, and in 1959 they were divorced.

Cooley was disciplined in the same year for drinking on duty, owing to an unfortunate falling-out with his superior. In 1960 he left the Amherst police force and moved to Pittsburgh, where he went to work for an armored car company. The work was undemanding and the pay was fair. In 1962 he began using his vacation time to visit circuses and carnivals in the east.

His reasoning was simple: if the kid kept on growing at the same rate, by the time he was twenty he would be nearly eight feet tall. He wouldn't be able to get an ordinary job anywhere; he couldn't even join the army. Sooner or later he would turn up in a sideshow.

Cooley struck up acquaintances with circus people whenever he got a chance, and discovered that the bible of the industry was a magazine called *Amusement Business*, published in Nashville. He subscribed to it, and read every issue from cover to cover.

Through the summer the carnival worked its way into Ohio and Indiana, turned north briefly into Wisconsin, then back into Ohio again, and from there to Pennsylvania and Maryland, then southward down the coast through New Jersey, the Carolinas, and Georgia, and so back to Florida. There were tearful good-byes, and the women kissed Gene. "See you next season," they all said.

Gene went back to his A-frame on Lake Brantley. At first he liked the solitude and freedom, the time to think. He finished a large wood carving and several smaller pieces; he made a few tentative experiments in poetry. But the winter was long; when the end of March came, he went back to the carnival with a sense of relief.

Some of the old faces were missing, and there were some new ones, even in the sideshow. The Fat Lady was gone; she had had a stroke during the winter. In her place there was a young juggler, a wiry dark-skinned man named Ray Hartz. He joined Irma in the bally, where he did a spectacular act with five whirling daggers. He could not use knives in the tent, where he worked so close to the marks, but he juggled apples, oranges, milk bottles. "He won't stay long," Wilcox predicted, "but he'll do to fill in until Ducklin can find another Fat Lady, or a morphodite."

Early in the season Hartz began teaching Irma to juggle; she picked it up readily, and within a few weeks they were practicing together in the back yard between performances, disturbing Gene's Scrabble games with Ed Parlow. Irma's husband, Ted LeFever, looked more and more tired every time Gene saw him; he was running the candy-apple stand all by himself.

One evening in Gene's trailer, Wilcox showed him what he called "the grift."

"All this more or less stopped about nineteen forty-eight, when carnivals became respectable, but I've run into oldtimers who used to do it. The classic way is with three walnut shells and a pea, like this." He showed Gene the "pea"—a little dark sphere of rubber. He put it under one of the shells and began to move them back and forth, changing their positions rapidly. "The idea is, I bet you a dollar you can't tell me which shell the pea's under. Where is it now?"

Gene pointed to the shell in the middle. Wilcox lifted it. "Right, and you've won a dollar. Care to try again?"

Next time Gene picked the wrong shell. "Bad luck, you've got to watch closer. Now don't take your eye off the shell with the pea." Gene picked the wrong one again.

"You see how it goes," Wilcox said. "You let the mark win just often enough to keep him enthusiastic, and he always thinks if he pays more attention he'll win next time. Then you begin doubling the bet, and so on, and a good grifter can take all his money away. You see, the pea is compressible: you can squirt it out under the shell and palm it, like this." He showed Gene the pea between his fingers.

"Then you squirt it back in under another shell the same way, and the mark never sees it because you do it so fast."

"So 'the grift' is another word for cheating?"

"Sure. In the old days, the idea was to separate the mark from his money, never mind how. Game of chance, pick his pocket, anything. You had to pay off the law, of course, and so it was really a sort of vicious cycle, I mean, without the grift you couldn't make the payments."

He took a deck of cards out of his pocket. "This is a more sophisticated version." He laid three aces face up on the table, put the rest away. "Here it's the ace of spades you're looking for, and just to make it easier for you, I'll bend it down the middle." He did so, and turned all three cards over; the ace of spades was slightly bowed, the other two flat. He switched the cards back and forth. "Where is it now?"

Gene turned over the bowed card: it was the ace of hearts. "How did you do that?"

"Simple, you just take the bend out of one card and put in into another one as you move them, but it takes a bit of practice."

"Let me see it again."

"Right, here we go."

Gene touched the three cards one after another, as if indecisive; he felt them change under his fingers. Then he turned over the middle card, the bowed one. It was the ace of spades.

Wilcox stared in disbelief. "Well, I'm damned. I must be losing my touch."

Gene reached out slowly and turned over the other two aces. They were spades, too.

Wilcox sat back and looked at him. "My God, here I am trying to teach you, and I'm an infant. Where did you learn that?"

"Just something I figured out myself."

Wilcox was full of enthusiasm; he wanted Gene to do a magic act in the sideshow. "You'd be the first giant magician—it would be tremendous. You could go on to bigger and better things."

"I'd rather not."

"Don't you want to be famous?"

"No, obscure."

Gene discovered that he had taken a dislike to the new juggler, whether it was because his practice sessions with Irma disturbed the quiet of the back yard, or because of Hartz's exaggerated deference, or because he felt sorry for Ted LeFever. It had been obvious all along that Ted knew Irma slept with other men, but it had never seemed to make any difference in their affection for each other. Now there was a new sadness in his face when he looked at Irma and Ray Hartz.

Irma still came to Gene every now and then, not as often as before. One night she seemed moody. "I don't know what to do. Ray wants to blow the show and take me with him. He has an offer from Circus Vargas for a double act. He had a partner before—she got married and moved to Canada, that's why he came here, but now he says I'm already good enough to start, and with him teaching me I'll get better and better."

After a moment Gene asked, "What about Ted?"

"He says it's all right, but I know it will hurt him."

"What are you going to do?"

"I don't know."

Later she told him she had decided to stay with the show, and Gene was relieved. But a week later, rising early in the morning, he saw her coming tousled out of Hartz's trailer. She gave him a mournful glance, and he knew she was wavering again.

He told himself that it was absurd to feel abandoned by somebody else's wife.

Somewhere along the line, something had gone terribly wrong. When he was a child, the world had been a big juicy apple that he was not tall enough to pluck. The boy-heroes in novels always had a series of tribulations to get through, and then they became men and everything was all right. Now he was twenty-one, legally adult, and it was not like that at all.

The worst of it was that the same thing seemed to happen to most people: not only the freaks in the sideshow, like Ed Parlow, but the ordinary people living their ordinary lives. Only Avila, of all the people he had known in New York, had seemed to have a sense of purpose that gave meaning to everything he did; the rest were drifting in sluggish channels.

He thought now of his childhood more often and with bitter regret. It was a cruel joke that you grew so eagerly, reaching for the sun, and then all the brightness went away.

At long last, he thought he had penetrated the secret of the grownups; it was something they could never tell a child, because it was emptiness and despair. He wrote a poem about this; it was very bad, and he tore it up.

The carnival people had their own names for some of the places they passed through. Two months into the season, they came to a West Virginia town they called "East Asshole."

"Is it that bad?" Gene asked.

"Oh, well, it's a *hole*," said Wilcox, "but that's not the reason. Two years ago there was some trouble here—local toughs got into an argument with a couple of the butchers, and there was a 'Hey, rube,' the only one I've ever seen. The constabulary came and cleared them off, but they arrested some of our people too and Ducklin had to go down and bail them out. Then the next night the local boys came back after dark and set fire to the Ferris wheel—did about fifteen hundred dollars' worth of damage. Ducklin wouldn't show here last season, but I suppose he thinks two years is enough to forgive and forget. I'd have given the place a wide berth for the next century if it was up to me, but it isn't. Anyhow, we're keeping an eye out, so don't worry."

In the summer of 1965, Cooley bought a Chevy station wagon and made a swing south into West Virginia. South of Parkersburg, in a little town called Elvis, he saw a carnival poster on a light pole: COMING JUNE 3, DUCKLIN & RIPLEY ATTRACTIONS—7 RIDES 7—SEE THE TALLEST MAN IN THE WORLD! At the bottom was a line, SPONSORED BY EAGLES LODGE.

Cooley went to a pay phone, looked up the Eagles, dialed the number. A woman's voice answered.

"Ma'am, you folks have a carnival coming to town next week?"

"Yes, we sure do."

"Well, I hate to bother you, but I'm just in town for the day, and my kids are after me—I wonder if you could tell me where the carnival's playing at now?"

"Well, let me see. I believe—let me look it up. Would you hold the phone just a second?" A pause. "Yes, here it is—they're playing this week in East Anglia, do you know where that is?"

"No, ma'am, I don't."

"Well, it's just about sixty miles from here. You head south on the state highway, and you can't miss it."

An hour and a half later he was in East Anglia, an uninspiring clapboard town with a railroad through the middle of it. He found the carnival on a lot near the tracks. He watched the talker gather a tip for the sideshow, admired the shape of the sword-swallower and the skill of the juggler; then he bought a candy apple from a sad-faced vendor and stood eating it while he waited.

After so many years, he did not expect to be able to recognize Gene Anderson. By the same token, maybe Anderson wouldn't recognize him, but Cooley believed himself to be distinctive in appearance, and he didn't want to take the risk. After fifteen minutes or so the little crowd emerged from the other end of the tent. Cooley strolled over and fell in beside a ten-year-old kid who was carrying a glossy photograph. "Is that the giant's picture?" he asked.

The kid glanced up. "Yessir. He's really big."

"Did he give it to you hisself?"

"He sold it to me. For a dollar."

"No, I mean did he hand it to you when you bought it?"

"Yessir." The kid started edging away.

"Listen," Cooley said confidentially, "I've got a boy at home that really wants a picture like that. Would you sell it to me for five bucks?"

"I want to keep it."

"Sure, but with five bucks you can go back and get another one. See, I haven't got time to go in there myself. I'll make it six bucks—what do you say?" He held out the money.

"Well—all right."

The photograph showed a clean-shaven young man dressed in a business suit; standing beside him was another man, the top of whose head was level with the handkerchief in the giant's breast pocket. The photograph was inscribed, "Best wishes, Big John Kimberley." Cooley took it back to his station wagon, got out his fingerprint kit and dusted it. It was easy to pick out the giant's prints from the rest—the thumbprint was over two inches long. He took the old Dog River flyer from its envelope in the glove compartment and compared the prints under a magnifying glass. They were the same.

Cooley went back to the carnival, bought a strip of tickets for the Ferris wheel, and waited in line. When his turn came, the young attendant threw out the clutch of his putt-putting engine, steadied the car, helped Cooley in, fastened the metal rod over his lap. The car lurched as he started the wheel and stopped it again almost immediately; Cooley hung a few feet in the air, looking down at the next car as the attendant settled a woman and two children in it. Up they went again, the car swaying, and Cooley clutched the lap rod; he hadn't been in one of these things since Paul was eight, that time in Portland, and he never had liked them. He knew the car was suspended on gimbals so that it always hung level, but if *felt* as if it was going to tip over, and what if the gimbals seized up?

If Paul was here he would enjoy this; he had always been crazy about rides of any kind. He would grin with pleasure and his face would get flushed, and he would be grabbing Cooley's sleeve, "Dad, do it again! Do it again!"

There was no front to the car; it was really nothing but a seat and a back and a footrest, and he could look down past the tips of his shoes at the car below where the woman and her two daughters were squeezed together with the metal rod over their laps, and then below them, as the great wheel revolved, to the empty car and then the one after that, and the next one where a young man and his girl had their arms around each other, each car smaller and farther away, each one hanging and swaying from the framework of the wheel as it turned. The cars were hung like baskets, the seat part was the basket and the footrest stuck out, and he could see that if it wasn't for the lap rod, if he could stand up on the footrest, the car would tip then, it would have to, and out he would go, like Paul, into air and distance.

All the new passengers were on the wheel now, and as it majestically turned, Cooley rose higher and higher, while the sunlit people below grew tiny and foreshortened until it looked like, if his legs were just long enough, he could step on them like ants. He could see the dirty canvas tops of the concession booths, and now, as he reached the apex of the wheel, he could look diagonally down over the sideshow tent and see the rear ends of a dozen house trailers and semis lined up there like patient elephants. One of those trailers must be the giant's, but which one? That was what he had to know, and it was worth coming up here to find out.

The Ferris wheel revolved and Cooley pursued his slow orbit, now backward and down, now forward and upward. After a long time the wheel stopped when Cooley reached the bottom; the attendant came over, and Cooley handed him another ticket. Up he went again. This time, as he approached the dizzy height of the wheel, he saw a flash of color down there beyond the freak tent. It was the top of a brown-haired man's head, coming into view as if he had been sitting there, hidden by the tent, and had just now stood up. The head moved toward the tent and vanished.

There was the evil thing, that brown oval in the sunlight, and it gave Cooley a jolt to realize that he had seen his enemy, that there had been a connection between them just for that moment across eighty feet of air.

He had used up three more tickets before the moment came

that he was waiting for. From the height of the wheel, down there in the area behind the freak tent, he saw the brown head appear again. This time it was moving the other way. The man's torso came into view, then his legs; he was wearing a brown suit, moving with long strides, and even at this distance Cooley could see that he was unnaturally tall. The man walked around the end of the last semi in the row, the one with the bright yellow cab. That one had to be his; the vehicle on the far side of it was a house trailer.

When the wheel stopped again, Cooley got off and handed his unused tickets to the first kid he saw.

"Gee, thanks."

"That's okay, son," Cooley said. He lit a cigar with a wooden match, looking at the flame bright and pale in the sunshine.

It was too bad that the giant was living in a converted semi, not a house trailer, because that meant no windows. One of his ideas, the one he had spent the most time thinking about, was to tape up a photo of Paul on a window, and then knock, and then light the match.

Along the ratty main street, a couple of blocks away from the carnival, there was a bank, a five and dime, a greasy spoon, a hardware store, and a decayed movie theater advertising a Glenn Ford double bill. Cooley bought two ten-gallon jerrycans at the hardware store, had them filled at a gas station, and asked directions to a lumber yard. It was out at the other end of town; Cooley went there and bought four two-by-fours. He paid the man in the shop a few dollars to cut them to five and a half feet, with a forty-five-degree bevel cut on the flat side. "It's for my kid," he explained, "he's building some damn thing, I don't even know what it is, and he don't know how to use a miter box."

"Well, sometimes the old man's got to help out the young ones," said the man, with a wink.

"That's right."

He stowed the two-by-fours in the wagon, parked it on a side street, and went into the greasy spoon for dinner. He was too wound up to eat much, but he bought a couple of sandwiches to go.

He already knew that the rear door of the semi had been replaced; that was standard in a semi conversion. The chances were that the doors on one side had been replaced too; there might be only one door, or depending on how the trailer had been made in the first place, there might be as many as four—double doors on each side. The door handles were probably about five feet off the ground, not any more than that, even for a giant, which meant that five and a half would be about right to wedge them shut, with the beveled ends of the two-by-fours jammed into the ground. Then the rags piled underneath, and the match. Gasoline made a hot fire; long before those two-by-fours burned through, the metal doors would be too hot to touch.

He parked on the deserted street back of the carnival lot and ate his sandwiches while he waited. A little after midnight the carnival closed down; the white lights on the Ferris wheel and the other rides went dark. Cooley was getting out of the wagon when he saw something that made him sit down and swear. In the dark lot there were two or three pale glimmers moving. Cooley took his binoculars out of the glove compartment and managed to get one of them in the field of view: it was a man with a flashlight.

That tore it. He had never heard of a carnival keeping a night watch before, but there they were. If he tried to get in there with four two-by-fours, two jerrycans of gasoline and a carton full of rags, they would catch him for sure, and even if he got away, the giant would have had a warning.

For a moment he considered the rifle. It was in the wagon, his Winchester .30-06, cleaned and oiled, with two boxes of soft-nosed ammo, and he could wrap it up in brown paper or something, take it on the Ferris wheel and wait for his chance. The range would be only about twenty-five yards, but how would he get rid of the rifle afterward? And what if the wheel happened to start or stop just as he squeezed the trigger?

All the excitement had drained out of him and he was suddenly tired. He started the car, drove to the end of town, found a tourist court and checked in. In the knotty-pine cabin, under the miserly yellow light, he looked at his road map. Between here and Elvis, where the carnival was going next, there were two possible routes, the four-lane state highway he had used coming down here, and a two-lane secondary route. Tomorrow he would see what could be done there.

Chapter Fifteen

Early the next morning Cooley drove out of town on the state highway. Forty miles out of East Anglia he came to an underpass; it was marked, "Clearance 11 feet 10 inches." Cooley turned off at the next exit, drove east until he came to the secondary route, then turned back toward East Anglia. The road was winding and hilly, with second-growth forests on either side.

After a few miles he came to a feeder road that connected the two highways. He drove down it to the state highway, and saw a sign, "Truck Route," that he hadn't noticed before. The carnival caravan would turn off here, it would have to— eleven feet ten was not high enough for the semis. He turned the wagon around, went back to the secondary road and headed for Elvis again, driving slowly. He was looking for a place where a truck and semitrailer would be sure to go off the road if you shot out a tire. What he found was something better.

Ten miles up the secondary route, he came to a broad gravel road that went up between cut banks into the hills. On a sudden hunch, he turned up it. Three miles brought him to a T where another road branched off. There was a heavy chain stretched between concrete posts, and a rusted metal sign: "Private. No Trespassing." Cooley parked on the shoulder, got out, and listened. The air was clear and still. He stepped over the chain and began walking up the road. When he had gone only a few hundred yards, he could see the black mounds rising above the treetops; then he knew where he was.

The road made a loop that brought it back under an enormous hopper projecting from a metal building that had once been painted green. Mammoth coal trucks were in a parking area off the road; beyond them was a little green house that looked like it might be a watchman's shack, but it was padlocked and empty.

Cooley went back to his car for a flashlight and a tire iron. He used the iron to prize open the door to the tower. He wanted to make sure that the hopper was full, and it was; it was loaded with pea coal, and that was perfect.

The whole thing, or anyhow the main part of it, had come into his head as soon as he saw the coal station. What he had in mind was complicated, and there were things that could go wrong with it at every stage, but if it worked it would be better than a fire.

He couldn't help thinking how great it would be if Jerry was alive and here to help him. There were a couple of places in his scheme that really needed two people, and there was one place where he couldn't see how to do it alone. He had it all figured out except that one part, where the semi came around the loop. The semi would have to stop in just the right spot, and he had thought about putting something in the road, a sawhorse, or a sign, or maybe a bonfire, but any of those things the driver would see from way back, and you couldn't tell where he would put on the brakes. If somebody jumped out on the road suddenly, that would be perfect, but Cooley couldn't do it because he had to be in the control room. That was where Jerry would have come in. But Jerry was dead, and so was Paul, and they couldn't help, unless maybe one of them came back as a ghost.

That was what gave him the idea, or else it was seeing the scarecrow in the field. The scarecrow was just an old shirt and a pair of pants, and a round head made of two pieces of cloth sewed together, the whole thing stuffed with straw. After Cooley saw it, he drove for half a mile in a sort of trance, then turned around and took the scarecrow off its pole.

In East Anglia that afternoon he bought a hacksaw, a can of medium-weight machine oil, a long-handled screwdriver, a staple gun, a reel of copper wire, some sash weights, a pair of wire cutters, and fresh batteries for his flashlight. At the five and dime down the street, he bought scissors, needles, and carpet thread. Nobody was around when he got back to his cabin. He attached the sash weights to one end of a length of wire, opened the scarecrow's body, and inserted the weights. He threaded the wire up through the top of the scarecrow's head, wishing it had brown hair, and formed the end into a ring. Then he went back to the car for Paul's photograph, the one he had meant to tape on the giant's window. It was an enlargement of an old snapshot; the face was almost life size. He cut the face out with scissors and sewed it onto the scarecrow's face.

At six o'clock he ate a slice of ham with red-eye gravy in the greasy spoon, then drove out of town. It took him a little over an hour to get to the coal station turnoff. The chain across the entrance was heavy; it took him half an hour to cut through one link. When he was finished, he pulled the chain out of the way, got into his wagon, and drove up the road to the coal station. He went all the way around the loop and parked just behind the hopper.

The next thing was the scarecrow. Cooley fastened the end of his copper wire to the loop at the top of the figure's head. Then he carried the reel up the outside stairway of the hopper, hoisted the figure until it hung a foot or two off the ground, cut the wire and fastened it to a rung of the stairway. The figure hung below, rotating gently. Cooley went down to look at it. He got into his car, turned on the headlights, and drove slowly under the hopper. The figure ahead was ghostly against the twilight. Cooley pictured how it would look if it suddenly appeared ahead of him; he jammed on the brakes, and now, in his mind, he heard the rattle and roar of coal falling from the hopper.

He backed up a few yards and turned off the headlights. He left the car there, climbed the stairway again and hoisted the scarecrow. He fastened another length of wire to the ring in the figure's head, passed the wire through a rung, and went down again, unreeling the wire behind him. He opened a window in the control booth, passed the wire inside, and reeled it in until the figure hung just above the bottom of the hopper. He cut the wire, secured it to a desk-leg. He studied the control board until he was sure he understood it. Then he picked up his tools and the rest of the wire, put them in the wagon, and drove back toward East Anglia on the secondary road. Before long he saw what he was looking for: a piece of white cardboard with a red arrow on it, stapled to a tree. The route man had been through here sometime in the evening, "arrowing the route" for the caravan.

Cooley stopped and got out long enough to pry loose the marker with his screwdriver. Most of these arrows were just for reassurance; there was no place to turn here anyhow. At the turnoff to the feeder road he found a cluster of three red arrows, and took one; at the state road there was another cluster, and he got one there. That made three, and he needed one more. He drove back past the coal station road until he found another one, and took it.

He stapled one of his arrows to a tree half a mile up the gravel road, then two more to indicate the turn between the concrete posts where he had cut the chain. He uprooted the "No Trespassing" sign and threw it into a bush. He put up his last arrow pointing straight ahead where the road looped back to form a Y. Then he drove back to East Anglia, parked on the street in front of the carnival, and waited. Only a few people were on the midway; the white lights of the Ferris wheel were revolving lonely in the darkness.

At midnight he heard the loudspeakers announcing that the carnival was over; half an hour later he saw the workmen swarming over the rides and booths, disassembling them to be loaded into trucks. About three o'clock he saw the caravan forming up. Three semis marked in the carnival's purple and orange pulled out first, then three cars with house trailers, then the semi with the yellow cab, the one that was Gene Anderson's. Cooley started his engine, turned a corner to get off the main street, and headed for the secondary road. He believed he had time enough to get where he was going ahead of the caravan, because it would take a while for them all to get onto the state highway, but he kept the speedometer at seventy and hurtled over the winding road behind the beams of his headlights.

Larry Scanlon unlocked the cab, swung himself up, and closed the door. He took a sip of the Coke he was carrying and set it down in the snack box. The yellow tag was hanging from the mirror, the signal they used to let Larry know that the giant was back in the trailer. He removed it and tossed it into the glove compartment. He had spent the last three hours helping to take down and load the loop-the-loop. A shower would have been good, but he would just get sweaty again, unloading and setting up in Elvis. The house trailer ahead of him was just pulling out; he started the engine, turned on the headlights and followed.

Once they were on the highway there was nothing to do but follow the taillights of the driver ahead. He finished the Coke and lit a cigarette. This was part of what he liked about carnival life—pulling out of town in the dead of night, heading for somewhere else, being awake and moving when the rest of the world was asleep. Back in Cleveland, the kids he had gone to school with were probably pounding their ears, with alarm clocks beside them to wake them for one more day at their boring jobs; or else they were in Viet Nam getting their butts shot off.

The four-lane was almost deserted at this time of night. Every now and then, when the road curved just enough but not too much, he could see the lights of the caravan strung out in the darkness, but most of the time his view was blocked by the house trailer ahead. After about three-quarters of an hour he saw the trailer's turn signals flash three times. He flicked the lever, passing the signal along, and reduced his speed.

The caravan turned off the highway onto a feeder road that led to a two-lane rising and dipping through the hills. There were so many sharp curves now that he frequently lost sight of the trailer ahead and the car behind him. As he came around one curve, he saw a moving light, and hit the brake. Someone was standing on the shoulder, swinging a flashlight with a red rim, and he saw that the flash was pointing up a steep gravel road. As he slowed to make the turn, he glimpsed the figure in the headlights; it was a short, heavy-set man, but his hat brim shadowed his face and Larry couldn't see who it was.

The semi had lurched a little as he made the turnoff and shifted down. After a minute the intercom hissed and crackled. "Larry?"

"Yeah, Mr. Kimberley. I wake you up?"

"Guess so. Where are we, anyway?"

"Beats me. There was a guy back there with a flashlight, so I turned off."

"With a flashlight? That's funny."

"Yeah." There was nothing in sight in the gravel road ahead, and nothing behind but the cloud of dust they were making. "This doesn't look right," Larry said. "Oh, wait a minute—" The headlights lit up a tree on his right; a red arrow was stapled to the trunk of the tree. "There's an arrow."

Headlights came up behind. "Guess it's all right," Larry said. "Here comes somebody behind us." The lights kept coming, drew up, and swung out to pass. In the dust cloud as it pulled ahead, Larry could tell only that it was a brown station wagon, not hauling anything, just a car.

"What about the guy with the light, could you tell who it was?"

"No."

The pale road unwound before them out of the darkness. The taillights of the car that had passed were nowhere to be seen, and there was still no one behind them. "There's another arrow," said Larry, with relief. On a tree ahead, two red arrows marked a turn. Larry swung the wheel. "Maybe this'll take us back to the highway."

Ahead, tall shapes were looming against the sky. The road made a Y; another red arrow showed him which way to go. The other road ran past a cluster of tall buildings with skeletal stairways going up and down; beyond them were black mounds, taller than the buildings. "Coal," said Larry. "This can't be right. Oh, *hell*." In the headlights, he could see that the road curved into a loop—it was going to lead them back to the Y again. He stopped the truck. "This is a mine or something," he said. "I don't get it. Some kind of a joke?"

"I'm coming up," the giant's voice said. The hiss from the intercom stopped.

In the side mirror, he saw the trailer door open. The giant came out, wearing his brown and white robe. He walked past the cab, crossed in the glare of the headlights, and after a moment rapped on the window. Larry leaned over to unlock the door for him, and he climbed in, ducking under the ceiling of the cab. He rummaged in the glove compartment, pulled out a road map, and spread it between them in the glow of the dome light.

Larry studied it a moment. "Here's the state road," he said. "This must be where we turned off, and then here's where we went north again on the two-lane. *This* road doesn't even show on the map." He looked up. "What do you think?"

"All we can do is go back the way we came, and just head for Elvis. We'll get there late."

"Yeah. Well—" Larry put the truck into gear and drove around the curve of the loop. Where the road straightened again, it led under the bulk of a tall structure on posts that straddled the road. "What's that?" the giant asked.

"A hopper. Where they load coal, I guess." As they drove under it, something white flashed toward them, a leaping figure, arms waving. Larry hit the brakes; the engine died. He had just time to see that the pale figure was a dummy, a scarecrow with a face, jerking and swinging in front of the windshield. Then the cab shook to an insane roar; the figure was gone behind a tumbling stream of darkness that cascaded past the windshield.

"Back up!" the giant said sharply.

The roar continued, like nothing Larry had ever heard. His arms were trembling, and he couldn't feel the gearshift lever. He got it into neutral somehow, turned on the engine, then shifted into reverse. When he let out the clutch, nothing seemed to happen. The cab rocked a little, but the roar continued and the dark cascade kept on falling.

"You're just spinning the wheels," the giant shouted in his ear. "Try forward. Hurry up!"

Larry slammed the gearshift lever into first. It was a moment before he realized that he had killed the engine again. He felt dizzy, and it was hard to focus his eyes: he was trembling all over. He got the engine started, let the clutch out and stepped on the gas. Nothing happened, except that the cab shuddered and slewed a little.

"Oh, God!" said Larry. His voice was stifled inside his head by the unending, maddening roar. He jammed the gas pedal down, again and again. The idiot lights went on; he had killed the engine once more. He reached for the start button, but the giant's hand covered his. "Don't," said the voice in his ear. "The exhaust stacks must be covered by now. Leave it off."

"What?" he said. "I don't—Oh, God, oh, God!" He wrenched his hand away, grabbed the steering wheel and tried to shake it, then thought of the door handle and reached for it, but it would not move. The giant's arm came around him, pinning him to the seat. "Easy," said the voice. "Easy. Take it easy."

The roar went on echoing unbearably in the cab, like an avalanche, a river of stone; darkness hurtled past the windshield, the side windows. "Easy!" Larry said. "Oh, God!" His mouth wouldn't work right, and when he wiped it with his sleeve, he found that his face was wet with tears.

Bits of the solid darkness were bounding upward from the hood. Larry stared uncomprehendingly; then he saw the edge of the black mass creeping up from the bottom of the wind-shield. It was rising all around them. Coal! They were being buried in coal! He screamed and fought, but the giant would not let him go.

Remorseless as sand in an hourglass, the darkness rose over the windshield. Now there was only a narrow stripe at the top where the black torrent was still falling. Now even that was gone. In the yellow dome light, the windshield and side windows were masked by a solid layer of tiny gray-glistening bits of coal. The sound had changed; it was more furious than ever on the roof, but muffled all around.

Then there was another change: the roar of the falling coal was receding above their heads, dwindling, distant. At last it stopped. Larry could hear nothing but the painful ringing in his ears. The giant held him firmly. "Listen," he said. "Listen. We're going to get out. You understand me?"

"Get out," said Larry. He heard how weak his voice was, but he couldn't help it. "How we going to get out?"

"I'll show you after a while. Right now we have to wait."

"Wait, why?"

"Because the man who did this is still out there." He let go of Larry. "Okay now?"

Larry wiped his face with his sleeve. "You know who did it?"

"I think so. It's a man who wants to kill me."

Larry looked at him in wonder. The giant's mouth was set in an expression he could not read: it was not anger or sadness, but something else.

He could feel his body still trembling; he was cold all the way through, as cold as if he were already dead. Through the ringing in his ears he could feel the silence. There was nothing out there, nothing but stillness; it was like being entombed in the heart of a mountain. After a moment he fumbled in his pocket for a cigarette.

"Better not," said the giant. "The air."

"Oh. How long can we—?"

"I don't know. Long enough, but it won't help if we fill the cab with smoke."

They listened to the silence. The giant said, "You remember that thing that jumped at us? What did it look like?"

"I dunno. It happened so quick. A dummy, I guess, like a scarecrow."

"The face? Did you see the face?"

"Yeah."

"Was it a kid's face?"

"Maybe. Yeah, I guess so. Listen, couldn't we break a window—"

"The coal would come in."

"Yeah, but we could pull the coal in and then get out the window."

"Unless there's too much coal. Even if there isn't, I told you, the man who did this is still out there. We've got to wait."

"How long?"

"Till he goes away."

"Okay, if you say so." Larry fidgeted. "I gotta piss," he said, and clamped his knees together. "Oh, Jesus."

"Is there a bottle or something?"

He remembered the Coke bottle, reached for it, and unzipped his pants. It was hard to direct the stream through the narrow neck of the bottle; some of it ran down outside and some sprayed. He offered the half-full bottle to the giant. "Do you want—?"

"No, I'll wait." Suddenly the giant raised his head. "He's gone."

"You sure?"

"Yes."

"What do we do now?"

"Wait awhile, just to make sure he doesn't come back."

After a moment Larry heard himself saying, "There was a story we read in school, the cask of something—"

"*The Cask of Amontillado?*"

"Yeah, that was it. Where they wall up this guy in the cellar?"

" 'For the love of God, Montresor.' I remember."

"Yeah, when he put in the last brick. That scared the hell out of me."

"Try not to think about it."

"Some kids locked me in a closet once, when I was little."

"Where was that, in Cleveland?"

"Yeah. I can remember how it smelled in there. Kind of dead air. Ever since then—"

"What did your folks do?"

"My old man's an engineer with the power company. He was sore when I dropped out of school Then he wanted me to volunteer for the army. Listen, it's getting real hard to breathe in here. Can you really do it, because if you can *for God's sake* will you do it?''

"All right." The giant turned away and put his hands on the window.

"That's jammed," Larry said.

"I know it. Shut up a minute."

Larry waited. After a few moments he heard a curious rustling sound. He leaned to look past the giant's body, and saw with disbelief that the particles of coal were sliding down past the window.

The giant let his head hang for a moment, took a deep breath, and straightened again. The rustling sound resumed. Suddenly a shaft of pale light came in at the top of the window. It was the most beautiful and unexpected thing Larry had ever seen. It widened into a wedge-shape, expanding slowly and steadily. "What are you doing?" he whispered.

"Getting rid of the coal," said the giant. He lowered his head for a moment, raised it again. The wedge of daylight steadily widened; Larry could see now that a funnel was forming in the coal beyond the door, particles pouring down the sides as if they were falling into a hole somewhere.

The giant opened the door and stepped out. Larry followed him. They were in a semicircular hollow space; beyond it the coal was still heaped chest-high. The buildings around them were silent and almost shadowless in the morning light; the sky was a pale greenish blue, and the air was scented with moisture. Larry filled his lungs again and again, experiencing the incredible fact that he was alive.

The giant was climbing the slope. Larry scrambled up after him on hands and knees, got over the top and down the other side.

The giant was a few yards away, staring at the front of the mound. After a moment Larry saw what he was looking at: a thin copper wire hung from a stairway on the hopper almost to the mound of coal. Another piece, not attached to anything, lay in loops on the road. "That's where he hung the dummy," the giant said. "He must have taken it away again. I was hoping it was still here."

He turned, and they walked around to the back. The mound of coal covered all but the last five feet of the trailer. The giant turned long enough to say, "See if you can find a shovel. They must have some around for cleanup.''

When he came back with the shovel, the giant was standing at the side of the mound. Directly in front of him, Larry could see that a little funnel-shaped space had formed high on the slope, exposing the top of the door. As he watched, the funnel deepened abruptly. There was a pause, and it deepened again.

The giant looked around and saw him. ''Dig,'' he said.

''It'll take me all day to shovel this. Why can't you—''

''I can't do much at a time. Shut up and dig.''

By the time they had cleared the door, it was full daylight. Sweat was dripping from Larry's chin; the giant looked haggard and ill. Inside, the lighted interior of the trailer was like a room in a cave. The giant climbed in slowly, took off his robe and began to dress. When he was finished, he wandered around the trailer and put a few things in his pockets, then took a suitcase out of the storage space under the bed. ''Let's go.''

''Aren't you going to put anything in that?''

''No, it doesn't matter.''

Out in the road, the giant put the suitcase down. ''This had better be good-bye. I can't go back to the carnival, and I wish you wouldn't either, because that's the first place he'll look. It would be easy enough for him to find out you were my driver. You understand?'' He took some bills out of his pocket and handed them to Larry. ''Take this and buy yourself a car, or get on the train and go wherever you want. And by the way, if there's anything in the trailer you want, help yourself.''

''What are you going to do?''

The giant smiled faintly. ''I'm going to find a place in the woods to sleep for about eight hours. After that—it's better if you don't know. Good luck to you, Larry.'' He turned and walked away.

Larry looked at the money in his hand. The first bill was a hundred dollars, and so was the next, and the next . . . there were thirty of them. When he looked up, the giant was already out of sight around the curve of the road.

Chapter Sixteen

In October of that year Gene Anderson landed in Le Havre, where he joined Le Cirque Tripp, a small traveling circus and sideshow. During the next few years he moved often from one circus or carnival to another; by the time he was twenty-six he had visited every country in Europe. He changed his professional name many times. In Great Britain he was John Livingston; in France, Belgium, and Holland, Peter Owen, *le géant gallois*; in Italy and Greece, Robert Lee. In his twenty-sixth year he grew only half an inch: he was then eight feet four inches tall.

On a post at the side of his booth Anderson always taped a little card with the names of his childhood pen-pals on it: Gerd Heilbrunner, Claudina Neri, Yves Morand. One day in Paris, a woman said to him, "Why do you have my name on your card?"

He looked at her intently. She was blond, slender, erect, with a thin aristocratic nose: not pretty but handsome. "Are you Claudina Neri?"

"I was. Who are you?"

"Gene Anderson. We used to correspond. I'm very glad to meet you."

She put her hand in his and withdrew it. "My God!" she said. "I had forgotten, I was a girl at school. Let me think, you lived in—what was it, Washington?"

"Oregon."

"You never told me you were a giant."

"I wasn't one then."

Two people were holding up photographs for him to sign. Claudina Neri wrote something on a card and handed it to him. "This is where I am staying. Come and see me."

They met the next morning at her hotel. Her name was Faure now. Her husband was Belgian; she had married when she was eighteen. They lived in Antwerp; she came to Paris once or twice a year for the shopping. There was also a villa in Nice, and she spoke of frequent trips to Rome, Florence, Athens. Her father was Italian, her mother German; she spoke French, English, Italian, German, Spanish.

"You are an extraordinary person," she told him at breakfast. "It is wrong of you to be so ignorant."

"I didn't have your advantages," Anderson said.

"If you mean the convent school, it was purgatory for me. I tried twice to commit suicide before I was sixteen. I was educated by force. You must educate yourself. Read, learn, think."

She made him speak French and corrected his mistakes; she also criticized his table manners. "A polite person does not use his fork like a shovel, to scoop food into his mouth, nor use his fingers to push food onto his fork."

They spent three mornings together before the circus left for Orléans, and after that Anderson saw her nearly every year. She seldom spoke of her husband, and Anderson met him only once, in the summer of 1968: a dark-haired man with pomaded hair, whose manners were almost too exquisite. She took him to the Louvre, which he disliked, and to the Jeu de Paume and the Orangerie, where he found all the Impressionists whose work was still excluded from the Louvre. He discovered, however, that very good postcard reproductions of Monet and van Gogh were for sale in the gift shop of the Louvre; he bought stacks of these and carried them with him for years.

They went to Notre Dame de Paris, in whose vast shadowy vault the rose windows stared down like celestial mandalas. Anderson was moved beyond speech. A woman near them was talking loudly and angrily in German.

"Everyone hates the Germans," Claudina remarked afterward, when they were sitting in the sunlight at a brasserie across the street from the cathedral.

"Because they invaded France?"

"No, just because they are Germans."

Once when she protested that he was paying too much at a restaurant, he said, "Don't worry about the money; I have plenty."

"More than they pay you in the circus?"

"Yes."

"Then why do you stay?"

"It's a community," he told her. "I'm accepted there; it's almost like having a family."

"There are other families." She introduced him to artists and writers, to Dubuffet, Genet, Arenas. Some of them became his friends, and gave him notes to people in other places. He bought paintings and sculptures, because he liked them and because he wanted to help the artists; he bought books, more than he could carry with him. He put them in storage, in Paris, Rome, Athens, Berlin. He was spending much more than he earned, and he disliked counterfeiting currency. In Turkey he bought cut diamonds at wholesale, thirty carats in all. He copied them, distributed the copies into bags, copied them again. Three months later, when he was in Amsterdam, he took his diamonds to a dealer.

"And where did you obtain these diamonds, Mr. Gordon?" the manager asked politely.

"In Ankara."

"And do you have an import license for them?"

"No."

The manager, a young man, rosy-cheeked, very well dressed, folded his hands on the table. "In that case, I could not offer you a very good price, I'm afraid."

"It doesn't matter. I want to sell them."

The manager stirred the pile of stones with his finger. "One hundred forty thousand guilders."

After that, he came back at least once a year and sold larger and larger quantities of diamonds. He put his money in numbered accounts in Switzerland. Later he began to invest in stocks and bonds, real estate, precious metals. There were many pleasures in the world for a young man with money; but even as he took them, he thought, *Is this all?*

For a few years after Avila's death he had continued to make occasional small wood carvings; then even that had stopped, and he knew now that he had never had a real vocation. He had left everyone he had loved behind him. Although he had many friends, he knew he could get along without any one of them; he was proud of this self-reliance, this invulnerability, and he despised himself for it.

During the late sixties and early seventies he spent a good deal of time in museums. One of his favorite places was the Alte Pinakothek in Munich, where they had Rubens' huge *Fall of the Damned*—all those plump pink bellies and buttocks tumbling through the air like clotted leaves on the wind. Another was the Musée Unterlinden, in Colmar. He kept going back there to see Grünewald's *Isenheim Altarpiece*, the only Crucifixion that he thought was worth a damn: Christ's body, not afloat in Disneyland like the one in El Greco, with its silly spigot of blood and its loincloth slipping coyly down like the tresses of the Botticelli Venus, and not like van der Weyden's Oriental monarch, lily in one hand, girdle in the other, robe flapping open across his muscular midriff, about to flap further—God the Great Flasher—but hanging under the weight of its pain, mouth open in a rictus and the sweat of death on its skin. It was not so much that he wanted to see it but that he could not stay away.

At a party given by a non-objective painter in London, he met a scruffy man named Hamilton who was drawing diagrams on the back of an envelope. "You see, here's the human population in the Middle Ages," he said. "See how it rises very gradually until you get to about seventeen fifty. Now it goes up more steeply. The population in nineteen fifty was about two and a half billion. By the year two thousand, it will be more like six billion."

The woman on the other side leaned over, spilling her Martini on Hamilton's knee. "Oh, sorry," she said. "But after all, Reggie, what's wrong with six billion people?"

Hamilton looked at her. "We can't feed that many," he said. "Even if we could, can we feed twice as many? Fifteen billion in twenty fifty? What about twenty-four billion? If we don't reduce our population ourselves, something else will reduce it for us."

"What might that be?"

"War. Famine. Plague."

"How grim." The woman got up, swaying a little, and called to a man across the room. "Donald, haven't you got any good records?"

"You see," said Hamilton, "they won't listen. I think it's the most extraordinary thing."

"Well, she's drunk," Gene said.

"Yes, but you're not, and you're not really listening either, are you?"

"Did you say you'd published a book about this?"

"Yes. It sold two thousand copies in England. There were more babies born than that on the day of publication. The main culprit," he went on, "is modern medicine. If you wanted to do something useful for humanity, you could go back in a time machine and kill Pasteur."

"Are you serious?"

"Oh, absolutely. Until the end of the nineteenth century there was really no effective medicine for anything. Doctors weren't healers especially, they were diagnosticians—their job was to identify the malady and tell the patient what to expect. Apart from that, and a lot of nostrums that didn't work, they just did palliative things—sent people on ocean voyages, and so on. Well, in the twentieth century we've wiped out one disease after another, and the result is that there is no effective check on population. But people are breeding pretty much the way they always have, and you see the ghastly result. You're, what, about twenty?"

"Twenty-four."

"Well, with reasonable luck, you'll live long enough to see the big smash. I put it about ten years into the new century. We can't go on as we are much longer than that."

"You'd rather see people die of things like cholera, and typhoid?"

"It's not a question of wanting people to die. We're all going to die. The question is *how many*. People are going to die of plague and famine and war. The longer we put it off, the worse it will be."

"What's the answer, then? Birth control, education?"

"Yes. The only answer, except the three I mentioned."

"Will it work?"

After a moment Hamilton put his envelope away in his pocket. "No. Probably not. But one's got to try."

One spring in Rome, when Claudina was there, she took him to see an extraordinary exhibit. It was not in a gallery but in a cellar hired for the occasion, under an abandoned brewery. From the lobby where they bought their tickets they went down a steep flight of stairs into an unpleasant earth-smelling gloom. An attendant held a curtain open. "*Per favore*." Beyond the curtain they found themselves in a long, high chamber with a wooden hand-rail running down the middle. The only light came from dim hooded lamps aimed diagonally upward from the floor. Above each of these lights, as their eyes began to adjust, they could see a monstrous incomprehensible shape projecting from the wall. As they moved slowly down the room, each figure in turn became clearer. There were five: a king and a queen in tenth-century costume, a goat-horned demon, a nude and obese woman with a hood concealing her face, a hawk-headed image of the god Horus. The figures were carved of some grainless wood, stained red-brown; each one sat on a carved throne fixed to the wall, not upright but projecting horizontally, so that the vast malignant faces stared downward; and the figures were so massive, so arrogant in their perverse gravity that Gene and Claudina felt a kind of vertigo, as if they themselves, not the carved figures, were standing impossibly on a wall.

Afterward they met the artist, a haggard young man named Gianfranco Peganuzzi. His smile was wolfish; his English was very good.

"Where did you get the idea for those figures?" Gene asked.

"It was something in *The Adventures of Augie March*, by Saul Bellow. His people were in a gallery in Paris, looking at some paintings from the Pinakothek, and Bellow wrote, 'These grand masterpieces were sitting on the walls.' At first I thought that was funny. Then I said to myself, 'Why not?' And then it grew."

He said that it had taken him five years to carve the figures; he had hollowed them out to reduce the weight, but, even so, each one weighed seven hundred pounds, and it had been necessary to attach them by means of bolts inserted through holes drilled in the masonry.

"Did you feel a dislocation, a nausea?" he asked.

"Yes," said Claudina, "very much. I understood then why there was a hand-rail. And after the exhibition, what will you do with them?"

He shrugged. "Maybe some museum will buy them, or some collector. Or maybe, if I get rich, I will build a gallery for them, underground—in a castle which I will buy, you understand—and leave them there. There will be no lights in the gallery. If you want to see them, you have to go there with flashlights." He grinned.

*   *   *

In 1972 Gene Anderson left the circus for good and took up residence in Athens, where there was an international community that he liked. Among his friends there was an Irish painter named Hugh Mulloy. Mulloy drank a good deal and quarreled with his wife, and sometimes when she locked him out he would go to one of his friends' apartments, climb down the fire escape, and get in through a window. They would find him the next morning asleep on the couch, or perhaps on the floor. People used to say, "Poor old Hugh." Everyone liked him, even when he was so drunk that he couldn't talk. He was an emaciated little man with ginger-colored hair and bright blue eyes. His favorite saying was, "Let's have another for the fun that's in it."

In the autumn of 1973 Gene was living in an old high-ceilinged apartment in the Patésia district; he had been there only a month or two. One night he had a bad dream, the kind in which the dreamer sees everything very clearly and knows what is happening, but is unable to move. In the dream, he was in an old house, perhaps a castle, with tall ceilings and casement windows. It was dark outside. Gene was lying in bed looking at one of the windows, and he knew that in a moment someone was going to try to get in and kill him. But he could not move; it was that kind of dream. He lay watching the window, and he saw a man's shape appear in the frame. Then he woke up with a jolt, covered with sweat, cold and shaking. The window in his room was partly open, but there was nobody there. He closed the window and turned on all the lights, and sat up until after dawn. For some reason the dream had made him think of the gigantic carved figures of Gianfranco Peganuzzi, and he wondered if they were brooding somewhere in the darkness underground.

About a week later, someone asked him if he had seen Hugh. His friends compared notes; it turned out that no one had seen him since the day before Gene's nightmare; and no one ever saw him again.

Gene believed he knew what had happened. Hugh had been to his new apartment only once, and didn't know where all the rooms were. He must have come down the fire escape on the wrong side, and tried to get into Gene's bedroom window instead of the window in the living room; and Gene, half-aware in his sleep, had destroyed him—made him nonexistent, thrown him out of the world forever.

He went to see Hugh's wife and gave her some money, and got away as soon as he could; he was unable to bear her gratitude. He flew to London and talked to a marine architect, who designed for him a sixty-foot cutter-rigged sloop with a cabin and galley tall enough for him to stand upright. He took instruction in sailing and seamanship; a year later, when *Sea Sprite* was ready, he hired a deckhand-cook named Richards and sailed across the Atlantic. From that day onward, he never spent a night ashore in a room that had a window that could be reached from the outside.

Chapter Seventeen

On the Gulf coast outside St. Petersburg there is a chain of islands connected by causeways to each other and to the mainland; the islands form a strip twenty-five miles long and in places no more than a few hundred yards wide: St. Petersburg Beach, Treasure Island, Madeira Beach, Redington Beach, Indian Rocks. The southern end is heavily commercialized, with many luxury hotels and condominiums; then, as you go northward, the tourist cabins on the ocean side become progressively smaller and shabbier, the beach sadder and more desolate.

Margaret Morrow, freshly arrived from Albany, found a tourist cabin, one of six with identical peeling green paint and pink trim, at the upper end of Indian Rocks Beach; the place was called Site O'Sea. The owner and manager was an old woman with frizzy lemon-colored hair who wore muu-muus and carpet slippers, and called Margaret "Dearie." The cabin was a single room with a tiny kitchenette, a sofa bed, and an air conditioner that hummed and dripped all day long. The windows, of narrow glass panes that overlapped each other like the siding on a house, were gummy with salt spray, and the sand drifted in under the doorsill.

It was hard to get used to the strong sunlight, the bright pastel colors like a child's painting, the cleanness of everything. Sand was everywhere, drifted against the sides of houses, scattering in the wind across the highway; it got into your hair, your ears, and, if you were not careful, into your food, but there was no dirt, no grime. On the beach, at certain hours, the gulls and terns gathered in convention—just standing around, blinking wearily, the gulls and terns in separate groups but side by side, like businessmen waiting for a tour bus. Cormorants sat on the pilings of the groins, spreading their huge wings to dry. The sun on the water was piercingly white, painful to look at even through dark glasses. In the evening skimmers glided over the shallow water, scooping up something with their open beaks; the sun spread vast robes of pink and gold over half the sky, and the wind rattled the dry fronds of the palm trees.

On her second day she bought a newspaper and rode the bus into St. Petersburg. After Albany, the wide streets seemed almost empty. She filled out applications in three employment agencies. On the third day she answered advertisements in the paper and was interviewed, but not hired, by an insurance company, a stock broker, and a home finance agency. The next day was Saturday. She spent the weekend writing postcards, swimming, and walking on the beach. In a grocery bag she collected several pounds of shells and pebbles.

On Monday she applied for a waitress job in a coffee shop in Treasure Island; the manager said he would let her know. Walking back toward the bus stop, she noticed a sign she had not seen before: it was an employment agency, a tiny place tucked in between a drugstore and a real-estate office.

The woman behind the desk was a fortyish blonde in a startling blouse of blue and yellow trapezoids. She looked at Margaret's application without putting down her cigarette. "Well, let's see. You haven't had much business experience, have you?"

"No, but I can type and take shorthand."

"I see you were a teacher before—why did you give that up?"

"Not cut out for it, I guess."

The woman gave her an indifferent look. "Uh-huh. How good is your shorthand?"

"Not very, but I can brush up."

"Well, here's a filing job—you say you don't want that— filing and bookkeeping. . . . Here's one, secretary, part time, some filing and bookkeeping. Salary open, that means it probably isn't much."

"What sort of place is it?"

"Not a place, it's the man's home. Occupation, investor. Do you have a car?"

"No—not yet."

"Well, it's back in the boonies, but it says here, 'Will pick up for interview.'"

"I'd like to try it."

"All right." The woman picked up the phone, squinting past the smoke of her cigarette. "Mr. Anderson, please. . . . Well, would you tell him that Mrs. Harrell of Suncoast Employment called. We have an applicant for the secretary job, and she'd like to be picked up for an interview. . . . Just a moment." She covered the phone. "Can you go out there this afternoon?"

"Yes."

"Yes, that will be fine. Her name is Margaret Morrow. Two o'clock?" She lifted an eyebrow at Margaret. "All right, thank you."

She put the phone down. "Somebody will pick you up here at two. The office will be closed until twelve-thirty, but you can come back here any time after that. Whether you get the job or not, please remember to check back and let us know; that's important."

Margaret went back to the coffee shop, had a sandwich and a glass of milk, then browsed in the tourist shops until almost two.

In the waiting room sat a man in a blue flowered shirt. He was partly bald, compactly built, tanned the color of mahogany. There was a cold cigar stub in his mouth. He got up and put on a blue straw hat. "Miss Morrow?"

"Yes."

He looked up at her. "Well, you're tall enough, anyhow. My name is Bill Richards. Come on."

He led her to a dusty blue Lincoln convertible parked at the curb. "I haven't seen one of these in years," she remarked as she got in.

"They just started making them again." Richards pulled out into the street, made a startling U-turn and headed north. "Been here long?" he said around the cigar.

"No, only a week."

"Figures." He glanced at her out of the corner of his eye;

his expression did not change, but she thought he was amused. "Get a little sunburn?"

"A little."

"Thought so." His muscular arms were covered with coarse black hair; his fingers were blunt and spatulate, but his nails were clean.

"Mr. Richards, what does Mr. Anderson do?"

"A little of this, a little of that." He gave her a faint smile. "Mr. Anderson," he said, "is a very big man."

They were running across the causeway, the water sparkling white beneath them; then around the curve of the road, past Spanish-looking villas with palm trees, up the gentle rise that passed for a hill in Florida. After a few miles the car slowed, turned to the left onto a macadam road that quickly became white dust, bordered with yucca and palmetto. They turned again, running now between fenced pastures where brown and white cattle grazed; then once more, into a road marked "Private." Up ahead was a real hill covered with trees, a wall, a cluster of rooftops.

They halted in a wide archway closed by a wrought-iron gate. Richards rolled down his window and spoke to a grille in the wall. "Irma, open up." Beyond his head, Margaret could see a lens swiveling to point at them. "Okay," said a metallic voice. The gate swung open, they drove through past flowering bushes, a vast stretch of new lawn with sprinklers playing on it. Where the driveway leveled off, the house was too close to see, but she caught a glimpse of tall stucco walls, wrought-iron balconies.

They swung into the cool shadow of a carport. Richards led her up three steps to an enormously tall door of carved wood; he opened it and ushered her into a huge kitchen where a blond woman was sitting with a telephone in her hand. "I understand that, Mr. Lyons," she was saying, "But Mr. Anderson wants me to tell you that if we can't get better service, we'll have to look for another supplier." She smiled at Margaret and pointed to a chair at the long table.

Richards had disappeared; he came back carrying a cardboard carton full of packages and letters, which he set down on the table, then went out again.

The blond woman put down the phone. She was in her forties, a little plump in a candy-striped blouse and blue shorts; her legs were bare and tanned. "I'm Irma Hartz," she said.

"You're Miss Morrow, from the agency?"

"Yes."

"Nice to meet you. Want to go to the bathroom or anything before we start?"

"No, I'm fine."

"All right, let's go." When she stood up, Margaret noticed that her brown feet were bare. She led the way across the kitchen. The chair at the far end of the table stood in a curious sunken area, a foot or two lower than the rest of the floor. They passed into a tiled hallway, down a gentle ramp, and emerged into a vast space with a cathedral ceiling; it must have been thirty feet high. There were Oriental rugs on the tile floor; the walls were oyster white. To their left a broad ramp rose to a balcony at the far end of the room. Under the balcony, through sliding glass doors, she glimpsed a colonnade and a garden with a fountain. The room itself was enormous, more like a museum hall than a living room. The middle part of it was sunken, with a wrought-iron railing around it.

She followed Mrs. Hartz down a hall lined with pictures to a room fitted out with filing cabinets, a desk, an electronic typewriter. "Sit down, honey, and let's talk." Mrs. Hartz took a seat behind a second, smaller desk, and peered at her over her glasses. "Your name is Margaret Morrow—just like it sounds?"

"Yes."

Mrs. Hartz wrote on a yellow pad. "Age?"

"Thirty."

"Married?"

"No."

"What was your last job?"

"I was a schoolteacher in Albany."

"Albany, New York? Why did you leave?"

Margaret was silent a moment.

"Honey," said Mrs. Hartz, "I don't want to be nosy, but I have to know all this stuff. If you were fired, you can tell me."

"No, I wasn't fired," Margaret said. "Maybe I was burned out. My mother died in February. She was bedridden for seven years. And—" She stopped and went on again, trying to keep her voice level. "I don't know, the middle school I taught in was consolidated with a high school that wasn't as good, and some of our programs went downhill. It stopped being fun.

One day I caught myself hating one of the kids. It scared me, I thought maybe I was cracking up. The only thing I could think of was just to get out of Albany, and I came here because of the sunshine.''

Mrs. Hartz wrote something slowly. "O-kay." She got up and came around the desk. "Have you ever used one of these gadgets?" she asked, indicating a dictation machine beside the typewriter.

"No, not that kind."

"It uses a little plastic disk, like this one. You put it in the machine here. Here's the 'on' button, here's reverse—'review,' they call it—here's forward, and this counter keeps track of where you are." She touched a button, and a man's deep voice said, " . . . items number three seventy-five, three eighty-one, five ninety-seven, and please bill to my account." She pressed the "off" button. "Why don't you fool with this awhile till you get the hang of it, and then type the first letter on the disk. There's a foot pedal under here, and letterheads, envelopes, carbon paper, and all that stuff in these drawers. I'll be in the kitchen. You can bring the letter out when you're finished, or if you run into any trouble, you can call me on this intercom—press number five." She turned and went out.

Margaret sat down, pressed the "review" button, then played the disk from the beginning. "J. R. Veillot Frères, dear sirs, referring to your catalog dated November 1983, I would like to order items number one fifteen, two seventy, three seventy-five . . ." She stopped the machine; where was the address? She would feel like a fool to call Mrs. Hartz for help so soon, before she had even started.

There was a rotary file on the desk: she looked under *V*, and found it: Veillot, with an address in New York. She typed the letter rapidly. The letterhead read "G. Anderson," and she put that under the space for his signature. She typed an envelope, looked over the letter and envelope for errors, and carried them back to the kitchen.

Mrs. Hartz was sitting where Margaret had first seen her; behind her, in an alcove, there was an intercom and a television screen. She looked up and smiled. "All done? Let's see." She took the letter and envelope. "Perfect," she said firmly. "Good as I could do. How's your shorthand?"

"Pretty poor."

"Well, let's try it." Mrs. Hartz picked up a stenographic notebook and pencil, handed them to her. "Ready?" She turned a page of the account book before her and began to read. "Two hundred twenty square yards wool carpeting at seventy-three dollars, sixteen thousand and sixty dollars. Four pairs damask drapes . . ." It was a long list. When she was done, Mrs. Hartz put out her hand for the notebook. "Can I see?"

Margaret handed it over: it was a mixture of half-remembered Gregg shorthand, abbreviations, and figures.

"That's a mess," Mrs. Hartz said, "but if you can read it back, what's the difference?" She handed Margaret the notebook again. "See if you can."

"Two hundred twenty square yards wool carpeting," Margaret began, and went through to the end of the list.

"Okay," said Mrs. Hartz. "Let's see if we can find the boss." She reached back to the intercom and pressed a button. "Gene, are you there?"

"Yes," said a voice promptly.

"You want to come in and meet Miss Morrow, or should I bring her out?"

A pause. "Bring her out. I'm too dirty to come in."

"Okay." Mrs. Hartz went to a closet, came back with a pair of sneakers without laces, and put them on. Margaret followed her through the sliding doors at the far end of the living room, across the colonnade to a long building behind the house. The interior was brilliantly lit by the glass panes in the north side of the roof. Down at the far end a bearded man stood at a workbench, cutting something on a jigsaw. Only when he turned off the saw and began walking toward them did she realize that perspective had misled her in that enormous room: the man was grotesquely, impossibly tall.

He picked up a bench casually with one hand as he approached; he put it down in front of them and sat on it. Even then, he loomed over the two women until he bent over to put his elbows on his knees, like a man leaning over to talk to children. That was almost worse, because his leonine head was so big and so close. His skin was deeply tanned, but not as dark as Richards'; bits of wood dust were clinging to his beard and to the bleached hairs of his arms and chest. He looked at Margaret attentively when Mrs. Hartz introduced them, and took her hand in his for a moment; his huge fingers were calloused and warm. His face was heavy-boned, perfectly in proportion except for his eyes, which were no larger than hers. His voice was unexpectedly quiet. "Three or four hours a day," he was saying. "Would that suit you?"

She stammered something.

"Fine, then. Tomorrow?"

"Yes, tomorrow."

Mrs. Hartz led her back through the garden. "Didn't Pongo tell you?" she asked.

"What?"

"Pongo—Bill Richards—the man who brought you out. Didn't he say anything?"

"He said Mr. Anderson was a very big man."

Mrs. Hartz snorted. "That's Pongo." They crossed the living room again, went through the hall into the kitchen. It was cool here; Margaret sat down gratefully at the table. She looked at the huge Spanish chair at the far end where the floor was sunken. How could she not have understood?

"Second thoughts?" Mrs. Hartz asked, coming over with a cup and a pot of coffee. "This is dark Colombian. Would you rather have something else? Tea, or a Coke?"

"No, this is fine. Thank you."

Mrs. Hartz sat down and put her elbows on the table. "Well, you can have the job if you want it. He likes you."

"How could you tell?"

"If he didn't, he would've let me know. Then it would be up to me to tell you to leave your number and pretend we'd call you later. Gene won't tell a lie if he can help it, but he doesn't care if I do."

Margaret sipped her coffee, put it down. "Mrs. Hartz—"

"Irma."

"Irma, would you take this job if you were me?"

"Sure. I'm here, aren't I? Any dumbbell could do the work; I did it myself until last week. But it doesn't hurt to be smart, no matter what you're doing, unless it bores you out of your mind."

"*You're* no dumbbell. Why only until last week?"

"We were living in the cottages in back, until the big house was finished. Then Gene wanted me to be the housekeeper, and I couldn't do both. Now, take your time, but tell me if you want it. He'll pay you twice what you're worth. What *would* you say you're worth?"

"Oh—I don't know. Ten dollars an hour?"

"Okay, twenty then, and he'll pay you for a full week no matter how much you work, so that's eight hundred."

"Eight hundred a *week?* That's too much!"

"I know it, but he doesn't care. Deal?"

"Okay."

"All right, now about transportation. You haven't got a car?"

"No."

"Pongo can take you back and forth until you get some wheels of your own. Don't know where he is now, though. I'll try his cottage." She leaned back to the intercom, pushed a button. "Pongo?"

"Yeah."

"You want to run Miss Morrow back into town?"

There was a perceptible pause. "Okay. Five minutes."

"Mrs. Hartz, I can just as well get a taxi—"

"It would take half an hour to get out here. Where are you living, in town?"

"No, on the beach, at Indian Rocks."

"Well, that's a forty-dollar fare. Relax, Pongo can do it—he likes to drive."

Margaret was waiting at the kitchen door when the Lincoln pulled up, looking dustier than ever. Pongo grinned at her around his cigar when she got in. "Make out okay?"

"I got the job."

"All right." The gate opened for them and they wheeled onto the long dusty road. "Surprised when you met the boss?"

She smiled. "Yes."

He glanced at her to see her expression. "He's not a bad guy to work for."

"Have you known him long?" she asked.

"Ten years, on *Sea Sprite*. She's decommissioned now, over in Tampa. Needs new rigging and some work on the engines. We went all over the world in her. Australia, India, Japan, everywhere. He says he's all done cruising now. Maybe he is."

Pongo let her out at the entrance to the cottages and asked what time she wanted to be picked up in the morning.

"Mrs. Hartz said she'd like me to start around ten, but please don't come. Honestly. I'm going to rent a car—you have so much to do already."

"Aw, that's all right," he said, but she could tell he was pleased.

Chapter Eighteen

When she arrived at the house the next morning, she found the gate open. Up by the kitchen door three black women in maids' uniforms were getting into a station wagon, and beyond that was a huge delivery van. Margaret pulled over to make room for the station wagon; the driver, a black man, gave her an expressionless glance as he drove past.

She parked her rented Mazda in the garage; Pongo's Lincoln was not there, but there were two other cars, a black Mercedes and a green BMW station wagon, plus a vast cream-colored motor home.

At the back of the house, two men in blue work clothes were carrying a crate from the moving van through an open doorway. A metallic screech came from somewhere inside, then another. She peered in and saw Anderson, bare-chested as before, surrounded by crates, with a wrecking bar in his hand. He waved when he saw her. "Margaret, I've got my hands full this morning. If you can go on and get started by yourself, I'll be able to talk to you later."

"That'll be fine," she said, and retreated around the corner to the kitchen door.

Irma Hartz covered the telephone mouthpiece with her hand when Margaret went in. "Can't talk now," she said. "Go on in, honey, and if you have any problems punch number five on the intercom." As Margaret left, she was saying in a steady voice, "I understand all that, Mr. Galloway, but Mr. Anderson prefers to handle his business affairs through an agent."

Margaret put her bag on the desk and sat down. The intercom on the wall had a great many buttons. There was a whisper of air conditioning; she felt the sweat drying on her forearms.

The disk was still in the machine. She rolled paper and carbons into the typewriter and began the first letter. Like the one she had typed yesterday, it was an order for items from a catalog, and so was the next. The third was a personal letter to someone named Justin, full of names she was not sure how to spell. She looked them all up in the rotary file, found only one. The fourth was a business letter about investments, and that was all. She turned the disk over, but got nothing but a hiss.

In the basket behind the dictation machine there was a disorderly stack of papers. Margaret lifted them out and began to sort them. There was a click from the intercom, and Mrs. Hartz's voice said, "Maggie, everything okay?"

"Yes," she answered, startled. "Good," said the voice, and the intercom clicked off.

The file folders in the drawers were neatly labeled, but there did not seem to be files for about a third of the letters she had. She filed what she could, put the others aside, and began to make a list of the file headings. She was typing it when the intercom clicked again and Mrs. Hartz's voice said, "Lunch in fifteen minutes, Maggie. In the kitchen."

"All right, thank you." She looked at her watch; it was a quarter after twelve. She finished the list, combed her hair, and put the finished letters into a folder.

Mrs. Hartz was sitting at the kitchen table; Pongo was doing something at the counter beside the stove. "Sit here, honey," said Mrs. Hartz. "Do you like this kitchen?"

"It's beautiful," said Margaret, and in fact, whether it was because the table was set with napkins and china, or because she had got the job and felt she was not quite a stranger here any longer, the room had a quiet beauty that she had not noticed before. The floor was red Spanish tile with a dull sheen, the walls cream-colored; black hand-hewn beams supported the ceiling. Copper and iron pots hung on either side of the stoves—two of them, side by side, each bigger than any kitchen range Margaret had ever seen before. Gadgets were lined up at one end of the counter—a Cuisinart, an espresso machine, two little convection ovens, and others that she did not recognize.

"I always wanted a *big* kitchen," said Irma Hartz. "If you knew how many meals I've cooked in the back of a trailer."

"Not enough cabinets," said Pongo. He put a little pastry shell filled with something pink at each place, sat down, and picked up his fork.

"Mm, this is great," said Irma with her mouth full. "What's in it?"

Margaret tried a bite; it was shrimp in some kind of sauce, meltingly delicious; the pastry was light as air.

"Shrimp," said Pongo, "truffles, shrimp butter." He swallowed a mouthful and looked meditative. "Could use more tarragon."

Gene Anderson came in quietly and sat down at the end of the table. He was wearing a short-sleeved white cotton shirt and white trousers. The plate and silverware in front of him looked of ordinary size until Margaret compared them with the others, and then she saw that they were a third again as large; the heavy silver knife was almost a foot long.

Pongo, who had got up when Anderson came in, put down a much bigger pastry in front of him. He poured wine from a chilled bottle and slipped away again; in a moment Margaret heard the sizzle of meat on the grill.

Anderson had already finished half his pastry. "Maggie, did you have any problems?" He pointed with his fork to the folder beside her on the table.

"Yes, a few. There's one letter that has names in it I'm not sure how to spell. I typed it anyhow, and I thought you could look it over—"

"Okay, let's do that right after lunch."

Pongo was up again, turning the meat on the grill, then collecting their plates. He put fresh ones down, went to the oven and came back with a steaming platter. "Red snapper," he said. "Irma, you want to serve it?"

The fish, of a kind unfamiliar to Margaret, had a delicate flavor of garlic and thyme. "Mr. Richards, where did you learn to cook like this?"

"Here and there," said Pongo. "Mostly there." He was up again, bringing an enormous steak from the grill.

"He's a sea cook," said Irma. "Call him Pongo, or he'll think you're mad at him."

"Wait till you see what he can do when he makes an effort," said Anderson. "Who'd like some of this steak?"

No one replied; Anderson put the steak on his plate and proceeded to cut it up and eat it. Margaret tried not to watch him, but she could not help being fascinated by the unhurried way he made the food disappear. He forked up a bleeding chunk, his strong jaws chewed it, and he was ready for another. When the steak was gone, he took a helping of fish and ate that.

"Sit still, Pongo, I'll bring the dessert," said Irma. She took their plates, brought a cool green mousse, and served coffee. Anderson's mousse was the same size as the others; he ate it in two bites and said, "Let's see that letter, Maggie."

She brought it to him and handed him a pencil from the counter; it looked like a dance-card pencil in his fingers. "This is all right," he said, "this is wrong, and this one." He crossed out two names and corrected them.

A bell sounded; Irma swiveled her chair to the intercom panel, glanced at the screen. "Expecting anybody?" she said to the room. No one replied.

"Yes, can I help you?" she said to the microphone. In the screen, Margaret could see a man in the open window of a car. A voice said, "Ma'am, I'm J. A. Coburn, of Smith and Barrows, here to see Mr. Anderson."

"Mr. Anderson doesn't see anybody without an appointment."

"Well, ma'am, I did write asking for an appointment, but unfortunately I didn't get an answer, so I just figured—"

"I'm sorry your letter wasn't answered. If you'll just go home and be patient, we'll take care of that as soon as we can." She turned off the microphone.

"Was there anything from him in that stack?" she asked Margaret.

"No."

"This whole county is full of people that would just love to sell Gene something. We try to stay out of sight, but you can't hide a place like this. People will talk. There's the builder and all the contractors, the cleaning women, the lawyers—"

"Irma, try to keep that damn gate closed, too, will you?" Anderson's hand was clenched around his napkin. "I know it's hard, when people are going in and out, but I hate to think somebody could just walk in here."

"*Yes*, sir," said Irma, in a tone nicely balanced between respect and irony.

Anderson got up. "See you all later." He walked out.
Pongo asked, "More coffee?"

Margaret took the misspelled letter back to her office and
retyped it. When she was finished, she put the new copy in the
folder with the other letters and carried it back to the kitchen.
Irma was at the table as usual; Pongo was banging pots in the
sink.

"Irma, I forgot to ask you where to put these letters when
I'm done—back in the office?"

"Oh. I never told you, did I. Come on, I might as well give
you the fifty-cent tour while I'm at it. Pongo, you going to be
here for a while?"

"Sure, go ahead."

In the hallway, Irma gestured toward the stairway with its
wrought-iron railing that led up to the back of the house.
"Here's where you go upstairs, if you don't like ramps. It
brings you out on the balcony up there, but we'll go the other
way." They walked through the living room to the corridor
and passed Margaret's office. Irma opened the next door.
"Library."

It was a big room paneled in walnut, with a fireplace, a long
table in the center with a few stacks of books on it, and empty
shelves all around. "Books haven't come yet," Irma said.
"*That*'ll be a job." She closed the door. "The rest of these
rooms down here are empty."

Next came a ramp, like the one in the living room but much
narrower. As they started up, Margaret was thinking with
respect of the architect who had designed this house. He had
had an impossible problem and had solved it beautifully: the
sunken areas in the kitchen and living room that made it possible for Anderson to talk face to face with normal people; the
ramps, because he couldn't use an ordinary staircase. To
Anderson, she thought, this must be like living in a house built
partly for dolls. "Munchkins," she said aloud.

"What?"

"I was just thinking. The Munchkins—you know, the little
people in *The Wizard of Oz*."

"Oh."

The door at the end of the balcony opened onto a study. All
the furniture here was scaled to Anderson's dimensions, the
desk, drawing table, couch, chairs, coffee table. The room

was almost as big as the kitchen, but it looked much smaller because of the ramp that rose around two sides.

"This part is all Gene's," said Irma. "This is his study, or den, or whatever you want to call it, and in there is his sitting room." Through the open doorway Margaret could see a huge cushioned Morris chair with a shelf on either side, on which books and papers were stacked, and a sort of tilted lapboard on a swivel which held an open dictionary. "What he likes is for you to come when he's not here, put the letters on the desk for him to sign, pick up anything in his out basket. When he *is* here, he hates to be disturbed, so always make sure before you go up. You can go in the sitting room, too, if you have a reason. Up there is his bedroom, and that's out of bounds. He even cleans it himself."

"That sounds awfully lonely," Margaret said after a moment.

"Maybe so." Irma led her back to the balcony and through a doorway into a long passage that ran the width of the house. "Most of these rooms are empty," she said. "Here's mine. Come in and sit down awhile—Pongo will mind the store."

They were in a cheerful living room with floral covers on the furniture, flowers in a vase, a huge TV screen. In one corner, over a little desk, was a duplicate of the intercom system in the kitchen. "Excuse me a minute," Irma said. She went to the intercom, pushed a putton. "Pongo?"

"Yeah."

"We're in my room. If you want to go somewhere before we get back, push the slave button."

"Okay."

Irma sat down opposite Margaret and put her feet up on a hassock. "Now let's talk," she said. "Anything you're wondering about—any questions?"

"I don't understand why he doesn't hire more people. You work so hard, and Pongo—does he do all the cooking?"

"And the marketing, and goes to the post office every day, and so on. I know what you're saying. Gene could have a staff of servants in here, security guards and all that, but he can't bear having anybody around that he doesn't know. He's spooky about intruders—you saw that. There isn't even a fire escape to his apartment up there. Building code says you have to have one, so he had it built, waited till after inspection, then tore it down and hauled it away."

"Doesn't he have any family, or friends, I mean besides you and Pongo?"

"He knows a few people here. He was out of the country for twenty years; when he got back he put a little ad in *Amusement Business*, but I was the only one that answered it. All the people he used to know in the carnival are dead and gone, or else scattered who knows where."

"You were in the carnival?"

"Carnival, and then in the circus. My husband and I had a juggling act—the Amazing Raimondis. Ray left me a little money when he died. I didn't have anything else to do, so I came down here to work for Gene."

"Ray was your husband?"

"My second. He died on Christmas Day, nineteen seventy-six. Heart attack."

"I'm sorry."

"That's all right. He was a real bastard. Speaking of Christmas," Irma said, "we have a rule here that you don't give anybody anything made by a machine. If you can make your own presents, Gene would like that, or if you can't, find something that was hand made by some one person."

"I see."

Irma gave her a bright glance. "Do you? Look, if you give him something that anybody can buy in a store, even if it costs five hundred dollars, that's like giving him money. He wants something he hasn't got." She lifted a heap of material from a workbasket beside her chair. "Like, I'm making him this quilt. The damn thing is ten feet long. Pongo will probably make him a belt or something—he does leatherwork."

Margaret bent to examine the unfinished quilt, diamonds and stars of pale rose, blue, white, corn yellow. "Oh, this is beautiful. But I couldn't do anything like that."

"You never know till you try," Irma said. She stood up. "Let's go on back—Pongo will be wanting to make his post-office run. Are you through for the day?"

"I guess so, there's nothing more on my desk. Oh, I forgot to look in his out basket."

"That's all right, I did. You go on home and relax."

The next day there were paintings hanging all along the balcony wall; Anderson was putting one up in the living room when she arrived. She found a disk in his out-basket upstairs, and several letters marked in his meticulous handwriting, "Tell him no." After some hesitation, she translated this into: "Mr. Anderson has asked me to acknowledge your letter of —— and to tell you how sorry he is that under present circumstances he does not feel able to accept your interesting proposal." She signed these letters, "Margaret W. Morrow, Secretary to Mr. Anderson."

"I thought it would be better, more of a polite brushoff, if these came from me," she explained at lunch. "And it's less work for you; is that all right?"

"Fine, Maggie. A little more polite than I would have been, but okay."

Pongo served another incredible meal: lemon soup, turtle steak, shrimp in mustard sauce, and a huge Greek salad with anchovies, black olives, and feta cheese, all in addition to Anderson's porterhouse. Margaret began to wonder what Pongo's dinners were like; if this kept on, she would have to start thinking about a diet.

After lunch Anderson went back to his picture hanging, refusing Margaret's offer of help. "You're not dressed for it," he said, "and anyhow it's a one-man job." Margaret typed two more letters, left them in Anderson's in-basket, tidied her desk.

On her way out she asked Irma, "Would it be all right if I walk around outside a little before I go home?"

"Sure it would. You'd better wear a hat, though. That sun is fierce, and you're burned already."

Margaret put on her dark glasses and went out into the glare. She got her wide-brimmed hat from the car, then strolled up past the garage and the storeroom. Above her the hill began, planted in ferns and flowering shrubs. On a tree with pale bark and narrow boat-shaped leaves she saw a brown lizard with a startling orange throat-pouch. The pouch swelled like a balloon, disappeared; the lizard bobbed its narrow head three times, then the pouch swelled again. It seemed to pay no attention to her until she was almost near enough to touch it; then it whirled and flicked out of sight around the branch.

The driveway curved off to the left and disappeared around the shoulder of the hill. Beyond it, a winding path covered with bark mulch led upward between waist-high shrubs. When she had climbed a few yards, she turned for a better view of the house. It was U-shaped around the garden, thirty feet tall except at the far end, where a sort of tower rose another twenty feet. The roofs were all of Spanish tile, and the house looked vaguely Spanish, with its wrought-iron balconies, except for the modern gleam of the glass doors that opened into the living room.

She went on into the cool shadow of the trees. First they were birches and maples, then young oaks, then pines of an unfamiliar variety, and some other trees that she could not identify. Moss and ferns grew thickly between the trunks; the bark-mulch was gone now and she was walking on a narrow dirt path; she might have been in a northern forest, except that everything was too perfect, too beautifully cared for.

Around the next bend she came upon an old man on his knees beside a wheelbarrow full of bulbs. He had been digging with a trowel near the trunk of a maple; he looked up alertly under the brim of his shapeless hat. "Afternoon."

"Hello," Margaret said.

"Visiting, are you?"

"No, I'm Mr. Anderson's new secretary. Margaret Morrow."

"Glen Hoke is my name. I put in all this here." He waved the trowel vaguely at the forest around them.

"You mean, the ferns, and flowers?"

"No, I mean the whole thing. Been working here a year. He's a crazy man. He built this hill, you know."

"He *built* the hill?"

"Sure. There's no hill like this in Florida. Brought in crushed rock and bulldozers, then topsoil. Must of been near ten thousand yards of topsoil. Then trees, and all the rest of it. You know what it cost him for this one tree?" He slapped the trunk of the maple beside him. "Seven hundred dollars. That's one tree."

"I didn't even know you could transplant a tree that big."

"You can, if you want to pay for it. The brook over there, have you seen that?"

"No."

"Drilled six hundred feet, put in a pump, dug a channel and lined it with rock. There's your brook. Seems like you could build a house where there *was* a brook."

"You don't really mean you did all this by yourself, do you, Mr. Hoke?"

"No, no." He looked impatient. "I had a whole crew in here, twenty men at one time. I'm a contractor, but hell, he pays me enough, and I take an interest."

"You say the brook is over that way?"

"Just follow the path. Nice meeting you, Miss."

The trail forked, and forked again; Margaret took the downhill branch both times, and presently found herself descending into a ravine cool with willows. She heard the brook before she saw it: it ran bright and transparent over red stones. It was narrow enough, almost, to jump over, but a little farther down there was a little Japanese footbridge, sunbleached and sturdy, looking as if it had been there forever.

After another few yards she heard the water change its tone, and saw that it fell over a miniature precipice into a thirty-foot pool, deep enough for diving at one end. Beside the pool, in a shaded grassy place, something white hung from a limb. When she came near enough, she saw that it was a towel.

Chapter Nineteen

Margaret stayed in the cabin at Site O'Sea until the end of the week, partly because she had paid in advance and partly out of a superstitious feeling that her job was too good to last. On Friday, when Irma handed her a check and said nothing but "Have a good weekend, honey," she began to believe in her luck. She went househunting over the weekend and found a furnished two-room apartment in Madeira Beach, overlooking the bay. She also found time to shop for clothes: modest, well-tailored sundresses, skirts and blouses in unobtrusive pale colors, several pairs of shoes and sandals, and two linen dusters with vast pockets.

When she came to work on Monday, she knew she had been right to wear a duster when she glanced through the open door of the library and saw Anderson on his knees beside an open carton, pulling books out in handfuls and looking at them. "Moldy," he said to her, holding one up to show her the pale corruption that had spread across the cover. He brushed his hand over it, and when he put it down, by some trick of the light, it looked better. "The whole carton is; not worth the trouble."

"I could get something from the kitchen and wipe them off."

"Okay."

She came back with a rag and a bowl of water in which, on Irma's advice, she had mixed a couple of tablespoons of vinegar.

"If I put these on the table," Anderson said, "could you

make a list of the titles and authors?''

"Sure." Margaret found a normal-sized chair, pulled it up to the table and sat down. "Where have they been, to get like this?"

"In storage in Europe, some of them as long as fifteen years." He put a stack of books on the table. "Dirty work."

"It's okay, I'm dressed for it." She held up the book she was looking at. "This is so beautiful. Is it a book about the Tarot?"

"Not exactly. It's a novel, but the Italian edition has these tipped-in reproductions of fifteenth-century Tarot cards. They are beautiful, aren't they? Nobody does that kind of work in this country."

Anderson went back to the cartons, stacked more books, and finally sat back on his haunches with a discouraged expression. After a moment she said, "Moving is awful."

"It isn't that, but I think I've bitten off more than I can chew. I'm no librarian; I'm going to have to hire somebody."

"To shelve the books, and catalog them? I could do that."

He turned and gave her a skeptical look. "Do you know the Dewey Decimal System?"

"They don't use that anymore, it's all the Library of Congress System now. No, I don't know either one, but neither do you, so what good would it be? What you want is a system you can understand, so you can find a book when you want it."

"So?"

"So, novels in one place, art books in another, biography, science, whatever. I'll put labels on the shelves, and each book will have a sticker to show where it belongs. Books you're through with, that you want reshelved, you can put at one end of the table and I'll take care of them. Yes?"

"Yes, Maggie. Do it."

"And, books in foreign languages, I'll put on another part of the table with little slips of paper in them. And you can write on each one what kind of book it is, and then I'll know."

"Okay."

Every day, seeing Gene was almost like seeing him for the first time: there was a shock of wrongness, as if someone had come through a magnifying glass. His hands fascinated her; they were tanned, shapely, unscarred, with neatly trimmed nails, and they were twelve inches long from wrist to fingertip. Since the first day, when they shook hands, he had not touched her. She found herself wondering what it would be like.

Gene's habits were regular. He spent his mornings in the workshop, where he was fitting together an intricate inlaid tabletop. In the afternoon, he read his mail and dictated replies or annotated the letters for Margaret's attention. Most of his mail orders now were for books, some new, some from collector's catalogs.

Every afternoon Margaret worked on cataloging the books. Gene was impatient to get them on the shelves, but he understood that it would save time to do the cataloging first. When she realized how long a job it was going to be she began working straight through to dinnertime. Pongo's dinners were even more amazing than his lunches: one day it would be turkey mole with guacamole and corn fritters, the next coq au vin and carrot soufflé, the next a Middle Eastern lamb and apricot stew, with chickpeas and olive oil flavored with garlic.

The first time she went back to the library for another hour's work after dinner, Irma gave her a curious ironic smile.

The house was even bigger than she had realized. There was a dining room, never used so far, with a table that would seat twenty. Under the back stairway was a room fitted out with a huge reclining chair that could be used for haircuts or dentistry. There was a central music system with outlets all over the house; you could play any record or tape by looking it up in the catalog and punching in the number.

Books with slips of paper in them began to appear in Gene's out-basket. The slips marked pages on which passages had been outlined in pencil; some were annotated in Gene's precise tiny hand. Guessing at his intention, Margaret typed the passages single-spaced, one to a page even if it was short, and indented Gene's commentary. All he said was, "Maggie, I forgot to tell you these ought to be punched for a ring binder. Punch them, will you, and after this use binder paper."

She could not discern any pattern in the things he was reading. Most were popular works on science or quasi-science; evolutionary theory, genetics, psychology, sociology, history. In one book he had written: "Is the problem that the gene's selfishness is not enlightened?"

At the end of the second week she made a down payment on a car, a three-year-old red Datsun. On the following Wednes-

day, after dinner, when Pongo had gone back to his cottage
and Anderson had disappeared for the night, Irma said to her,
"Gene thinks there's no point in your driving back and forth
every day when we've got so much room here. If you want to
move into one of the cottages, or upstairs, it's okay."

"That's incredibly generous," Margaret said. She tried not
to show what she knew: this meant that she had been accepted
as a member of the household.

"Maybe not," Irma said with a faint smile. "It probably
means he'll get more work out of you. Go upstairs if you
want, look in the empty rooms and see if you find one you
like. Then I'll give you the cottage keys and you can go back
and look them over before you make up your mind."

The upstairs apartments were like Irma's, each with a sitting
room, bedroom, kitchenette, and bath. Each one was furnished in a different style, some formal, some cozy.

In the cool evening she walked back to the cottages. There
were three, well separated and screened by hedges; the first
had lighted windows, the others were dark. She opened the
door of the middle cottage and went in.

"Cottage" was a misnomer. The living room was forty feet
long and had a twenty-foot cathedral ceiling; it was luxuri-
ously furnished, and so were the four bedrooms, one downstairs, three up, each with its private bath.

As she walked back, the door of Pongo's cottage opened
and the beam of a flashlight hit her in the face. It dropped immediately. "Sorry," said Pongo's voice. "Didn't know it was
you." He was in the darkness beside the open door; she could
barely make him out.

"What would you have done if it was somebody else?" she
asked.

He stepped into the light and showed her the gleam of metal
in his hand. "Boom, boom," he said, grinning around his
cigar. "Like to see my place?"

"All right."

Pongo's living room was smaller than the other: it was
crowded with furniture and bric-a-brac. The paintings on the
walls were of cowboys and Indians. Beside the sofa was a
black leather armchair, obviously too big for anyone but
Gene. In a brass cage nearby, something small and brown
leaped at the bars and stared at her with bright eyes.

"What's that?"

"Marmoset," said Pongo. "His name's Gwendolyn."

"He's cute," she said dubiously. "Does he bite?"

"Like a tiger," said Pongo. "Sit down, have a beer." He poured from a chilled bottle into a Pilsener glass. The beer was dark; even the foam was coffee-colored. "Kulmbacher," he said. "You ever have this?"

"No. It's good."

Pongo took a long draught, set his glass down. "You moving out here?"

"I don't think so. Irma told me I could use one of the apartments upstairs, or else a cottage, but they're too big for one person. I wouldn't know what to do with a four-bedroom house."

"Might have guests later. You could move in with me."

"Right, and I could do your cooking and cleaning."

"Feed the marmoset," he said. He passed her a bowl of macadamia nuts.

"Pongo, I'm going to get fat as a pig. Can't you serve something lighter for lunch, or else something not so good?"

He looked pleased. "Maybe. You're not fat yet."

"What does your name mean, Pongo?"

He grimaced. "Monkey."

"Oh."

"He gave it to me. It's all right around here, but if we go to Tampa, call me Bill, okay?"

"Okay."

She moved into the apartment next to Irma's; her rent was paid for the rest of the month, but it didn't seem to matter. Irma said, "If you don't like the furniture, the drapes, anything, go pick out something you do like—Gene will pay for it."

"I haven't got *time*, Irma. Anyway, this is lovely the way it is."

"Working your tail off, aren't you?"

"Well—if I didn't, I'd feel I was taking the money under false pretenses."

"I know, but are you getting any sleep?"

"Not much, lately."

"Want some pills?"

"No, I can't use them. It'll be all right."

*   *   *

Pongo did not cook on weekends; there was a cold buffet for anyone who wanted it. Sometimes they all drove to Tampa in Gene's enormous motor home and had dinner at the Columbia, a Spanish restaurant with many high-ceilinged rooms. They ate behind a potted palm that gave Gene some protection from curious stares; the management brought out a special chair for him and laid a place with his own china and silverware. The chef, a brown, smiling man named Ruiz, always came to the table afterward for low-voiced consultations with Pongo and compliments from all the rest.

Margaret did her necessary shopping over the weekend, or drove down to the public beach and swam, or went to a movie. Often, if she had been having a bout of insomnia, she simply stayed home, slept late, and lazed around the house in the afternoon.

One day Anderson came into the living room and found her reading a paperback novel. He sat down beside her; when she put the book down on the end table, he picked it up and examined it curiously. The cover depicted a young woman with pinkish hair and a scoop-necked violet gown who was being embraced by a young man in a business suit. Their upper portions were painted with a sort of pasty realism; below the shoulders, however, they dissolved into a scribble of black and brown over which the artist had laid a few strokes of moldy green with his palette knife. From the positions of the two faces it was apparent that the young man was thrusting his nose into the young lady's left eye-socket. She appeared to be enjoying this penetration.

"Rebecca West, *Harriet Hume*," Anderson read aloud. "This is an old paperback, isn't it? Where did you get it?"

"At Haslam's, downtown."

"Is it any good?"

"The first twenty pages are really awful, until you start to see what she's up to."

Anderson laid the book down. "Why did you read the first twenty pages?"

"I'd read *The Birds Fall Down* by the same author, and it was so good that I couldn't believe she was being this awful by accident. And she isn't. It's a work of art."

"If you're awful on purpose, that makes it art?"

"Sometimes. What about Picasso?"

"Good point." He nudged the book with his forefinger and

stood up. "Maybe I ought to read it. Will you put it on my list?"

She did not quite smile; she had done so on Friday.

At the door he turned to look at her. "Don't be too clever, Maggie," he said, and was gone.

One day after lunch when Margaret and Irma were lingering over coffee in the kitchen, the gate signal rang. Irma leaned back to the intercom. "Yes? Oh, Piet!" In the little screen, Margaret could see a gray-haired man looking out of a car window. "Come on up, sweetie, I'll tell Gene you're here." She pressed the gate button. "That's Piet Linck," she said to Margaret. "He's an old friend." She pressed another button. "Gene?"

"Yes, Irma."

"Piet is here."

The stocky man who entered a few minutes later was gray all over—his tropical suit, his close-cut hair, his eyes. He gave Margaret a measuring glance when Irma introduced them. His voice was faintly English, but with a suggestion of an accent she could not identify. He was carrying an odd-shaped bundle wrapped in brown paper and tied with twine; he put it down to hug Irma.

Gene came in and the two men shook hands. "Piet, it's good to see you. Sit down. Irma, can't we give this man some coffee? Where's Pongo?"

"Out in back. Don't get in an uproar." She brought a cup, poured coffee.

"How was your trip?" Gene asked.

"Very good. I had some business to do in Minas Gerais, that was rather boring, but on the way here I spent four days in Colombia."

"Medellín? Did you see Rodrigo?"

"I did, and he sends his fraternal embraces. By the way, I have a present for you." He reached down for the bundle on the floor; Irma made room for it on the table.

Linck opened a pearl-handled pocket knife and began to cut the cords. Under the brown paper the object was wrapped in newspapers; Margaret could see Spanish headlines between the strips of tape. Linck cut the tape, pulled the papers away. Inside was a carving of pale brown wood, unstained and unvarnished.

"I got this in Cali," said Linck, turning the sculpture for their inspection. "They make them out of the roots of trees, and whatever form the roots take, that's what the artist uses. Here, this long loop becomes the snake biting the man's head, you see. Very ingenious."

"I like it," said Gene, bending close. "My goodness, he got everything in, didn't he? Here's the magic eye. Here's the book of wisdom. Sort of an allegory of human evolution, except that it goes from top to bottom—this guy up here has a tail. Did you get it from the artist?"

"Yes. He is an *indio*, his name is de La Cruz Saavedra. He wanted six hundred pesos for it; I pretended to misunderstand him and gave him double. Then he was happy and I was happy."

"What's it like in Bogotá now?"

"Awful." Linck shook his head. "Worse every year. Something very bad is going to happen there. I stayed there overnight only because I was invited to a reception at the ambassador's residence."

"The Dutch ambassador?"

"No, the American one. Have you been in that place, Gene? No? It's amazing. The entrance hall is bigger than your living room, with a rotunda for a ceiling, and all around this rotunda there are little blue light bulbs. The reception was for the novelist Eleanor Theil, a very nice woman, we had an interesting chat. Well, at this reception I also met a psychiatrist who is interested in occultism. He was flying back to Cali the next day and he offered me a ride and lunch in his club. The lunch was rather dull because the doctor wanted to talk about von Däniken, but afterward I wandered around town, and that's how I found this carving. Incidentally, I also brought you two small Boteros—I'll show them to you later. If you don't want them I have another buyer in mind."

Pongo turned up and helped Linck carry his bags upstairs; it appeared that he was a frequent house-guest. Now that she had had an opportunity to study him, Margaret decided that the main impression he gave was one of sturdy roundness, like an animal's. His hair was brushed close to his round head; his hands were not plump but rounded, with thick, blunt fingers. He rarely gestured; his whole aspect was of watchful calm. He had a way of looking down when he spoke, and then darting a glance at your face to see how you had reacted. His speech sometimes seemed more American than British, and at dinner he gave a startling imitation of a Texan. He did not seem to fit into any model of a foreigner, and that made her a little uneasy.

After dinner Gene carried him off to his tower room. Several hours later Linck came into the living room where Margaret was reading. He stood with his hands in his back pockets, looking around. When she glanced up, he remarked, "This is an amazing place. It was not finished last time I was here. Do you find it a little overwhelming?"

"It was at first."

Linck sat down beside her, taking a flat tin box out of his pocket. "Do you mind if I smoke this?" he asked, showing her the box. In it were slender brown cigars, hardly bigger than cigarettes.

"No, please go ahead."

"May I offer you one? They are very mild."

She smiled. "No, thank you."

Linck lighted his cigar and sat back, puffing blue smoke. "I believe I am getting a touch of agoraphobia," he said, with a glance at the ceiling. Anyhow, it's good that Gene finally has a house built to his own scale."

"Have you known him long, Mr. Linck?"

"I met him in Amsterdam, in nineteen sixty-seven. He had some business with the family firm, and one of the employees told me about him. Then we did some business, and then we became friends. We have seen each other I suppose ten or a dozen times in the last twenty years. By the way, please call me Piet. It is spelled differently, but it sounds the same."

"Piet."

"Piet actually is my middle name; my first name is Coenraad, or Coen for short, but it is spelled C-o-e-n and pronounced 'coon,' and that confuses Americans."

"It's too bad people won't take the trouble to get it right."

He shrugged. "Not many people can manage Dutch noises. I have a friend named Schildt, he has lived in this country for many years now. He pronounces it 'Skildt' now, because he says"—his voice dropped and became guttural—" 'Doesn'd id zound like schidt?' "

She laughed, and he smiled for the first time. "Maggie, I hope we will be friends," he said.

"I hope so too."

Chapter Twenty

—Con su permiso. The porter wheels up
His cart, dumps litter beside the trash can.
Smiling taxi drivers ask, —¿Amigo? —Si, amigo.
The telephones demand special coins. The seats
Have been stolen. Children are asleep
Under corrugated cardboard. They wake,
Stand in a circle like football players.
—¿Donde vamos a robar hoy? The particles
Are too small to be seen, a miasma of the mind.
Over the tilted city, in bright sun, the sky is gray.

—Gene Anderson

Next day Gene announced that they were all going to the
beach for a party. After a light lunch Pongo packed a huge
picnic hamper; they set out a little after two in Gene's motor
home, drove across the causeway and up the line of islands,
past the funereal row of hotels and condominiums, to a public
easement on Redington Beach, where the sea-front was still
lined with private houses on ample lots. They walked through
yucca and sea-grape and found themselves on a deserted
beach. To the south they could see a few tiny black figures,
small as ants; to the north, no one at all. Almost on the hori-
zon, a white pleasure boat was trudging northward.

Anderson walked through the gentle surf until he was thigh-
deep, then dived and disappeared; they saw him after a few

moments stroking out toward the breakers. A bottle-green wave curved over him; he dived again and reappeared, a dark moving dot on the white glare.

Margaret and Irma swam nearer shore; Linck and Pongo were still busy putting up a shelter on four poles near the seawall. The water was only a little cooler than the air; Margaret felt it as a caressing softness on her body. When she came out, the sand was hot underfoot and the sun warm on her head; she was deliciously cool in between. Walking along the shore with Irma, she saw Anderson coming in with powerful slow strokes. He rose dripping like Triton, waded ashore, and walked up to the shelter.

Margaret trudged up through the loose sand. Pongo and Linck were in the water now, Pongo with a mask and flippers snorkeling in the shallows, and Linck performing a decorous side-stroke farther out. Anderson was sitting cross-legged in the luminous blue umbra of the shelter. Margaret sat down on the blanket beside him. "This is so beautiful," she said.

"Yes."

"I still can't get used to the colors, and how clean everything is. It's like a child's drawing, almost."

"Some people would call it gaudy."

"It seemed that way to me at first, but now when I remember Albany, I realize how drab it was. All those muddy colors, gray and brown, and the grit and grime over everything."

Linck came trudging up toward them, his broad gray-haired chest glistening with moisture. "That was very pleasant," he said, dropping beside them. He reached over and opened the cooler. "What do we have? Heineken's, all right." He brought up a bottle with a rustle of ice, offered it. "Maggie?"

"No, thanks. Do we have any Coke?"

"Almost certainly." He handed the bottle to Gene, rummaged in the cooler, found a Pepsi for Margaret and another beer for himself. "You have chosen a good place," he said. "It is very beautiful here."

"So Maggie was just telling me."

"How easy it is to know beauty when you see it, and how hard to define."

"Aquinas said that the three requirements for beauty are wholeness, harmony, and radiance."

"That is in Joyce's *Portrait of the Artist as a Young Man*, isn't it?" Linck asked. "Yes. But the Latin is *claritas*, which is better translated 'clarity.' "

"No, I think radiance is right."

Margaret looked up at Anderson; he was staring out at the bright ocean. " 'Clarity' seems to be much simpler," he went on slowly. "But then what you're saying is that a work of art must be clear. To whom? That's a prescription for poster art. No, I think it's radiance—a shining. That's where the mystery comes in. You can understand wholeness, the unity of a work, and you can understand harmony, when all the parts work together. But where does radiance come from?"

"At the moment, I should say from the sun," Linck said comfortably, and took a long draught from his glass.

Irma was strolling back along the water's edge. They saw her stop and talk to Pongo, who was standing up in the shallows with his mask on top of his head. Something she said made him laugh.

"As for poster art," Linck said, "I have seen some very good posters. Toulouse-Lautrec made them, for instance. Even if you mean posters advertising toothpaste, it may be there are people who find them beautiful. If so, why not? Do we all have to admire the same things?"

Gene gave him an ironic glance. "*Retro me, Sathanas,*" he said.

"Well, really," Linck said, "you may treat this as frivolous if you choose, but beauty is relative, isn't it? I know a man who sincerely believes that Boston bull terriers are beautiful, whereas to me they are simply a mistake."

"Depends on how you define the term. To some people, beauty is just whatever is desirable or useful. My father would look at a painting of some old barn and say, 'Why can't they paint a picture of a nice house?' "

Margaret said, "I've known people like that. My mother's housekeeper couldn't see anything beautiful in snow, because she hated it."

"Sure," said Gene. "And then there's physical beauty in people. It varies a lot from one culture to another, but it all comes back to what the person is good for—bearing children, or fighting off tigers, or whatever. But there are other kinds of beauty you can't explain that way. Beauty in nature that doesn't seem to have any function, it's just there. Geometric beauty. Patterns."

"If by patterns you mean things like a butterfly's wing," said Linck, "or the veins in a leaf, those are certainly functional. In the butterfly it's a matter of species recognition, or sometimes misdirection, and in the leaf—''

"All right, but have you thought about coquinas?"

"I'm sorry?"

"You haven't seen them? Maggie, have you?"

"No, I don't think so."

"Well, if I'm not mistaken, Irma has just found some." He raised his voice. "Irma!"

She looked up; she was on her knees in the strip of wet sand above the water. Anderson beckoned. She came toward them with her hands cupped together, and Pongo followed her.

"Let me see," said Gene. Irma held her two hands over his palm and took them away. In his hand was a heap of little glistening shells, seed-shaped, each no more than half an inch long. Some were white, some pale yellow, some pink; others had delicate ray patterns of blue or violet alternating with white. Gene stirred the pile with his finger while the others bent close.

"Pretty little things," he said. "They live along the beaches here, and use the tides to move back and forth. When the tide starts to go out, you'll see them coming to the surface and washing out in the water, hundreds of them. Shore birds eat them. So what are these patterns and colors for? Not for camouflage. If you wanted to hide from shore birds, wouldn't you be the color of sand?"

"I would certainly try to be," said Linck.

"So that leaves species recognition. But these little creatures have no eyes—they can't see their own patterns. They are beautiful, and they are blind."

They had been so absorbed in what he was saying that nobody noticed the intruder until he was in front of them. It was a man in brown bathing trunks, well built, a little pudgy around the waist; his long hair was wind-blown.

"I'm sorry," he said to Gene, "but I don't suppose your name is John Kimberley?"

"Yes!" said Gene. "Who are you?"

The man smiled and took off his sunglasses. "Mike Wilcox. My God, is that Irma? What are you all doing here?"

Irma squeaked, shot forward and embraced him. He freed one arm to shake hands with Gene.

"I could ask you the same question," Gene said. "Come and sit down. Irma, leave some for the sharks. Mike, this is Margaret Morrow, and this is Piet Linck. That's Bill Richards down in the water." They made room under the canopy;

Irma, her eyes brighter than Margaret had ever seen them, sat next to Wilcox and held his arm.

"Mike and I were in the carnival together—what, twenty years ago?" said Gene.

"It can't be. You know, this is amazing luck. I almost didn't come out this morning; I was really more drawn to the idea of sulking in my room with a bottle. What *are* you doing here?"

"I live here. What about you?"

"I was playing a club on Treasure Island. Not a great success, I'm afraid."

"Doing magic?"

"Yes. It was all right, actually, until my assistant broke her knee. I offered to go on alone, but the manager wouldn't have it. I think he felt the customers were more interested in her legs than my card tricks."

"You're free, then?"

"At liberty is more like it."

"Come home with us, then, and we'll talk. Where's your assistant?"

"In hospital, poor old bird. I've got to hang around until I see she's all right."

"Stay with us, we've got plenty of room," said Irma. "Mike, I can't believe it's you! Have you seen any of the old gang?"

"No, not for donkey's years. I used to get a note now and again from Ed Parlow. He told me about Ray—that was hard lines."

"No, it's all right."

"Are you, ah—?" He glanced from Irma to Gene.

She laughed. "I'm the *housekeeper*. Gene is rich now—wait till you see."

"This calls for a celebration," said Linck. He was rummaging in the cooler. "Aha," he said, and drew up a frosted bottle. "I thought this might be here." He poured five small glasses and handed them around.

"What is this, gin?" Wilcox asked.

"No, jenever." He pronounced it as if the first letter were a *y*. "It is like gin, but much better. This is the new kind, I think. We have the old and the new. Some like one, some another."

Margaret tried a sip; the liquor was like icy water, and tasted almost as innocent.

Pongo came up glistening wet, carrying his mask and flippers, and was introduced. Linck handed him a glass; he sat down on a towel just outside the canopy.

"Well, I must say this is superb," said Wilcox, with a broad grin. "Wait till I tell Nan. Gene, whatever became of you, after you blew the show in West Virginia?"

"I went to France and joined a circus."

"No! How long were you in Europe?"

"Almost ten years, but I left the circus in seventy-two."

"Just before me. I was there from seventy-three on."

"Did you ever work the Circus Romano?"

"Yes! My God, now I come to think of it, they told me they'd had an American giant in the sixties. But the name was different, and you were long gone by then."

Pongo unpacked the hamper, and they ate huge sandwiches of cold chicken, Westphalian ham cut in paper-thin slices, raw Bermuda onion, cole slaw.

"Working a circus is quite different to carnivals," Wilcox said. "I don't know if you've found that."

"Oh, yes," said Irma.

"Because of the animals?" Margaret asked.

"Well, partly. It's a difference in attitude, though, I think. A circus is, well, you know, a traveling entertainment—it's a theatrical performance really, except too big for a theater. But you're right, the animals do make a difference. I used to like being around the elephants—bulls they call them, I don't know why."

"Aren't they bulls?"

"No, they're cows as a rule. Bulls are too hard to handle. You know, animals are near the top of the heap in a circus, right up with the aerialists and so on. I remember once in Georgia, we were showing a little town where they had a home for retarded children—we did a special matinee there, and so on, and when we got to the next town we discovered that one of the inmates had joined us. Well, the circus sort of adopted him, kept him for years, and the point I was getting at, they treated him like an animal, which is to say, several ranks above a common working hand."

"Was that with Clemens Brothers?" Irma asked.

"Yes, and you know, Clemens housed him with the workmen, gave him a little spending money—never paid him any wages, as far as I know, but he was sort of a privileged character. The working hands got paid, but they were the lowest of the low.''

"That's the truth,'' Irma said. "Once when I was with Vargas, I saw a workman get laid out with a stake because he spit at a llama that had just spit at him.''

"That's terrible,'' Margaret said.

"Well, the workman had probably been hired a week or two ago down on Skid Row, and the llama was worth a thousand dollars.''

Pongo brought out lemon tarts for dessert, coffee hot from the thermos, brandy. The sun was low by the time they finished, and a little group of people walking northward along the tide line cast shadows like spears. "This beach is getting too crowded,'' Gene remarked as they came closer. There were half a dozen in the group, all very young, the boys bare-chested, the girls in T-shirts and cutoffs. They stopped and looked up toward the shelter; after a moment one of them detached himself and walked up through the dry sand.

"Could you tell me what time it is?'' he asked, halting a few feet away.

"Just a minute.'' Margaret got her watch out of her bag. "Five-thirty.''

"Thanks.'' The boy needed a haircut; his body was slim and muscular, and very red across the shoulders. He was looking curiously at Gene. "Are you in the circus?''

"I used to be. I'm retired now. Where are you from?''

The others had been drifting closer as they spoke. "I'm from Schenectady,'' the boy said. "My name's Carl. This here's Scott, he's from Schenectady too''—a tall boy with sandy hair, also sunburned—"and this is Karen, and Christine, and Rebecca, and Tony, they're from Cincinnati.''

"My name is Gene Anderson. What are you all doing here?''

The boy shrugged. "Nothing to do at home, I guess. Nothing to do down here, either, but the beach is pretty nice.''

"We were in St. Augustine,'' said one of the girls, a frightened-looking blonde, "but we heard they were going to spray the garbage cans with poison.'' One of the boys gave her a nudge with his elbow; she pushed him away.

"Haven't you got any money?'' Gene asked. They shook their heads.

"Pongo, see what's in the hamper.''

Pongo opened the lid, looked in. "Couple of sandwiches."

"Push it over here." Gene reached in, withdrew two wrapped sandwiches that looked small in his hand, and offered them. "Are you hungry?"

"Gee, yeah, thanks."

Gene reached into the hamper again, drew out two more sandwiches, then another two. The young people crowded up, sat in a row and began to eat. Gene passed out soft drinks and bottles of beer. "Were you really getting food out of garbage cans?" he asked.

"Sure. People throw all kinds of stuff away—you wouldn't believe it. I mean good stuff, not rotten or anything."

"And they sprayed poison in the cans?"

"It's true," Irma said. "I heard about it on the radio last week. It made me sick. I can't believe how rotten some people are."

Margaret moved closer to the girl who had spoken about the garbage cans; she was one of the youngest of the group, not more than fourteen or fifteen; the bones of her shoulders were visible through her unicorn T-shirt.

"My name is Margaret," she said. "You're Christine?"

"No, Karen," said the girl, with her mouth full. "That's Christine over there. Hi."

"Have you been away from home long?"

"Couple of weeks, I guess."

"Going back there sometime?"

The girl shook her head. "They don't want me anymore."

Margaret felt her eyes blurring. She reached for her beach bag, found her wallet and a tube of suntan lotion. She pulled out the bills without trying to count them. "You'd better take this," she said, handing Karen the tube of lotion. "And this." She pressed the money into the girl's hand. "Will you share it with the others?"

"Oh, yeah. Gee, thanks. Thanks a *lot*."

The sandwiches were gone; Gene handed out lemon tarts and poured coffee. The corners of the children's mouths were sticky yellow; their voices grew loud and cheerful. When Pongo collected the empty cups and began packing things away in the hamper, they glanced at each other and stood up.

"We've got to be going now," said Carl. "Really appreciate this—that was really good food." The others came up to shake Gene's hand, and Karen kissed Margaret quickly on the cheek.

"Be careful," said Margaret, in a voice she did not recognize.

"We will. Good-bye!"

The children walked away, some with their arms around each other; they turned once or twice to wave. Beyond them, over the ruddy ocean, a line of pelicans was moving north. The birds drifted motionless for a long time. First one, then the next, beat its wings for a few strokes; then they drifted again.

"What's going to happen to those kids?" Margaret asked.

Linck said quietly, "They will survive, some of them. They are surplus children. We have them in Amsterdam also. In Bogotá there are thousands, sleeping in the streets. It's nothing new."

"Can't somebody do something about them?"

"There are various ways. One way is to put them into monasteries and convents. Another is war."

She turned to Gene. "Couldn't you—?"

"Take them in? Give them jobs on the grounds crew, or something like that? Yes, I could. And then what would I do with the next batch? There are hundreds of thousands of unwanted teenagers in this country alone."

After a moment she said, "I'm sorry."

"No, it's all right. I understand how you're feeling. 'Surplus children' is an ugly phrase. But that's what they are. Years ago I met a man who was beating the drum for population control. That was in the sixties. He was right, but he couldn't get anybody to listen to him. It's this funny idea we have about the future, that it's somebody else's problem."

"There are some very good organizations," Linck said.

"I belong to about thirty of them," said Gene, "but it isn't enough. It isn't working. Let's go home."

Later that evening Irma found Margaret in the patio, staring at the fountain. "Still thinking about those kids?"

Margaret nodded. "I know he's right—he can't help them all, but it just seems—"

"That if he wasn't a son of a bitch, he would have done something?"

"I didn't mean it that way."

"That's the way it is, though. When you get right down to it, Gene doesn't give a damn. Maybe it's because he was an only child. Or it could be that just because he was so big, he never could make friends with the other kids."

"It sounds terribly lonesome."

"There you go. Feeling sorry again for the poor rich man."
She smiled. "I was, wasn't I?"

"Sure you were, and so was I. That's what drives me
crazy."

Chapter Twenty-one

Margaret was not quite sure what to make of Wilcox. He had fitted himself unobtrusively into the household, as if he had always been there. Under his easy flow of talk there was a feeling of reserve, of something not spoken. Was that it, or was it the deceptions he practiced on them all, with evident enjoyment, when he picked silver coins out of their ears or made fans of cards appear and disappear?

One afternoon she found him in the living room playing with some ping-pong balls on a marble-topped coffee table. One of them fell off, and he said, "Damn." He looked up. "Maggie, come and watch this, will you? I need the audience."

She sat down across from him. "What is it?"

"A new thing I'm trying. It may not be any good." He gathered up the balls in one hand, dropped them in a row on the table. While they were still bouncing, he passed his hand over them: it was the same row of bouncing balls, but now there were five instead of four. He did it again; now there were six. She couldn't see where the extra balls were coming from, although she leaned over to watch. Another pass, and there were five balls; then four; and finally a single ball tapping on the marble. Wilcox picked it up, tossed it into the air; she distinctly saw it rise, but it never came down. He grinned at her.

"How did you do that?"

"Tricks of the trade."

"I think that's so *frustrating*."

"Because you're not sure if it's real magic or not?"

"Well—I know it isn't."

"But there's always a moment when you're not sure, isn't that true? I think that's the point. You know, when I was nine, I was a bit slow for my age, and I absolutely believed in magic. I thought it would be a great thing to learn how to do it, so I asked my mother to bring me a book from the library. Well, it was a disappointment at first, because what I had in mind was turning flowerpots into bicycles, or whatever, and this was all about deceiving people with matchsticks and rubber bands. But once I got over that, it began to be very interesting, especially the close-up work. The big stage illusions, the ones that mystify everybody, are actually quite easy. Those are mechanicals, you know, like the glass box on wheels—a girl gets in, they cover it with a cloth and whirl the box around, then whip off the cloth and she's gone, or else the magician himself pops out. All the big theatrical illusionists are using that now—you've probably seen it yourself."

"Yes, on television."

"Well, the only skill involved there is the skill of the people who invented the trick. Aside from that, it's all showmanship. People don't care so much about skill, they just want to be amazed. They like to believe in magic, just for a moment; I think that's what it's really all about."

Wilcox borrowed Irma's car every afternoon to drive into St. Petersburg and see his assistant. After ten days she was discharged from the hospital, and Wilcox brought her out to the house to say good-bye. Her name was Nan Leach; she was a tall, slender blonde, handsome rather than pretty; her right leg was in a brace, and she walked by swinging her leg from the hip. "It's still pretty stiff," she told them. "I'm supposed to have therapy when I get home."

Her right leg, stretched out in front of her with the foot on a hassock, was not quite so shapely as the other; it was swollen around the knee, and the calf looked shrunken.

"That's a shame," Gene said. "Let me see. Do you mind?" As the others watched, he knelt and put his fingers on her knee.

"No, that's all right," she said with an air of faint surprise, glancing at Wilcox.

Gene stroked her knee for a moment, then drew his hand away suddenly. Her body jumped a little.

"I'm sorry, did I hurt you?"

"No. It's all right, it just felt funny." She looked at Wilcox again. "We'd better go."

Wilcox kissed the women, Irma a little more thoroughly than Margaret. "Come back, Mike," said Gene.

"I will, in a month or two."

One afternoon a few days later, she found Pongo setting the table in the dining room. "Seven for dinner," he explained. "We could handle it in the kitchen, but Gene wants to be fancy."

"Who are the two extras?"

"Couple of professors from the university. I'm going to give them fish—brain food."

At dinner time, when she came in, the others were just gathering around the table. Gene, at the far end, was listening intently to a slender, dark-haired man. His voice was high-pitched; he had an accent that Margaret could not identify. "No, that is not the problem," he said. "That is not the problem. We understand pretty well how the universe began. First there was the primordial atom, which exploded in what we call Big Bang."

The other newcomer said, "But isn't it true that the math shows that if that happened, the universe never would have formed galaxies and planets—all that matter would have just kept on expanding indefinitely in a big sphere?" He was a rumpled, pudgy young man with a faint brown mustache.

"That is a very good point," said the dark-skinned man. "Yes, and therefore we must assume a discontinuity either in the primordial atom, or in the way it expanded during the first few milliseconds." There was something odd about his vowels; he said "univarse," and "primardial."

"Maggie, let me introduce you," said Gene. The others turned in their chairs, and the two newcomers stood up. "Margaret Morrow, my secretary. This is Nirmal Coomaraswami, a famous theoretical physicist—"

"I am not so famous as all that," said Coomaraswami, laughing nervously. "Very glad to know you."

"And this is Stan Salomon, he teaches biology at the University of Florida."

"Margaret." His hand was plump and cool.

She took the empty place next to Salomon. "We were talking about the creationism controversy," he said. "You know, whether God created the universe or whether it just happened."

"Yes, and that is what science cannot tell us," said Coomaraswami. Pongo put a bowl of soup in front of him; he glanced at it in apparent surprise. "We know what happened," he went on, "and we know when it happened, with a very high degree of certainty. But creationists want us to say why it happened. This is not a scientific question."

Pongo finished serving the soup and sat down across from Irma.

"That may be," said Salomon. "But the origin of man *is* a scientific problem, and that's what bothers me. Did you know," he said to Margaret, "that we have to give equal time now to the creationist theory in biology classes?"

"No, really? I think that's awful."

"It is not awful. It is not awful," said Coomaraswami. "We should examine both theories and see how well they explain the facts. Then let people decide for themselves."

"It's religion in the schools," said Salomon.

"That is not necessarily so."

"Creationism isn't religion?" Salomon demanded.

"No, not necessarily. The Bible account of the creation is a myth. In Hindu religion there is also a creation myth, slightly different. All over the world there are these creation myths. But even if we say that a myth is not true, that is not to say that creation cannot be true."

Margaret was watching him in fascination. His skin was no darker than Pongo's, but it was a different color, a ruddier brown; his crisp black hair, faintly glossy, clung to his neat narrow head. His fingernails and the tips of his fingers were pink.

"That's nonsense," said Salomon, with his soup spoon half raised to his lips. "The evidence for evolution—"

"Yes-yes, I know, but please let me finish. Of course there is evidence that living organisms have evolved from other organisms. There is no question about that, and that is a very good point. But it is possible to say that organisms were created by God, and then evolved into other forms, or that there are a limited number of forms—sort of Platonic ideals —that organisms can evolve into."

"The fossil record—" began Salomon, but fell silent because Anderson was speaking.

"I remember," he said slowly, "in one of Hemingway's letters he talks about a new kind of shark that appeared in the ocean off Cuba. Nobody had ever seen it before. They were black, with no dorsal fin, and their stomachs were full of swordfish swords. I couldn't help wondering, what if creation is still going on?"

Early one morning, before it was light, she went into the courtyard. The fountain was making a lonesome sound. A red spark glimmered not far away. "Oh," she said, "is that you, Piet?"

"Yes, it's me." He rose and came toward her. "You couldn't sleep?"

"No." .

"You have been looking a bit tired. Do you often have insomnia?"

"Fairly often."

"Have you tried hypnosis for it?"

"No. Do you think that would work?"

"Well, we can find out if you are a good subject, at least. Do you want to try now? Wait until I turn on the fountain light. Now stand there, please, and close your eyes."

Margaret did as she was told, feeling foolish.

"Now I want you to be aware of your right arm," said Linck's voice. "Feel how relaxed it is; it is very relaxed and soft, there is no tension in it. Your right arm is very relaxed, and now it is becoming lighter. It wants to rise because it is so light, almost as light as a balloon, and now it is rising, you can't stop it from rising, and you don't want to stop it. It is lighter and lighter, your arm is rising because it is so light . . ."

His voice went on, remote and almost inaudible, talking about her arm. She could feel her arm coming up a little, but she was not sure where it was. And his voice went on.

"You can open your eyes now," he said.

To her surprise, her right arm was extended almost at a right angle from her shoulder. She lowered it, feeling even more foolish.

"That was very good," Linck said. "You are a good subject, much better than Gene."

"Oh, have you hypnotized him?"

"No, because he is a very bad subject. But if you want to do something about your insomnia, I don't think we will have any trouble."

They had their first session that night in Linck's sitting room upstairs. Linck had her stare at the illuminated crystal of a clock in the darkened room, and suggested to her that her eyelids were growing heavy, that she was becoming drowsy, that she could not keep her eyes open. After she closed them, his voice went on, and she felt herself drifting deeper and deeper into a black velvety space in which she was aware but bodiless and without anxiety or volition. He told her that she would remember everything he said to her unless he ordered her not to, and that she would always awake from trance feeling refreshed and cheerful. He told her that in future she would always go directly into trance when he said, "Go to sleep, Maggie."

In their second session, two days later, Linck told her to imagine herself in an elevator descending very slowly down an endless shaft; each time the elevator passed another floor, her trance was deepened. He repeated his previous suggestions, and told her that when she went to bed she would feel relaxed and drowsy, and would have no anxiety about getting to sleep. That night she slept nine hours.

In their third session, Linck gave her a "sleep blanket": he told her that whenever she wanted to go to sleep, she could imagine a warm blanket being pulled up gradually over her body; when it got to her chin, she would fall into a deep natural sleep. And it worked.

Gradually and gently the world was slipping into winter. They turned off the air conditioning, opened the sliding glass doors to the garden and the clerestory windows in front. Loose papers blew like birds around the living room until Gene brought out a boxful of glass paperweights to put on them.

One afternoon she found him in his workroom, bent over the drawing board. "Gene, these letters ought to be signed."

"Okay." He laid his brush aside. A half-finished drawing was in front of him; others were spread out to dry on the table. They were delicate pen sketches with a wash of sepia: faces, floating hair, oak leaves. "What are those for?" she asked.

"Christmas cards." He scrawled his name at the bottom of a letter, picked up another one.

"Oh, my. I wish I could do that."

"Can't draw?"

"No. I can draw a pig, and that's about all."

"Let me see your pig." He pushed a blank card toward her.

"I don't want to spoil this."

"That's all right, there are plenty more."

Margaret took the pen he gave her and made a pig: a sort of bucket shape on its side for the head, then a round body, four stick legs, and a curlicue for the tail.

Gene looked at it without comment. "Would you like to make some cards? I'll show you a way without drawing."

"Yes, I'd love to."

"Get rid of these letters and I'll meet you in the dining room."

When she got there, Gene was spreading newspapers over one end of the table. When he was finished, he began taking jars of paint out of a shopping bag. "This is tempera—it'll wash off, but it's messy. Get me some spoons from the kitchen, will you, and some little bowls, and a glass of water."

"How many spoons?"

"Half a dozen."

Gene arranged the open paint jars, bowls, and spoons in the middle of the table. "Sit down and I'll show you what to do. First you fold a card in half, like this. Then you drop a little paint on it, wherever you want." He dipped up some red with a spoon, then blue, then a few drops of yellow. The paint stood up in blobs on the shiny white card. "Now you just fold it over." He demonstrated, pressing the card down vigorously with the heel of his hand.

He opened the card. The paint had spread and run together in a symmetrical winged shape; there were veins in it and subtle shadings where the colors had blended.

"My goodness, that's beautiful!" Margaret said.

"Try it."

Her first attempt made a sort of cabbage shape with yellow eyes. She tried again, with different colors, and got an orchid. Gene was mixing colors in one of the bowls to make a brownish violet. He spooned some of this onto a folded card, then added a little water. When he opened it, it was a veined brown-violet shape, like a block print, with delicate traceries around it. "Oh, let me try that," she said.

Irma wandered in after a while, then Pongo, then Linck, and they all sat around the table until nearly dinner time, making Christmas cards. As the colors dried, new patterns became visible in them. "Look at this rabbit," they said to each other, or, "Here's a demon standing over a tree." When they counted them, they discovered they had made more than a hundred cards, each more beautiful than the others.

Later Margaret said, "I know I can't draw, and I certainly can't paint. So where did the beauty come from?"

"Well, folding the card makes the design symmetrical, of course, and that's part of what we mean by beauty. Then the colors mixing on the card gave you all kinds of subtle gradations, and the surface tension of the paint made it form veins and so on. Remember that you chose the colors, and where to put them; that makes your cards different from anybody else's."

"Yes, I saw that. Irma's are big splashy flowers, and yours are like misty watercolors."

"Sure. And Piet's are dark and brooding because he uses so much black. So don't say you didn't do it, because you really did. But the rest of it came from just the physical properties of the paint and the card—if that's beautiful, it's because the universe is beautiful."

"Like the coquinas?"

"Maybe."

"But what's it for? Just for our benefit?"

"I don't think so. There's beauty in the universe that nobody ever saw until the invention of the microscope. Crack open a stone, or split a piece of wood, and you'll see beauty. But what if you never cracked that stone, or split that piece of wood?"

"Isn't that a little like, if a tree falls in the forest when nobody's there, is there a sound?"

"Well, is there? Depends on what you mean by sound. If it's just waves of compression and rarefaction in the air, then the answer is yes—if it's what you experience when those waves hit your ear, then the answer is no. A long time ago I used to think that when we make art we're celebrating the natural world, praising it, and that's what it's all about. What I think now is that we're here because we can make a kind of beauty the universe can't make by itself. The natural world can make a crystal, or an ocelot, or a poplar tree with the wind blowing through it, but it can't make a painting, or music, or stories. And there's a kind of beauty that we create in intellectual things, maybe—mathematics, physics."

"You don't think that's just there, and we're discovering it?"

"Oh, no. Mathematicians will tell you that mathematics is not descriptive except by coincidence. It isn't a science. And even physics—somebody, I think it was Leon Cooper, once said that when God created the world, he didn't bother to make any fine structure. A tree was just a tree, until somebody cut one down, and then he had to hurry up and create the rings and so on. And when somebody invented a microscope, he had to create all the fine structure that you can't see with your naked eye—cells and corpuscles and bacteria. And when we invented more and more powerful instruments for looking at the insides of atoms, of course he had to make electrons and protons and neutrons. And now it's quarks and leptons and so forth, and that's why particle physics is such a mess, because God is making it all up as he goes along."

Chapter Twenty-two

Tom Cooley left his job in 1976, moved back to Amherst where he still had friends, and retired on a small pension. With this and his income from several rental properties he had acquired in the sixties, he was financially secure, and for a number of years his health was good. He went on annual hunting trips with his cronies, did a little fishing and continued to read *Amusement Business* from cover to cover.

In the fall of 1982, camped in the Adirondacks, one evening he felt tired and out of sorts. The next morning he missed a clear shot at a six-point buck; the gun seemed to dip in his hands at the moment he squeezed the trigger. On the way back to camp with his friends, he slipped and fell heavily. The next day he noticed that he was having trouble holding things. When he tried to chop some kindling, the hatchet flew out of his hand and narrowly missed Al Jacobs' leg.

Cooley realized that something was seriously wrong. When he got back to Amherst he went to a doctor, who sent him to a V.A. hospital for tests. In December the doctor told him, "Mr. Cooley, what you've got is something called amyotrophic lateral sclerosis. You may have heard of it as Lou Gehrig's disease. It's a progressive muscular weakness, and there just isn't any treatment for it. I'm sorry to tell you this, but that's the way it looks."

"How long have I got?" Cooley asked.

"I'd say three or four years, five at the outside."

A few months after this interview, Cooley found a notice in the back of *Amusement Business*: "Big John Kimberley would like to hear from carnival friends, 1964–65." There was a box number in St. Petersburg, Florida.

Cooley's hands were now so weak that he could see the time coming when he would not be able to dress and feed himself. His legs were also affected; he could not walk far without tiring. Dr. Seward had been after him to go into the V.A. hospital again, but Cooley knew that once he did that he would never get out again.

There was no way he could aim and fire a gun, or use any other weapon. He thought of letter bombs, but that was too chancy; someone else might open the letter. He thought of poisons, of fire, of bacterial cultures, and rejected them all. He slept badly. In his dreams, Gene Anderson was guillotined, drowned, garroted, crushed by falling trees, and always he stood up again unharmed.

One evening he called a taxi and went to see Al Jacobs. They talked a little about hunting; then Cooley brought up his problem in a casual way.

"What are you telling me—you want to wire some guy's car? That's easy."

"No, not a car. I was thinking maybe under a chair."

"With a timer?"

"No, that's no good. I've got to be there when it happens."

"Right in the same room? You could do it with a shaped charge, if that's what you want. The explosion goes straight up. You could be sitting next to him, and it wouldn't knock your hat off."

"How would I fire it?"

Jacobs shrugged. "Dozens of ways. The simplest thing would be just a wire and a push-button. Or you could use a radio control—no wires."

"What would it cost?"

Jacobs scratched his chin. "Tom, it wouldn't be easy for me to get this stuff. The radio control, if you decide to go that way, I'll have to make that myself. Say five thousand."

Gene Anderson stood at his window, looking down at the lights along the driveway and in the parking area. The gate was open; here came a car, black behind the cones of its headlamps. Another was turning off the highway behind it. He had just finished dressing, in a suit and tie; it was the first time he had worn such an outfit in more than a year.

Behind him, on his writing chair, were some penciled notes headed "Toward a New Religion." He had not shown these to anyone, even to Maggie. It was curious and a little unsettling to think how his attitudes had changed over the years, as if belief were a function of metabolism. In his teens, he had dismissed religion as a mental aberration; now, although he found the answers of organized religion full of absurdities, the questions absorbed him.

He had one advantage over all the others who speculated about the unseen world: he knew that it existed. Several times, by accident, he had managed to bring through from another world some object which was not merely a copy of something existing in this world. Among these was a little volume by Marco Pallis which did not appear in any catalog or index. In this world, Pallis had written many works on metaphysics and religion, but not *The Phenomenology of Mind*.

Gene treasured this book, in its warped boards and faded green cloth, because it was itself evidence that the author's central postulate was true: the universe was an infinite manifold in which every possible thing existed: "God is free to do, and must do, everything that is possible." Somewhere in that vast flowering of creation, that n-dimensional dandelion globe of branching and rebranching realities, there were worlds in which Gene Anderson had never been born, others in which he was not a giant, others in which he had not killed Paul Cooley. . . .

He looked at his watch; it was time to go down.

The housewarming party, in his opinion, was an evil of doubtful necessity. "You can stand them for one evening," Irma had said, but he was not sure about that. They had invited all the local people who had had anything to do with the house, and their flowery wives. Little Larry Einarson, the architect, was there, and Russell Beck, the prime contractor, along with a crowd of subcontractors; then there was Dan Ankeny, the real estate broker; Sidney Webber, of St. Petersburg Trust and Guaranty; and various friends and relatives whose names he had not quite caught. The men were red-faced, painfully close-shaven and recently barbered; one or two of them were already glassy-eyed.

When he stood up, Gene's head was on a level with the heads of people on the raised portion of the living room, and when he sat down he was about as tall as people standing beside him, and that should have been all right, but people were still uneasy in his presence; they came over one or two at a time and said a few words—usually the same few words—then looked embarrassed and went away.

Maggie, in a white dress that showed off her tan, was talking to the publisher of the St. Petersburg *Times* and his rotund wife; Pongo and Irma had been here earlier but had disappeared. Hired waiters came and went with trays of highballs; a few people had brought plates from the buffet into the living room and were dripping vinaigrette sauce on the rugs.

"Mr. Anderson, please tell me, *where* did you get that marvelous wood carving? Is it one of yours?" The art critic of the *Times*, a pale young man with black-rimmed glasses, was pointing to a modern-looking piece that resembled the buttocks of a woman.

"No, I got it in the Seychelles," Anderson said. He did not add that the "sculpture" was the fruit of a coconut palm.

"Well, it's simply marvelous. I'd like to do a column about it, and of course, about all the other wonderful things you have here. I know how you feel about publicity, but—"

"I'd really rather not. You understand."

"Of course." The critic, whose name was Phelps or Phillips, shrugged with manly regret and drifted off, munching a canape.

A gray-haired man with a solemn expression was coming toward him. "Hello, Cliff," said Anderson. "Did you just get here?"

"Yes, my plane was late, but I've got that information you wanted. I could of phoned, but I thought you'd rather have me tell you in person."

"Yes, of course."

"Can we go someplace private?"

Anderson stood up and looked around. There were people on the balcony, in the dining room; there were even a few sitting on the benches in the garden. "Come on," he said, and led the way back through the hall to the infirmary, where he sat on the end of the examination chair and offered Cliff Guthrie a stool.

Guthrie said, "First off, I ought to tell you that I had to spend all the money you gave me. There was the guy in IRS, and then we had to find somebody in the Veterans Administration, so it was expensive."

"That's all right."

"Well, we located him. There are plenty of Thomas Cooleys, but this one was born in Portland, Oregon, and the dates match, and he gives his occupation as retired police officer, so it's got to be him. He's sixty-nine now. He's living in Amherst, Massachusetts, and he was in a veterans' hospital for a while last year. Sorry if that's bad news."

"No, it's okay," Anderson said. "Thanks, Cliff."

In the kitchen, the phone rang and Irma answered it. "Yes, it is," she said. "Who is this?" She listened a moment, then put the phone down.

"Who was it?" Pongo asked.

"I don't know. Some man asked if this was John Kimberley's residence, and I said yes, because that's the name Gene used in the carnival; then he hung up. That's funny."

"Maybe he'll call back."

Margaret found herself standing beside a large gray-haired man with mournful eyes. "My name is Cliff Guthrie," he said. "I haven't seen you around here before."

"No, I'm new. Margaret Morrow—I'm Gene's secretary. Have you known him long, Cliff?"

"About a year. I was an examiner with IRS. We were auditing his returns, and I saw him several times. After I retired last March, I came around just to pay a social call. He was pretty cordial, considering what a rough time we gave him."

"And now he invites you to his parties?"

"That's right. I've done some work for him, too." He stared at the highball in his hand. "It isn't the work, though —that isn't why. I just like to be around him."

"I know what you mean."

Anderson moved across the living room, past a group of men talking about fishing: " . . . thirty-five yards of hundred-

pound test, and, man, I mean he *snatched* it . . . '' At the end
of the raised area Linck was holding forth to a little group:
''Yes, even the pumpkin. Do you know that carriages and lanterns have essentially the same shape? If you look at a carriage
with two lanterns, there it is three times, one big one and two
little ones. And even in automobiles, up to about nineteen
thirty. Well, it has been shown that this form is based on the
seed-pod of a Chinese plant.''

Anderson paused to listen. Linck's group included one of
the insurance people, the publisher Orris Kilian and his wife,
and a man whose name he had forgotten—one of the subcontractors, probably. The publisher's wife was saying something
about the mystery of folk tales. Linck answered, ''I think
what you feel when you say a story like that is mysterious is
that there's another story behind it. For instance, Beauty and
the Beast. That is mysterious, because it is covering up another
story, the Amor and Psyche myth, and that one is mysterious
too, perhaps, because it's covering up still another story that
we don't know about.''

''Who was the man who made that movie of Beauty and the
Beast?'' the publisher asked.

''Cocteau.''

''Cocteau, right. Wasn't he a fag? Why do you suppose so
many—''

Anderson moved on. He knew the question and the answer
already. He walked through the garden, past a man and a
woman seriously engaged in kissing; he let himself into the
dark workshop, out again at the back, and began to climb the
hill. Behind him the house spilled its yellow lights out over the
garden and the lawn: it was like someone else's house, in
another country. The trees closed around him with their cool
breath. He climbed as far as the footbridge, crossed it, and sat
down on the far side, looking at the stars.

He remembered nights in the South Pacific when there had
been, incredibly, more stars than this. It was really better to be
on the ocean, he and Pongo the only sparks of human life in
the great vacancy; then you saw the world clearly and knew
just how large it was. But even here, knowing that St. Petersburg and the beaches were only ten miles away, it was good to
look up at the night sky and feel the great globe massively
turning under his body. The earth turned under the stars, and

as it turned the little sparks that were human souls dimmed and brightened, like candles lighted and snuffed, endlessly, over and over, around the turning world.

If it was true, as the physicists seemed to be saying, that consciousness did not merely observe reality but helped to create it, then perhaps science was an impiety, and the original sin might have been, not eating the fruit of the tree, but cutting it down—forcing God to disclose the structure of the rings which until then had not existed.

And if Western civilization were to be destroyed, if all that knowledge were lost in the cataclysm that was surely coming, would the universe then revert to a simpler model? The sky a crystal hemisphere over a flat earth? Sometimes he felt he could almost believe it. What if it were only human knowledge and belief that held the whole fabric together: with that gone, would time unroll again to the beginning? Would God walk again in the garden, in the cool of the evening?

It is a little after two o'clock. Pongo is in his living room, watched by the marmoset as he turns the pages of a bikers' magazine. Here is a photograph of a man with the usual beard and tattoos straddling a Harley-Davidson; swastikas and silver dollars are sewn to his black leather vest. Behind him stand two long-haired young women, bare to the belly. All three are smiling. The two women have big fruity breasts, pale and soft in the sunlight. The message seems to be that if you are a real man, you will wear black leather and ride a big bike; then the big-chested women will crowd around you and smile. Pongo's right buttock is itching, but he is too lazy to scratch it. He thinks about an afternoon at the Club de Pesce in Cartagena—'73 was that, or '74? They were sitting on the terrace in the shade of the flowering trees, looking out across the bay at the rusty hulk of a Colombian naval cruiser. It was hot even under the trees, but there was a little wind from the water. The smiling *indio* waiter in his purple jacket had just served them a pompano en papillote, brown and tender in the husk of charred paper. He remembers the smell of the fish, and the water too bright to look at. Now he sees the two women sitting down at the next table, in the sun. Gene, with his back turned, does not see them. He tries to capture that first moment, but it will not come clear—just the two women sitting down, and that one has glossy dark hair, the other a cap of short champagne-colored curls. The sun is behind her, and he sees that one breast is outlined clearly through her thin orange blouse; it is almost a perfect half-sphere, like a little grapefruit, and the nipple, thick and erect, is the size of a pencil eraser.

Irma, upstairs in the big house, is looking at one of the ads in *The New Yorker*. Two tanned young people stand under a tree. They are both barefoot. The young man leans on a branch with his forearms crossed over an open book; the flap of the book jacket has been folded in to keep his place if he should decide to put the book down. There is a ring on the third finger of his left hand. He looks patiently at the young woman, who hangs onto the branch with one hand, while, with the other, she brushes a hibiscus blossom against her chin. She does not look at him, but at something off-camera, perhaps the sunset (this would account for the pumpkin color of their skins); perhaps she is making up her mind whether to give the young man any reason to put down his book. She is a slightly disheveled blonde with a biteable lower lip. Her adolescent breasts are concealed by two triangles of cloth, one blue, one violet. She also wears a gauzy floral skirt in the same colors. Behind them are two wicker chairs and a low wicker table on the brown-sugar sand; on the table are two artfully decorated rum drinks, maybe rum Alexanders, each with its straw; a pair of sunglasses; and another hibiscus blossom: beyond all that lies the baby-blue sea.

Margaret is sitting on her bed with pillows behind her. She has just had a shower, and feels cool and clean. She picks up a copy of *Cosmopolitan;* on the cover is a vapid teenager in a purple dress with the zipper pulled down to reveal the inner slopes of two melony breasts. One has been retouched to look much smaller than the other: why is that? She opens the magazine toward the back and finds photos of women in purple woolly wraps, a purple mohair sweater, a purple knitted tam. There is a two-page cigarette ad showing the Golden Gate Bridge at sunset. The water is purple The eye-shadow in the cosmetic ads is purple. She reads a mail-order ad: "Yes, CONNECTING will show you how to find love *the day you receive it*—not after you've lost 20 pounds, not after you've spent money on a new wardrobe, not after you've been rejected by fifty other men, but the *day you receive it!* Just the way you are." Then a diet article.

Linck is in the bathroom, a room he thoroughly approves of because it has a tub long enough to stretch out in, a rubberized headrest, and a reading light. He runs his bath, hot with a little admixture of cold, until it is within a few inches of the drain; then he turns off the hot, turns the cold water on full. Probably because of the frostbite he suffered as a child, his toes are less tolerant of heat than the rest of his body, and he has worked out this method of dividing his bathwater into zones.

When the tub is full he steps into it, carrying his bathtub book—today it is *The Pound Era*, by Hugh Kenner—and lowers his buttocks with care into the water. When he is seated in the tub with his legs drawn up, he propels himself gently backward and lowers his body, with grunts of pleasure, until it is submerged.

In the few moments after he sits in the tub and before he lies down, he has noticed, as he always does in this house, that the light from the wall behind him makes visible certain curious turbulent shadows in the water. At first he supposed that oils from his skin, liberated by the heat, were swirling out into the tub; but by holding his forearm a few inches under the surface, he has been able to determine that the shadows come from a level higher than his submerged body, and it is now his opinion that these squirming ideograms are caused by the sudden admixture of the hot and cold zones of the bathwater.

It is interesting how often the bathtub has figured in the history of science, politics, and art: Archimedes, for instance, and the Shang emperor about whom he has just been reading, who inscribed on his tub the characters that Pound translated, "Make it new." Why on his tub? Was it because the emperor, like Linck himself, this person, this physical body who lies here now submerged and displacing water like Archimedes, liked to philosophize in his tub?

Now the shapes at the bottom of the water have paled almost to invisibility, but they are still there, no longer ideograms but slowly elongating serpents. The Manichaeans believed that God was visible in light, Satan in darkness. In the struggle between them, the elements had been mingled; the whole world was a mixture of darkness and light, good and evil. At certain moments Linck finds this a very plausible theory, the more so because without this mingling there would be no contrast and no borders; the perceptible universe could not exist.

On the bottom of the tub there is another shadow, a drifting chain of three lozenges, each one surrounded by two bright arcs, mathematically perfect, that intersect at the points of the lozenge. When he looks for the source of this shadow, he finds that it is a floating hair. It is curious, he thinks, that this marvelous and perfect appearance should be generated by nothing more than a hair, probably a pubic hair.

Alone in his room in the secure yellow-white light, Gene Anderson takes three coins from the cup on the desk. He throws them six times: they yield the hexagram Tui, "The Joyous, Lake."

He finds it in the text. Tui is the hexagram of "the joyous" and of success, which comes through gentleness. When men's hearts are won by gentleness, says the oracle, they will accept hardships and even death. This is the Judgment. The Image, the second trigram, tells him that knowledge becomes a vitalizing force through stimulating conversation with congenial friends.

There is a moving line, an old yin, in the third place. This tells him that if a man is empty inside, idle pleasures will fill the void. The next two lines are old yang. The first tells him that inner peace can come only from the renunciation of base pleasures; the second, that danger comes in the form of "disintegrating influences" even to the best of men.

As always, the *I Ching*'s response is apposite, and as always, it is ambiguous. He forms another question: "What is this danger?" and casts the coins again. They yield the hexagram Pi, "Union." Again the response is apposite: it says that for union to take place, there must be a central figure for the others to rally around: but if that man has no real calling, he will only bring about confusion.

Year by year the layers of coldness have folded around him, numbing the pain to a distant pinprick. Sculpture, painting, that whole world, is now like a nest of bright objects laid away in cabinets. People are interesting, clever little mechanisms, with their bright eyes, their flushes and smiles.

It is not that they are unintelligent. Taken one by one, they are as smart as they need to be, but in their numbers they are a terrible swarming mass, grinding everything to smaller and smaller bits.

For months he has been carrying in his mind the solution to humanity's problem—a way of saving the world. He knows it is possible, and he is almost persuaded that he can do it himself. When he examines his motives, he sees that for the most part they are selfish: the lust for glory; the desire for great accomplishment, for a sense of superiority; the urge to save his own life. On the other side, he is afraid of giving up his peace and privacy, perhaps forever; he is afraid of failure; he is afraid of revealing himself as a megalomaniac and narcissistic fool. Which is worse, to save humanity for the wrong reasons—or to let it perish through cowardice?

Chapter Twenty-three

The cab driver let Cooley off in front of the railroad station in Springfield. It was black dark, and cold. He went into the station carrying the attaché case; it weighed only about five pounds, but it felt like fifty. He sat with it between his knees until the train pulled in. The conductor helped him up the steps. "There you go, Gramp."

There was a three-hour wait between trains in New York. On the Florida train, the heat wasn't working in the dining car, and the food was worse than he remembered, but his compartment was comfortable; an "economy bedroom" was what they called it now. He slept fairly well, and at eleven the next morning he was in Tampa. He got a cab and went looking for a motel. The first one was not what he wanted: the lobby was too small and too crowded. "That's a fleabag," he told the driver when he came out. "Isn't there a decent motel in this town?"

The next one was just right; it had a big lobby with a lot of furniture and planters, and there didn't seem to be many people around.

Cooley had lunch in the coffee shop and made a phone call from his room, then went down to the desk to check out.

"You're not staying with us tonight, then?" the clerk said. He looked disapproving.

"No, something's come up. A friend of mine's going to come for me in an hour or so—I'll just wait over there out of

199

the way. How long's it take to get to the airport from here?''

"About twenty minutes, sir."

The lobby was empty. At the far end there were two big wing chairs facing each other. Cooley knelt on the floor, opened the attaché case and lifted out the explosive device. He had to get his legs under the chair, supporting the device on his knees, before he could attach it the way Jacobs had shown him. When he finished, he was sweating and dizzy. He closed the attaché case, which also contained his toothbrush and a change of underwear, and sat down to wait.

They were finishing lunch when the phone rang; Irma leaned over to answer it. "Anderson residence. . . . Who shall I say is calling?" After a moment she punched the hold button and said, "His name is McIver, and he says it's about your parents."

"McIver," said Gene reflectively, and shook his head. "Put it on tape, Irma, and turn on the speaker." When she had done so, he took the phone and said, "Mr. McIver, this is Gene Anderson. What's this about my parents?"

The voice that came into the room was thin and high-pitched, an old man's voice. "Gene, you don't remember me I guess, but I used to work with your father in Dog River when you was a boy. You know they moved away about a year after you left."

"Yes. Mr. McIver, how did you find me here?"

"Well, I have a friend in St. Pete, he's in real estate, and when he happened to mention your name and said you was a giant, why, I figured that's got to be the same Gene Anderson that I knew back then."

"What is your friend's name?"

"His name is Russ Lafler. Now I don't know if you know, Gene, that your parents both died in Chehalis in nineteen fifty-six."

"Yes, I know that."

"Well, I have reason to believe that their death may not of been accidental. I don't want to talk too much about this on the phone, but there's certain information I have that I think you'd like to know. I'm in Tampa for a day or two, staying at the Costa Brava Motel, do you know where it's at?"

"I can find it." Gene nodded at Irma, who took the Tampa

directory from the shelf and began turning the pages. "Would it be convenient if I came over this afternoon, say in about an hour?"

"Yes, that'd be fine. I'll be in the lobby, Gene, because from what I hear you wouldn't fit into a motel room too good."

"I appreciate that. In an hour then, Mr. McIver."

At Gene's nod, Irma turned off the phone. "What was that all about?"

Gene's face was stony. "There was a man who worked with my father—his name might have been McIver, I don't remember. Irma, see if you can find a Russ Lafler under real estate."

They looked at each other silently. Irma opened the St. Petersburg directory to the yellow pages. After a moment she said, "Here's an Aldridge and Lafler Realtors."

"Call them."

She punched the number. A woman's voice said, "Aldridge and Lafler, serving the Suncoast, may I help you?"

"I'd like to speak to Russ Lafler, please."

"I'm sorry, he's out of town till the twenty-first."

Gene nodded; she said, "Thank you," and turned off the phone.

For a moment no one spoke; then Pongo asked, "You think this is some kind of scam?"

Gene spread his big hands on the table. Margaret, watching him, thought she had never seen him look like this before. He said slowly, "It might be. Or maybe that really is McIver. But I don't think so. I think it's a man who tried to kill me in nineteen sixty-five. It's been twenty years; he's an old man now. I thought I was all through with him. Irma, call information in Amherst, Massachusetts, and get a number for Thomas or Tom Cooley. What time is it there?"

"Same as here—we're in the same zone." She made the call, wrote a number on her pad, and looked questioningly at Gene.

"Dial it."

They heard the buzz of the ringing signal. Then a woman's voice: "Hello?"

"Mr. Cooley, please," said Gene.

"He ain't here."

"Can you tell me where to reach him?"

"He went to New York Sunday. I told him, but would he

listen to me? No. Why would he listen to me, I'm just his damn housekeeper. You call back next week." The telephone clicked and buzzed.

"What are you going to do?" Irma asked.

"I'm going over there."

"That's dumb. Let me call the police."

"And tell them what? He hasn't committed any crime that I can prove. He's an old man—they'd laugh at me. If they question him and let him go, what will he do next?"

"I'm going with you," said Pongo. "I'll bring the Monster around—give me a couple of minutes."

Pongo backed the motor home out of the garage, drove it around to the cottage, and got his gun. He tucked the gun under his waistband, put on a Madras jacket to cover it, and a hat to go with the jacket.

Gene was waiting outside the kitchen door. "All dressed up?" he said as he got in.

"Sure. Social occasion."

Gene was silent and glum on the way over to Tampa. It was a fine winter afternoon, cool and clear. Pongo pulled into the motel parking lot; there were only a few cars there. The motel was two stories tall, with stairs and balconies all around. They walked in; the lobby seemed empty. "I'll ask at the desk," Pongo said. The desk clerk, a slender young man, was looking at them with round eyes.

"Wait a minute," said Gene. He nodded. "Over there."

At the far end of the lobby, partly concealed by a planter, there was a pair of green upholstered chairs. In one of the chairs an old man was sitting quietly, looking at nothing.

"Is that him?" Pongo asked in an undertone.

"I don't know."

The old man looked up as they approached. His bald head shone; what hair he had left was wispy and white, as fine as milkweed floss. His skin was baby pink, with an underlying waxy pallor. He watched them without expression through his rimless spectacles.

"Are you Mr. McIver?"

"That's right." The old man put out a flaccid hand. " 'Scuse me if I don't get up; I've got some trouble with my legs."

"This is Bill Richards, Mr. McIver." Gene sat down facing the old man, and Pongo pulled over another chair.

"Glad to know you," said McIver in his piping voice. "Now, Gene, I s'pose you know that whatever I tell you is between us. Your folks are dead and gone, nothing we can do about that. But it just kind of nagged at me, you know—" He was craning his neck and blinking as he looked up at Gene. "My gosh, they told me you was big, but I didn't have any idea. How tall are you, anyway?"

"I'm a little over eight and a half feet, Mr. McIver. Now about this information you say you have—"

The old man sighed and groped for something in the pocket of his jacket. The jacket was too big for him, and so was his shirt collar. There was something wrong with his hands: they were limp and hung unnaturally from his wrists. "Back in 'fifty-six," he said, "I was visiting your folks in Chehalis." He seemed to be struggling to grasp something in his pocket; at last he brought it out, holding it awkwardly between thumb and two fingers. It was a pack of cigarettes. "Smoke?" he said, holding it out.

"No, thanks," said Gene, and Pongo shook his head.

The old man fumbled a cigarette out of the pack and put it in his mouth. "I was staying with them when it happened," he said. "This isn't easy to talk about, Gene, but you know the house burned down and they was both killed in the fire."

"Yes."

The old man reached into his other pocket and brought out a heavy chrome lighter. When he tried to press the lever down, his fingers slipped; they seemed to have no more strength than a baby's. "Would you mind?" he said, holding it out. "Tell you the truth, it isn't just my legs—it's my hands, too."

Gene lit the lighter and offered it. The old man leaned forward, but did not touch his cigarette to the flame. "Now, Mr. Anderson," he said, "keep your thumb on that thing if you want to stay alive." His voice had changed; it was a little deeper and firmer. "If you take your thumb off," he said, "there's a plastic bomb under your chair that'll blow sky high. And if you try to get up, that'll make it blow too."

Pongo reached under his jacket, put his hand on the gun.

"Don't do that, Pongo," said Gene without looking around. He bent forward and blew out the lighter flame; his thumb was steady on the mechanism. "You're Tom Cooley," he said.

The old man blinked, then chuckled a little. "Didn't think you'd recognize me."

"I didn't. It's been thirty years—you must be close to seventy, and you're ill. What's the matter with you?"

"Not a damn thing that concerns you," said the old man, coloring a little. "Well, I guess it does, though, because if it hadn't of been for you, my boy Paul and my cousin Jerry would be alive, and my wife too, probably. You killed them, all three."

"If there's a bomb under my chair, and if it blows up, it'll kill you too," said Gene.

"It's what they call a shaped charge. It'll blow straight up, right through your ass, Mr. Anderson. Probably cut off your legs and leave 'em flopping on the floor, while the rest of you goes splat on the ceiling. Yes sir, just a big red smear on the ceiling." He took the unlit cigarette out of his mouth and dropped it.

"Did you kill my parents?"

The old man snorted. "Hell, no. I wasn't even there. That was just a story, but it got you here, didn't it?"

"What do you want?"

The old man smiled, with a gleam of false teeth. "Just want to watch you hanging from the ceiling, and your legs flopping on the floor."

Pongo moved slightly; the old man turned to look at him. "That bomb is armed now," he said. "Touch it or try to move it, and that'll set it off too."

Gene closed his eyes. One hand held the lighter steady; the other dropped between his knees, near the skirt of the chair. "Careful!" the old man said sharply.

After a moment Gene withdrew his hand; his eyes opened. "I want you to know," he said, "that Paul's death was an accident. About your cousin, I don't know what happened. I think he shot me."

"Well, you sure as hell shot him," said the old man. A curious look of anxiety came into his eyes.

"No," said Gene. He set the lighter down on the arm of his chair. The old man's eyes bulged in horror, and his body jerked once.

Gene was bending forward, groping with one hand under the chair. After a moment he brought out a cylindrical object about the size of a Frisbee. He held it up solemnly, then opened his hands: the thing was gone.

"God almighty!" said the old man. His body was trembling all over. "How did you—Where—?"

Gene's lips and nostrils were compressed; he was breathing unsteadily, and his eyes had a distant look. Slowly he bent forward and took the old man's arms. "What's wrong with you?" he said.

The old man tried to pull away but could not; his eyes squeezed shut, his face flushed, and his head dropped forward; he was sobbing angrily and helplessly. "Here," said Gene, as if to himself. "Here. And the legs too?" His hands began to move down the old man's thighs.

"Wait," he said after a moment. He knelt on the floor and leaned his body close against the old man's, pressing himself against his chest and arms and legs. Over his shoulder the old man's face stared madly, his glasses awry, eyes bleared. His mouth opened and shut, opened and shut.

"Excuse me, is there anything wrong here?" It was the desk clerk.

Pongo turned his head. "No, everything's okay."

Gene slowly leaned back again, running his hands down the old man's shoulders and arms, then his legs. "Let's see now," he muttered. "Stand up."

The old man stared at him, then at his own hands. There was a change. They looked like hands now, and not like flaccid yellowish gloves. He put them together unbelievingly, then laid them on the arms of the chair and slowly got to his feet. He took a step, then another. Tears began to leak down his face. "Did you—did you—?" he said.

"Mr. McIver, do you want me to call a doctor?" the clerk asked.

"Maybe that's a good idea," Gene said. His face had lost its distant expression; his eyes glittered. "Let's get him up to his room."

"Mr. McIver has already checked out," the clerk said.

"Give us another room, then. Pongo, take care of it."

Pongo went to the desk with the clerk. When he got back, the old man was sitting down with his glasses pushed up on his forehead, hands covering his eyes. "Son of a bitch, God damn," he was saying in a breathless voice, over and over.

Pongo put a hand under his arm. "Come on, let's go."

They got the old man into the elevator and along the corridor. Pongo said, "The doctor'll be here in about ten minutes." He opened the room door, led the old man inside, and made him sit in a chair. He was laughing and crying, with his hands over his face.

After a while there was a tap on the door; Gene opened it. The man who stood there was slender, with a bald brown forehead and a dark mustache. He looked up at Gene in surprise, then at the old man. "I'm Dr. Montoya," he said. "Is this the patient?" He set down his bag and looked at Cooley. "What happened here?"

"He had a shock," Pongo said.

Montoya bent over the old man. "I'm the doctor. How are you feeling?"

"Feeling!" said Cooley, and looked up. His cheeks were still wet with tears. "I'm feeling *fine!*" He began to laugh, his face contorted as if in pain.

"Will you wait outside while I examine him, please?" Montoya opened his bag.

They stood in the corridor. It was clean and bright. The dry, cool air had a flowery scent of antiseptic. After a long time the door opened and Montoya stepped out, carrying his bag. "I gave him a tranquilizer," he said. "I don't know yet if he should be hospitalized or not." He gave Gene an appraising glance. "You're a pituitary giant, aren't you?"

"Yes."

"Are you in the circus?"

"No. Retired."

"I want your name and address." He took out a black notebook. When he had finished writing, he said to Pongo, "And yours."

"It's the same."

Montoya put the notebook away. "Mr. Anderson, this man told me he was cured just now of amyotrophic lateral sclerosis. He does not show any sign of that disease. Did he seem confused or delusional to you?"

"No. He had it, and I cured him."

Montoya's eyebrows went up. "You cured him? How did you do that?"

"I put my hands on him."

"You are telling me that you cured this man by laying on of hands."

"Yes."

"Mr. Anderson, I find that very hard to believe."

"I know."

Montoya took out his wallet. "Here is my card. I am going now, but I think someone should stay with him for a little while. If there is any problem, call me."

"All right. Thank you, Doctor."

Montoya nodded stiffly and walked away toward the elevator. When he was gone, Gene opened the door and they went in.

Cooley was standing at the window with his hands clasped together, squeezing hard enough to turn his fingers pink and yellow. He looked up; his face was no longer contorted, but his eyes were red.

"You all right now?" Gene asked.

"Sure," said Cooley in a low voice.

"Are you hungry?"

"No." After a moment Cooley added, "Just leave me the hell alone, will you?"

Gene's eyes were still bright, but his expression had changed. "Pongo, wait for me in the Monster," he said.

Pongo stepped out; the door closed behind him. He listened a moment, then walked down the stairs.

"Is everything all right?" the desk clerk asked.

"Sure."

"Do you know how long Mr. McIver will be staying?"

"Beats me."

Pongo walked out to the parking lot, got into the mobile home, lighted a cigar, and waited.

In a few minutes he saw Gene coming toward him. The giant climbed in, sat down in the chair beside the driver's seat.

"What did you do?" Pongo asked.

"I talked to him. I told him I wasn't expecting any gratitude, but if he ever tried anything like that again, I would probably kill him. After a while he cried again—different kind of crying, not so much anger. I think he's going to be okay." He leaned over and hugged Pongo for a moment. "Let's go home."

Pongo started the engine and maneuvered the motor home

out of the lot. "You could have killed him, in the lobby, but you cured him instead. How come?"

"I didn't know I was going to do it. I didn't know I *could* do it. It was—" Gene hesitated. "It felt just like a big hand pushing me in the back."

Chapter Twenty-four

All the rest of that week, the household was in a state of tension. Pongo had told the others briefly what had happened at the Costa Brava Motel; Gene would not discuss it. Irma stayed in her room Tuesday morning and let messages pile up in the answering machine. Margaret broke a pencil and threw the pieces at the wall.

On Thursday Gene and Pongo went into Tampa again in the morning and did not come back until mid-afternoon; Irma and Margaret had cold turkey sandwiches for lunch.

That afternoon, at Gene's direction, Irma called Cliff Guthrie, Nirmal Coomaraswami, and Stan Salomon, and invited them for the weekend. On Friday, Gene and Pongo went into Tampa again. That afternoon, after the others had arrived, the gate signal rang. Irma said, "Yes—Oh, Mike!"

"Yes, it's me, luv. Can I come in?"

Wilcox entered beaming a few moments later. Irma hugged him and introduced the others. "You didn't bring Nan?"

"No, she's getting married actually. How is everyone?"

"Frantic," said Irma. "Gene has some big secret that he won't tell anybody about. I'm glad you're here."

Pongo came in a little after three. "Gene's in his room," he announced. "Says he won't be down for dinner, but he wants to see everybody in the dining room at nine o'clock."

"Pongo, what's going on?" Irma said. "This is too much."

"He went into the hospital and stayed two hours. That's all I know." Pongo got a slab of beef out of the refrigerator and began doing things to it.

At dinner, Cliff Guthrie said, "Nirmal, you look kind of tired. Is everything okay?"

"Well, it is not really okay. Some things I don't like are happening at the university. A good friend of mine, you probably don't know him, but he is quite well known in his field, and he happens to be gay. The university dismissed him this week for moral turpitude."

Linck nodded. "These swings in attitude are a very effective way of weeding out deviants," he said. "The door opens, people come out of the closet; then it shuts, and they are outside. What will your friend do now?"

"I don't know. He probably cannot get another job teaching. I have another friend who is gay, a philology professor; he was fired in November, and the last I heard he was tending a bar in Detroit."

"I don't think there has ever been an administration in this country that I have disliked so much," Linck said. "They are militarist, they are bigoted, and they are very ignorant. This adventurism in Central America and Africa—that is only the beginning."

"How long would you say we've got before the world blows itself to hell?" Salomon asked.

Linck shrugged. "On days when I am optimistic, I think we may last as much as thirty years. By then I will be eighty-four, and it won't so much matter to me. But if there is any advance warning, I think I will try to get out of the northern hemisphere."

"Why the northern hemisphere?" said Wilcox.

"Because if the Soviets and the West bomb each other, they are capable of making the northern hemisphere uninhabitable. I will go to Bolivia, probably. My first choice would be Australia, but there are too many military installations there. Bolivia is an unimportant little country."

"I have heard people talk like this before," said Coomaraswami, "and it is really bizarre, because people are saying, well, the world is going to be destroyed by atomic war, and they all agree, yes, it is going to be destroyed, and then they talk about something else. It is like people going down a river on a raft, and they say, tomorrow morning we will all go over the falls and be killed, and then they play pinochle or something."

"What should they do instead?" Margaret asked.

"Well, I think they should at least talk about some ways of getting off the raft."

"Suppose you were the President—what would you do?"

"Probably I could not do anything; the problem is global."

"If you were God, then?"

"Well, if I were God," said Coomaraswami, "I think I could make some very good improvements just by changing the rules a little bit. For instance, I could change the rate of radioactive decay so that an atomic explosion would not be possible. Or I could do something even simpler, I could change the rules in such a way that there would be no transparent solids in nature."

"How would that be an improvement?"

"Well, think about it. If there were no transparent solids, then you could not have windshields in cars or airplanes, and you would not be able to travel very fast. We could not have modern bombers or fighter planes. People would have to travel less and stay closer to home; then they would mind their own business more. Also we would not have cameras or telescopes, and that would keep us from killing each other at long distance."

"We wouldn't have eyeglasses, either, or windows."

Coomaraswami shrugged. "No, well, then it would be more of an advantage to have good eyesight, and therefore there would not be so much myopia and astigmatism. And people got along very well without glass in their windows for thousands of years."

Gene paused outside the dining room. His throat was dry, and that was absurd, because it was his house, his friends and companions, and yet he felt that he was about to attempt something ultimately perilous. That was where the excitement came from. It was one thing to solve a problem in a daydream, and it was another to translate it into reality. For that, he needed to persuade other people—real, living people, the people he had never understood. Would they be indifferent? Incredulous? Would they laugh?

Their heads turned as he walked in and took his seat; he could tell by their expressions that they saw him as somehow changed, as a new enigma. That was good.

Mike Wilcox was sitting between Margaret and Nirmal; he raised his hand slightly in greeting.

"Hello, Mike. When did you get here?"

"Just this afternoon. I'm not sure I'm meant to *be* here actually—I didn't know there was going to be a meeting."

Gene pulled his chair out and sat down. "It's all right, I want you to hear this. Has anyone told you that I healed a man named Cooley, Monday afternoon in Tampa?"

"Well, Irma did say something. I can't quite follow it."

"He had amyotrophic lateral sclerosis—Lou Gehrig's disease. I healed him by touching him. I know how this sounds, but reserve your judgment. The doctor who looked at him afterward is named Montoya. I got hold of him Wednesday and talked him into taking me through the intensive-care unit at Tampa General. He didn't want to do it, but I put some pressure on through the head of the fund-raising committee; I'm one of their heavy donors. He took me in there Thursday morning. It was an awful place—I had no idea. It's one big room partitioned off with portable screens—people yelling in pain, blood on the nurses' uniforms, blood on the floor, just a madhouse. Anyhow, we went down the row. I healed an old man with a massively bleeding ulcer, and a woman dying of cancer, and a girl with a crushed larynx. I'm getting follow-up x-rays, but I know I did it. I healed them. Yesterday I went in and tried it again. I healed three patients; that seems to be about my limit—after that I feel as if I'd been running uphill."

There was a silence.

"Had you ever done this before?" Salomon asked.

"I'm not sure. I remember once in Greece, a friend of mine hurt his toe. He was barefoot, and he tripped and hit the doorsill. He thought his big toe was broken, and I looked at it and touched it, and it was all right. I didn't think anything about it then—just thought he'd made a fuss over nothing. The only time I ever tried to heal anybody was years before that, in New York, when my best friend was dying of a heart attack. I couldn't do it; I didn't know enough. If I had, I could have saved him. There were things I could have done—open the airway, chest massage, mouth-to-mouth breathing. It wouldn't have taken a miracle, just somebody being there who knew the right thing to do. But I didn't know. After that, I never tried again, until Cooley."

Wilcox cleared his throat. "I'm not sure if this means anything," he said, "but you remember looking at Nan's leg, before we left? Well, when I got her home, she went down to start her physical therapy the next day, and when they took off the brace, the knee was completely mobile—not a thing wrong with it. They told her to go home and not be a nuisance."

"So. Maybe I healed her too. If so, I wasn't aware of it." Gene folded his hands on the table and leaned forward. "Now I've got to demonstrate something, because I want you to believe me. Pongo and Irma have already seen this, the rest of you haven't. Nirmal, will you hand me something from your wallet—something you think would be hard to duplicate?"

"Hard to duplicate?"

"Yes. Not a pack of cigarettes, not a coin. Something one-of-a-kind. Don't worry, I'll give it back."

"I am not worried, but I am confused. Will this do?" Coomaraswami handed over a credit card with a broken corner.

"Sure. Now watch." Gene laid the card on the table, covered it with his big hand for a moment. His hand moved sideways across the table. When he lifted it, there were two credit cards. He handed them to Salomon, who stared at them a moment before passing them to Coomaraswami. Margaret and Cliff Guthrie got up to look over his shoulder. Both credit cards had the same embossed twelve-digit number, both said "N. K. COOMARASWAMI" on the front; both had the lower right-hand corner broken in the same way.

"May I see?" said Wilcox. He took the two credit cards and looked at them closely.

"Mike, could you do that?"

"Yes, with a little preparation."

"Could you do it the way I did—not knowing in advance what Nirmal would give me?"

"Oh, yes. Not at all difficult."

Gene sighed. "All right," he said. He reached into his pocket, took out a little cloth bag with a drawstring and slid it down the table. The others stood up to see better as Wilcox opened the bag and drew out an oblong bar of bright gold. On the surface of the bar was the embossed legend, "CREDIT SUISSE, 500g GOLD, 999.9."

"Have you ever seen one of those before?" Gene asked.

"No, never. My lord, that's heavy. What's it worth?"

"About seven thousand dollars, I suppose. I haven't followed the market lately. Have you got a penknife?"

"A knife? Yes."

"Scratch your initials in it, or any symbol you like. Pongo, will you get a grocery bag from the kitchen?"

"Aha," said Wilcox good-humoredly. He took a knife out of his pocket, opened it, and carved the initials "MBW" on the bar.

Pongo came back and handed him a brown paper bag. "Examine it, please," said Gene. Wilcox turned the bag over in his hands, opened it, and peered in.

"Now put the bar in the bag. Take it out again. Now fold the top of the bag and hold it with both hands. Raise the bag a little, so it doesn't touch the table." Wilcox followed instructions, watching Gene with a glint of amusement in his eyes.

Gene stood up. He walked down the table until he was behind Wilcox; then he reached over and lightly touched the side of the brown paper bag. The bag dipped suddenly in Wilcox's hands and hit the table with a solid thump.

Wilcox had turned pale. He opened the bag and looked in, then drew out a gold bar and laid it beside the first. They gleamed in the middle of the table, each one with the same initials scratched in it.

After a moment Wilcox looked up. "I'll give you a thousand dollars if you'll teach me that trick," he said.

Gene sat down again. "Mike, if I can do this, what do I need your money for? Haven't you ever asked yourself how I got so rich?"

"Well, I did wonder—"

"I bought diamonds and copied them, just the way I copied that gold bar, and sold them to Piet's firm in Amsterdam."

Linck was nodding. "It's true. Millions of dollars' worth, over a period of years. It was very profitable to us."

"I still think it is a trick," said Coomaraswami, laughing weakly.

"Why?"

"Because it is impossible."

"Have you ever heard of the 'many-worlds' explanation of quantum physics?"

"Yes, of course. That is Hugh Everett's theory. He says that when two things can happen, at the particle level, both things do happen, and so you get a kind of splitting of reality into two separate worlds. It is a very interesting theory."

"And it's true. I've known it all my life. I can see into those other worlds, a little bit; I can reach in and turn them. I haven't created anything, I've just taken that gold bar from another world and moved it into this one. And I now know that I can heal people the same way."

He went on, "This is what I've been waiting for. A couple of years ago, in Japan, I woke up one morning and realized I was almost forty years old, and I had a power that I'd never done anything with except to kill people and make myself rich. So I came back here and built this house. I wanted a place where I could sit still for a while and get things straight in my head, and I wanted a place where I could spend the rest of my life in reasonable comfort, if I couldn't figure out anything better to do."

"And now you know what you want to do?" Irma asked.

"Irma, I knew what I wanted to do *before*—I just didn't see how to do it."

"And what is that?" asked Linck.

"Save the world." He sat back and looked at them. "Why not? The problems are not that difficult. I mean, most of these things are *obvious*: we have to reduce population and pollution, we have to have world-wide disarmament, and so on. People aren't *dumb*. They know their institutions are pushing them into stupid and destructive things, but nobody wants poverty, and nobody wants to get killed. Suppose you could get, let's say, sixty percent of the people on earth into one room and talk to them, show them how to get out of this mess. If you could convince them, and then send them home, do you think they wouldn't change the world?"

"That's a very large number of people," said Linck.

"Sure it is. Three billion. But let's take some arbitrary numbers. Suppose I can sign up ten thousand people a month through public appearances, and suppose each one of those can recruit one more person a month—how long would it take to get up to three billion? Has anyone got a calculator?"

"That is not necessary," said Coomaraswami. He thought a moment. "At the end of eighteen months you would have about two and a half billion people, and of course, doubling at that rate, at the end of the nineteenth month you would have five billion. But that is not a reasonable rate of increase. People can only recruit other people who live in their own locality, you see. Pretty soon, if you have a rapidly growing organization, everybody is trying to recruit everybody else. That is why pyramid schemes always collapse."

"What would you say was a reasonable rate of increase?"

"That depends on a lot of factors. But I would say that if you have good organization and very enthusiastic people, a million at the end of the first year would be a reasonable goal, and then perhaps ten million the second year, and so on. Most organizations of this kind reach a point of diminishing returns fairly early, but supposing yours did not, then I would say it would take at least ten years to reach three billion."

After a moment he added, "Gene, you know, what you are talking about sounds a good deal like what some other people are already doing—Barry Commoner, for instance, the Planetary Initiative, and so on. They are doing all right, but they are not sweeping the world. Why do you think you can succeed where they are failing?"

"Because I can do something they can't do. I can really heal the sick. Think about this a minute. I'll have people with incurable ailments. Paraplegics, people with cancer. They'll be screened by physicians, we'll do before and after x-rays. I'll heal them publicly, you'll see it happen. And people will listen to me."

"And what will you tell them?"

"That's what I want you all to think about. Tomorrow we'll meet again after breakfast, if you're willing. Good night." He stood up and left the room.

The rest looked at each other. No one seemed to want to speak. At last Wilcox said, "There's your question again with knobs on, Maggie. What would you do if you were God? I'm not sure I want to know."

They got up and separated, Pongo and Irma to the kitchen, Margaret and most of the others to separate corners of the living room. Wilcox went into the garden by himself; through the glass doors they could see him pacing up and down. After a while he went up to his room. One by one, the others joined Linck in his pool of light at the end of the room. Conversation was desultory until Salomon said, "Did you see in the paper that there's another expedition to Ararat to find the Ark?"

"No, but I am not surprised," Coomaraswami answered. "It seems to me they have found it three or four times in the last thirty years, but it always gets lost again."

"Maybe so, but I think the reason for this expedition is interesting. It's a little fundamentalist group in Florida—they say they have to find the Ark in order to measure it, so they can find out how long a cubit is."

"Why a cubit?"

"Because until they know how long a cubit is, they can't rebuild the temple in Jerusalem, and until they do that, Christ can't come again."

"Have they got government funding?" Linck asked drily.

"Not that I know of, but it may come to that. You know, these people give me a royal pain. Of all the ways there are of being wrong, I think theirs is the worst."

"What do you mean by that? What way are they wrong?" Cliff Guthrie asked. "I'm a Baptist myself," he added.

"Well, Cliff, no offense to your religion, but they're wrong because they claim to know what the answers are. They say the Bible is literally true because it's the word of God, but that can't be, because the Bible is full of contradictions. There are two accounts of the Creation in Genesis, two genealogies of Jesus, two different accounts of the death of Judas Iscariot."

"I never heard that before."

"Well, it's true—you can look it up."

Linck coughed delicately. "In justice to the Christians, I should say that they have explanations for all this. They say that the second chapter of Genesis merely expands on the first chapter, for instance, and that one of the genealogies is Jesus' father's line, the other one his father's mother's line. And they say that Judas hanged himself, and then the rope broke and he burst his bowels over a stone."

"Yes, but the Jews *never* reckoned descent through the female line. We aren't even told who Mary's father was."

"According to the Coptic Gospels, and I think also in Pseudo-Matthew, her father was Cleopas," Linck said apologetically. "But that gets us into a terrible muddle, because Hegesippus says that Cleopas or Cleophas was an uncle of Jesus, who was married to *another* Mary, who also had three sons with the same names—James, Joses, and Simon. And then, some authorities say that Cleopas is a Greek form of the name Alphaeus, which turns up in some of the Gospels as the name of one of the disciples, and these names are also a terrible muddle. For instance, in the Gospel of Matthew the disciple who is a publican"—he bowed slightly toward Cliff Guthrie—"is called Matthew, in Mark he is Levi of Alphaeus, in Luke he is just Levi, and John does not mention him at all. And so on. I sometimes think that when we read the name

Cleopas or Alphaeus in the Bible, it is a code word meaning, 'We don't know this person's name.' ''

Later Guthrie found Linck alone in the garden, lighting a cigar.

"Piet, there were a couple of things you said before that I didn't quite understand. Those gospels you mentioned, I never heard of them—the Coptic, and Pseudo-Matthew?"

"They are apocryphal gospels. They were not included in the canon, but some of them were quite widely read—more so than one or two of the canonical gospels, perhaps."

"And you read these, what, in the original languages?"

"I do read a little Coptic and Greek," said Linck mildly, "but that is not necessary. You can find them in a translation by M. R. James called *The Apocryphal Gospels*."

Guthrie produced a small notebook and wrote it down. "The other thing," he said, "I noticed you looked at me when you were talking about the publican, and I had a feeling I was missing something."

"Don't you feel that we are all Gene's disciples, Cliff?"

Guthrie stared at him. "But what's that got to do with—A publican is a bartender, isn't it?"

"Yes, quite right, but at the time the King James Bible was translated, it meant a tax collector."

Chapter Twenty-five

All around him, the other worlds sheaved away in layers of gray mist. There were worlds in which the Chinese had colonized North and South America, in which the Christian religion did not exist, in which giant sloths and tapirs roamed the Great Plains. Even closer to home, there were things even more bizarre in their own way: there was a world in which Shirley Temple had been appointed an ambassador, and Ronald Reagan was President of the United States. Most of the time it seemed to make no difference at all who was president, premier, or chairman; the world drifted in its massive way toward the same catastrophe just the same.

There were worlds in which it had already happened: there were rotting corpses along the highways, beside the lines of abandoned cars. The cities were fields of rubble, like vast firebombed junkyards.

Since the idea had occurred to him, or rather since the first moment when he had known with an electric tingle in his nerves that he was going to take the risk, he had thought carefully about groups and their dynamics. He already knew that the only comfortable place in a group for him was at the center; he had formed groups around himself again and again solely for that reason, and not because of any impulse toward hospitality or benevolence, although he was glad enough to let people think those were his reasons.

Others liked to be near the center of power but did not care for the responsibility or the risk of managing a group of their own. And there were still others who liked to be on the fringe, to be told what to do. He did not understand it, but it must be so, or every adult human being would have his own group, with a membership of one.

He ate in his room, and did not go downstairs until the others had had time to finish breakfast. He found them in the dining room, with pads and pencils in front of them. They fell silent and their heads turned as he walked in.

"Good morning," he said. "I hope you've all been thinking about what I said last night. You probably have some questions, but I'd like to hold those until later. What I want us to do this morning is to have a brainstorming session—does everybody know what that is?"

"Sounds like a fit of lunacy," said Wilcox.

"Brainstorming is a way of getting ideas," Coomaraswami explained. "The rule is, you have a certain problem to talk about, and you try to generate as many ideas as possible, never mind whether they are good ideas or not: that you can decide later. But I am not quite clear what we are going to talk about."

"All right," said Gene. "The problem is this: the organization that we talked about last night has to be a political movement, even if it looks like something else, and yet it can't be a nationalist or ethnic movement—it has to be universal, or it won't work. That suggests to me that we must have a very simple core message. It has to be something that even a child can understand, and something that can be expressed in any language. Yes, Stan?"

"When you say the idea has to be simple, that rules out things like 'Support scientific education,' for instance."

"Yes, and also it's not enough to be simple. 'Save the whales' is a simple idea, and a good idea, but it's not universal —not everybody can do anything about saving the whales."

"So, then, you just want something that will improve people's behavior generally, is that it?"

"Maybe."

"What about, 'You shall love thy neighbor as thyself'?" Irma asked quietly.

"That has been tried," said Linck. "Unfortunately it always turns out that most people love themselves better."

"Not always," Salomon retorted. "I'm tired of hearing that you can't change 'human nature.' People who say that usually assume that whatever behavior their own society produces is natural. So if you grew up in a highly competitive and cynical society, you think that's human nature. But the Pueblo Indians were not like that, for instance—they were cooperative, nurturant, nonaggressive. To them, *that* was human nature.''

"Remember that we're not going to criticize these ideas now, just try to get as many out as we can. Maggie, are you making notes?''

She nodded. Linck, she saw, was also writing on his pad; one or two of the others were doodling.

"So, then,'' said Coomaraswami, "what we are looking for is an idea that will make people behave better toward each other? How about 'Be kind'? That is simple enough—two words.''

"Before we go any further,'' Salomon said, "I think I see something missing. It isn't enough for your idea to be simple and universal; there also has to be some reward for the person who adopts the idea. It *could* be something just as simple as 'Be kind.' And if everybody heard that and said, 'Great, I'll be kind,' it would make a big difference. But how are you going to get them to do it? What's in it for them?''

"We could give them a dollar whenever they're kind to somebody,'' Wilcox said with a grin. There was a ripple of laughter.

"Maybe that's not such a dumb idea,'' said Salomon slowly.

"How, Stan?'' asked Linck. "There isn't enough money in the world.''

"No, not money, but—'' Salomon was sketching on the pad in front of him. He tore off the sheet and held it up: he had drawn a circle in which a scribble of a face appeared, and around the edge he had lettered: YOU WERE NICE TO ME.

"Call them 'Gene's dollars,' '' he said. "Hand them out at meetings, maybe five or ten to a customer. The idea is, they give them to people who are nice to *them*. And so on. An instant reinforcement.''

The group was silent for a while.

"Instead of tokens, we could pass out our own credit cards. People could get them punched, or something, when they were kind to somebody else.''

"Rubber stamps—you could stamp somebody's forehead.''

"Free balloons.''

"Or gerbils—they breed like crazy, so that would take care of the manufacturing problem."

They branched out into suggestions about the meetings:

"There should be music."

"Not rock."

"No, something very quiet, to give a kind of feeling of expectancy."

"Moog would be best."

"You need ushers to lead people to their seats, and so on. Give them something distinctive to wear."

"Not a uniform. Smocks, maybe, or little vests."

"The lighting is important. It has to be bright enough so they can see the healing, but it ought to be diffuse, kind of golden."

"How do they sign up? There has to be a long table at the front, and people to take down their names and addresses, give them membership cards or whatever, and maybe little leaflets—"

"If you want the organization to grow, you're going to have to pick out leaders right away, and help them set up the local chapter or whatever."

"What does the local chapter do? If it holds meetings when Gene's not there, you can't have the healing every time."

"They could take applications for the next time he *is* there."

"What about having films of Gene healing? That would be the next best thing."

"Yes, and videotapes for TV."

"You need somebody to speak at meetings, and they have to know what to say."

"There should be a manual for heads of chapters."

"Not only that, I think we need a training course. You need the manual, and you've got to train the people who train people."

"Dinners and picnics."

"Little envelopes for donations."

"We have to think of ways to encourage recruiting. Announce the number of new members every meeting, and tell who signed them up."

"Give them special badges or something for recruiting ten people or more."

"Put their names on a big bulletin board."

"About publicity—we should arrange for all the interviews we can get, naturally. And I think Gene should write a book."

"Thanks a lot," said Gene.

"Well, I think so. And, I'm looking ahead now, there ought to be some TV specials, and maybe a weekly newspaper column."

The discussion came back to "Gene's dollars."

"I think we should use paper money instead of coins. Otherwise it's a bottleneck. You've got to get a wax model made, then dies, and you've got to find a manufacturer, and we're going to need *billions* of them. Paper is quicker, cheaper, you can get more run off whenever you need them. It doesn't have to look like real money—it shouldn't, in fact."

"It ought to be a little bigger than real money, so people don't get them mixed up."

"You could have little folders for them, so you could pull one out whenever you want it."

"It shouldn't look like any foreign currency, either. Make it an unusual color, pink, for example."

"How's this? I was thinking about the printing costs. Put a portrait of Gene on the front, and all the stuff we were talking about, and then on the *back*, divide it up into spaces for signatures. Everybody who gets one signs it before they pass it on, and when you get one that's full, you can turn it in for ten more."

Eventually Gene called a halt, and Margaret read the list of suggestions aloud. There were murmurs of agreement for some of them, silence or rude noises for others.

"Gene, how big an organization are we talking about here—I mean how many professionals? I think we ought to see what we're getting into."

Linck said, "I have been making a list as we went along. I can't tell you numbers of people, but perhaps it will help if we just see how many sections there are. We need first of all a planning section—we need economists, demographers, and God knows what to draw a master plan for at least the first five years. We need an executive section. A personnel section, to find and recruit the people we need. A training section. Then there is housing: someone has to find office space and arrange for leases and so on. Legal section, probably quite large. Publicity section, that will be very important. Transportation and liaison. At some point we will probably need a political section, with lobbyists in Washington and in other countries. Security. Public relations. Procurement. Accounting. That is thirteen sections so far, and probably there are others I have forgotten."

"Translation," said Margaret.

"Yes, a very good point. That would come under the heading of an information section, I think, but we will also need interpreters."

"Let's talk about some of the legal problems," Cliff Guthrie said. "Is this going to be a not-for-profit corporation, or what? Do you want to incorporate it as a church, for the tax advantages?"

"Not a church," Gene said. "There are one or two things I won't do, and one is to let anybody put a halo on my head."

"Then probably it has to be a scientific and educational corporation, but I.R.S. doesn't like to hand out that designation. Then there's another thing. A non-profit corporation can't engage in political activity of any kind. That means lobbying is out."

"Here's something we haven't talked about. The organization has to have a name—what are we going to call it?"

"Maybe an acronym, something with the initials G.E.N.E.?"

"General Exodus of Nuclear Energy."

"Why not just something descriptive like, A World at Peace?"

"Peace is a good word, but a lot of people are using it."

"There are some other words we can't use either, like Crusade. Popular. People's."

"How about 'A World for Mankind'? Then you could have a great logo, with the *W* and the *M*."

"What happened to womankind?"

"I like the idea of getting 'World' into it, and I like the *M*. World of Miracles."

"Let's keep this simple. Remember whatever we pick has to be translated into a lot of languages—you don't want any ambiguities."

"The World Movement."

"Sounds like a giant laxative."

"One World would be perfect, but that's been done."

"As far as the initials are concerned, they've got to be different in every language anyhow, so let's not get hung up on them."

Wilcox suggested a committee to look into the question of names; Gene promptly appointed him the head of it, and then said, "Let's break for lunch. Afterward, I'd like to spend the rest of the afternoon talking to you in the library, one at a time—or if two or three of you want to come together, that's all right." He got up and left the room.

The others got up more slowly. As they straggled out, Stan Salomon said, "Do you realize that when we went in there it was just a game, and when we left we were committed?"

Gene's place was still vacant at lunch.

"You know, it is possible, what he is talking about," said Coomaraswami. "It really is possible. It took about a century for the Islamic movement to spread through North Africa and Spain, and it took a lot of fighting also, but imagine what Mohammed could have done if he had been able to go around the world on jet planes, and preach by television. It is very much easier now to persuade a lot of people very quickly. And if you tell them something sensible that they want to hear, and you also can demonstrate a kind of supernatural ability, then you sort of get them both ways, because you are giving them something practical, and also something transcendental. I am willing to believe that he can do it. The only question in my mind is, will it be a good thing or a bad thing?"

"How could it be a bad thing?"

"Well, I have a picture in my mind of the world Gene wants—fewer people, not so many big cities. And I think it may be a world in which it is not possible to do physics."

"Come in, Mike."

Wilcox sat down and crossed his legs nervously. Gene was in his outsize black leather armchair; between them was a table with a coffeepot, cups, sugar.

"Coffee?"

"No, thanks. You know, all this has more or less knocked my pins out from under me. I mean, all my life I've been going on the assumption that magic is a highly specialized form of deception. Now I have to get used to the idea that there really is a sort of magic."

"There isn't anything magical about it," Gene said.

"Well, if you say not. Anyhow, I'm curious about something. What's your limit, I mean in size? Could you make an elephant appear, for instance?"

"No. I think the limit is somewhere around my own size,

and I haven't even got very close to that. Why do you mention elephants?"

"Just something that crossed my mind. I'd like to talk about these meetings of yours. Stop me if I speak out of turn. I suppose you've never spoken in public before? Are you nervy about it?"

"Yes, a little."

"How long will your speech run?"

"About an hour."

"Pardon me, but that's not enough. When people come to a meeting, or the theater or whatever, they expect to be entertained or jawed at for two hours, more or less."

"I don't think I can make it last that long."

"No, that's what I'm getting at. There's got to be something else to fill up the evening, and my idea is to use magic. I can get some really spectacular illusions from New York if you say the word. An hour of magic, an hour of lecture—do the healing, and there you are."

"What sort of illusions?"

"The famous glass box on wheels, for one. I take it money is no object?"

"Right."

"Well, I know a man who will rent us one if we make him an offer he can't refuse. I can get his stage crew as well. It will pack the customers in, I promise you."

Gene said, "Mike, I'm grateful, but if we use fake magic, won't people think I'm a fake too?"

"Not with the healing. We could make a point of that, in fact—the contrast. Anyhow, it's quite likely that some people will call you a fake, whatever you do. The point is, the people who've seen you won't believe that, and people who haven't seen you will come because they're curious."

"Come in, Cliff. Coffee?"

"No, thanks."

"Cliff, there's one good reason why this can't be a church. I want to thank you for that suggestion; I know you were thinking of what's best for me and putting aside your own religious feelings. But we can't do that, because a church can only grow at the expense of other churches. We can't get three billion people in ten years that way. This has to be a movement that anybody can belong to, Christian, Jew, Moslem, whatever."

"That's right. I wasn't thinking."

"And I hope I can say what I have to say without tearing down anybody's religious beliefs. If you catch me doing that, tell me."

"I will. But I'll tell you one thing."

"Yes?"

"If I had a choice between you and the Baptist Church, I'd follow you."

"What's the matter, Cliff? What happened?"

Guthrie had a curious look on his face. "He touched me on the forehead," he said.

"Coffee, Piet?"

"Yes, please." Linck sat down, took out a cigar, and settled himself comfortably. "There are some practical details that I want to discuss with you, and then I have a frivolous question."

"Good."

"Practical things first. You realize that you are going to need a large number of professional people of very high caliber. The best place to recruit them would be New York. If you wish, I'll go there and talk to some headhunters, do some preliminary interviews."

"Yes, Piet. Thank you."

Linck waved his cigar. "I have nothing else to do. I have to go back to Amsterdam for a week or so in July or August, otherwise I am free. Now for the frivolous question. Frivolous is not the right word, perhaps, but it is just something I'm curious about. Don't answer if you would rather not. Have you ever had what people call a religious experience?"

"Funny you should ask," Gene said. "Years ago, when I left home, something did happen. I was eleven at the time. Out in eastern Oregon one night I hitched a ride with an old man who got suspicious of me and left me off on a dirt road in the middle of nowhere. It was getting late, and it was cold. I didn't know where I was. I started walking down that road and I came to a forest. It wasn't like any other forest I've ever seen. Tall pines and little twisted junipers, spaced pretty widely apart, growing in white sand. That place scared me, it was so quiet. There wasn't a sound, no insects, no birds, nothing. Then it began to rain, and in a funny way that made it easier to take, because of the sound. I walked into the forest a little way, out of sight of the road, and lay down curled up around the trunk of one of those trees, and went to sleep there.

"Sometime just after dawn I woke up and the rain had stopped, the place was deathly still again. And then—this is the hard part. I don't know how to explain it. I felt, I sensed, that there was somebody up there, and then I heard a voice. Not a voice, but a—I don't know what. Telling me something. It was a word, or maybe a number—some number too big to grasp. Just the one thing, the big voice that wasn't a voice. And I heard what it said, and I couldn't understand it. Not because the voice wasn't speaking clearly, but because my head was too small for what it was saying."

He shifted in his chair. "That was all. I started walking again, and got to another road, hitched another ride, and I wound up in San Francisco."

"And you've never gone back there?"

"No. I don't know if it would be worse if I went back and it happened again, or if it didn't—if nothing happened. I know where that place is—I looked it up later. It's called the Lost Forest, in eastern Oregon. It's a place that shouldn't be there, because those are Ponderosa pines, growing in sand, in a place that never gets more than about six inches of rainfall a year."

"And you still don't know what the voice was trying to say to you?"

"I know. But I don't know what it is that I know. My head still isn't big enough."

"Irma, I've got to talk to you."

"Come in the pantry, honey. What is it, did he touch you on the forehead too?"

"Yes, but that's not it. He told me he's going to need a personal secretary, and an appointments secretary, and a press secretary, and at least two office managers, one for here and one for downtown, and he asked me to choose."

Irma cocked an ironic eyebrow at her. "You want me to guess?"

Margaret picked up a cocktail napkin and began to shred it. "Irma, I *know* I should have said I wanted to be an office manager. But then somebody else would have been with him all the time."

"I understand," Irma said. "Isn't it hell?"

Chapter Twenty-six

From the St. Petersburg *Times*:

"An Evening of Magic and Mystery," presented Friday through Sunday at the Sherman Theatre, is a puzzling mixture of entertainment and propaganda.

At the Friday performance, stage illusions, offered by a magician who called himself the Astounding Willy, dominated the earlier part of the evening. Ghostly heads floated out over the audience, there were showers of rose petals, and many things appeared and vanished, including cards, coins, pigeons, and the magician himself.

As a climax of this part of the evening, the Astounding Willy stepped into a large glass box on wheels, which was then covered with a drape by his assistants. When the drape was removed, Willy had disappeared, and in his place was Gene Anderson, eight feet six inches tall, billed as "The World's Tallest Man."

Emerging from the box, Anderson, a former circus performer who has made his home in Pinellas Park for the last two years, spoke to the audience about peace and brotherhood. At the end of his lecture, he brought up a young man in a wheelchair, allegedly suffering from muscular dystrophy, and healed him, or appeared to heal him, by miraculous means.

On leaving the theater, members of the audience were handed application forms for an organization called "Peace, Prosperity, and Justice," and were also given pink play money to exchange with each other.

The performance will be repeated tonight and Sunday.

Margaret pasted the clipping into a scrapbook, along with copies of the newspaper advertisements, flyers, and handbills. Within a few months the scrapbook was full, and she began filing clippings in the first of a series of fat folders.

Coomaraswami had taken a leave of absence from the university to set up a think-tank in Orlando; it was beginning to issue position papers on renewable resources, birth control, the economics of a declining population. "It turns out there are a lot of things you can do," he said. "For instance, if population is declining, there is a lot of work just in tearing down large buildings that you don't need anymore, and salvaging the materials, and so on. Then the demographics are different too, so there is room for new products and we need different services. It is not hard to keep people working if you just look at the needs and opportunities."

One evening, after a private talk with Gene, he reported that Gene had touched him on the forehead. "You know, when he touched me, I felt as if I could feel those two marks of his fingers on my forehead afterward. It was really strange. I think it was just something he did, but it was really extraordinary how I felt about it."

"You don't think he can—rearrange your brain, or anything, do you?" Wilcox asked.

"No, no." Coomaraswami waved the suggestion away. "I am sure my brain has not been rearranged. As far as I can tell, I am thinking as clearly as ever. Maybe a little more so. Just before I came in here I had the idea for a really marvelous physics paper. But, you know, something happened when he touched me. I can't explain it. But I feel now that it made everything definite in some way. As if he had confirmed a decision. And, really, I am very happy about it, but still it is strange."

The "kitchen cabinet," as Irma called it, still met on weekends when Gene was at home, but now there were new faces in it: lawyers, managers, publicity people. The head of the new legal staff was Brian Altman, who looked more like a choir boy than a corporation lawyer.

After St. Petersburg, Gene and Mike Wilcox took their show to Tampa, Orlando, Miami, and Savannah, setting up local organizations in each city. Arrangements were being made for a national tour beginning in June—not in theaters, this time, but in stadiums and civic centers.

"How will you manage the magic part in a big stadium?" Linck asked Wilcox. They were in the kitchen, with Irma, Pongo, and Margaret; Linck had just returned from a New York trip. Gene was in his room.

"It can't be done," Wilcox said. "I mean, I suppose you could do an elephant, but Gene doesn't want anything like that. We're giving up the magic. It was fun while it lasted, and it served its purpose."

"Is he relieved about that?"

"No, in a funny way I think he liked the idea, because he hates these comparisons with Jesus, and the magic made him different."

"How is that?"

"Well, I mean, Jesus at least wasn't a magician."

"Perhaps not, but he was crucified for being one. Don't repeat this to Gene, please, but when Jesus was brought before Pilate, you probably remember, Pilate asked the Jews, 'What is this man accused of?' And they answered, 'If he were not a doer of evil, we would not have brought him before you.' Well, you know, this sounds at first rather like the trial scene in *Alice in Wonderland*. But 'doer of evil' at that time was a common term for a magician."

"Good heavens."

"The story is only in John, not the other three gospels. But it is a convincing story to me, because it makes good sense of this episode. In the other gospels, the charge against Jesus is blasphemy. If that had really been the charge, he would have been stoned to death under Mosaic law, not turned over to the Romans. Under Roman law, blasphemy against the Hebrew god was not a crime. But the practice of magic was, and the penalty was crucifixion."

Wilcox said after a moment, "I never heard that before, and I've read a good bit about magic. Why isn't there a little footnote or something to explain it in the Bible?"

"The meaning of 'doer of evil'? I suppose because the translators didn't know it. There are many mistakes in the English bible—and in the Dutch one, too. Every translation is different. Did you know that in the French Bible, where it says in the English version, 'Blessed are the meek,' it says in French, *'Heureux sont les debonnaires'*?"

"*Debonnaires!* That's very good. Maurice Chevalier at the

Pearly Gates. But there's something else that bothers me. You know, Gene won't hear of any idea that he's the Second Coming or anything like that. You seem to be suggesting that he really is. I'm curious to know if that's what you actually think.''

"No, and that's why I asked you not to mention this to Gene. I don't believe in reincarnation, you know. I think that when we die the universe takes us apart and uses us to make other things. That's just my opinion. But I also believe that there are patterns in the universe, and perhaps sometimes they repeat. Why not? The Platonists and Pythagoreans believed in the 'magnus annus,' the great year, when history would begin to repeat itself. I don't think for a moment that Gene is Jesus come again. But just consider a few things. His father was a carpenter. He has the power to heal and to make things appear and disappear. 'Gene' means 'born,' and 'Anderson,' well, you could interpret it as 'the son of man.' ''

"I don't like talking about it behind his back this way," said Irma.

"I don't either, but he has only told us that he doesn't want us to talk about it to him. He hasn't said that we mustn't talk about it among ourselves. Well, never mind that, but there is something more important. How can we do our duty to him unless we try to understand what is happening? I assume that you all feel as I do, that we have a duty to him. To help him and protect him as far as we can. Would you agree?''

Their heads were nodding.

"Well, we can't predict the future, but sometimes we can see a pattern. That's really all I am saying.''

In the spring Gene Anderson continued his tour. He was traveling now in his own Lear jet, with a modified motor home waiting for him at every airport. Plans for a European tour had preoccupied him through the winter. He was studying Russian and Polish with a young man named Kozlow, who reported that his progress was excellent. There was talk of buying a short-wave radio station in West Germany, perhaps a TV station as well.

On the evening before the rally in Houston, the group assembled as usual in the living room of Gene's suite. Through the open window came the sound of a car radio at full volume:

You're the one,
Gene Anderson,
You are the one.
Oh-oh-oh-oh-oh!
Anderson,
You are the one, oh-oh!

"That tune is driving me crazy," said Linck. "I have heard choral versions, one with a brass band, an organ version, and I don't know what all. It goes around and round. I can forget it quite easily, but then somebody plays it again."

"Let's begin," said Gene. "Anything earthshaking today?"

Lisa Finn, the public relations director, showed them a religious magazine, poorly printed on coarse paper. On the cover was a drawing of a Gene's Dollar which had been altered to give him a Satanic appearance. The headline was "The Mark of the Beast."

"This kind of thing isn't too important—these people are always calling for a crusade against somebody. Here's something that worries me a little more, though." She held up a newspaper, opened to a syndicated column. The headline was "Against America."

"Let me read you a little of this. 'Gene Anderson is telling us to give up competitiveness, reduce our population, reduce consumption, disarm ourselves—in other words, to give up all the things that make this country strong. The rosy future he paints for us is one of villagers baking their own bread, milking their own cows, and patching their own pants, probably under the eye of a commissar appointed by the Kremlin. Is Gene Anderson the Anti-Christ? Maybe. Is he Anti-American? No doubt about it.' "

"Piffle," said Brian Altman.

"Maybe so, but it's the kind of piffle they seem to like in Washington. You know that Senator Monroe has introduced a bill making it a criminal offense to promulgate the doctrines of a cult."

"How can they do that?" asked Cliff Guthrie. "I thought there was something in the Constitution against any law about religion."

"The bill isn't directed against religions, only against cults."

"Well, how do you tell the difference?"

"The bill sets up a Federal Commission on Cults. So a cult is anything declared to be a cult by the commission—meaning anything the Moral Majority doesn't like."

"Brian, how serious is this?" Gene asked.

"Not very. In my opinion, the bill won't pass, and if it should, it will be struck down by the courts—this cult commission is a transparent device to evade the Constitution. In any event, they're obviously out to get the Moonies and Hare Krishnas, Church of Scientology, people like that; I don't see how it affects us."

"Lisa?"

"I think we ought to oppose it on principle, just the same. I could get together with a couple of lobbyists and work something out."

"How much?" Gene asked.

"Oh—sixty, seventy thousand. Maybe a little more."

"Okay, let's do it. Next item?"

From Art Buchwald's column:

The other day my friend Garfinkel handed me a pink dollar bill. "What's this?" I said.

"A Gene's Dollar. I gave it to you because you did something nice. You were starting to light your cigar, but when you saw me coming you put the match out."

I examined the dollar; sure enough, it said: "YOU WERE NICE TO ME."

"What can I do with this?" I asked.

"You can give it to somebody who's nice to you."

"Suppose everybody is nasty to me?"

"Then you get to keep the dollar."

I lit my cigar and puffed smoke at him. "If I put this out again, do I get another dollar?"

"No, because I've only got one more and I'm saving it for my girlfriend."

I puffed steadily; he coughed and turned a little green. Finally, as he got up to go, he handed me another bill: on the top it said "Garfinkel's Dollar," and on the bottom, "YOU WERE LOUSY TO ME."

They were in Roanoke a month later when news came that the Anti-Cult Bill had been passed by the Senate and the

House on the same day. On the following day it was signed into law by the President, who appointed a five-man commission. At the end of the week the commission announced its preliminary list of organizations proscribed as cults. There were thirty-six; among them was the Anderson Movement.

"They really railroaded it through," said Brian Altman. "Under the statute, anybody who promulgates a proscribed doctrine or induces anyone to join a proscribed organization can be brought up on criminal charges. I hate to say this, but I think we'd better cancel the rest of the tour."

"There will be ten thousand people waiting to get into the civic center tomorrow night. The network crews are here; we've got three people lined up to be healed."

"How can this be happening?" Margaret asked. "You know the Moral Majority is a *minority*."

"Yes, but it's the kind of minority that runs a lynch mob," said Lisa Finn. "I saw this happen thirty years ago—a lot of good people were afraid not to quack when everybody else was quacking."

"How's the hate mail running?" Gene asked.

"Pretty high. Worse the last month or so. Some death threats."

"I can't believe this country will throw away its greatest traditions overnight," said Cliff Guthrie.

"Let me tell you about those traditions." Lisa Finn tapped with a pencil on the table for emphasis. "Most of the civil rights we take for granted are *recent*. Women didn't even get the vote until nineteen twenty. In the forties, thousands of Japanese-Americans were rounded up into concentration camps. The traditions you're talking about say that couldn't happen—so does the Constitution—but in fact it was very easy. The President said do it. That's all it took. Don't think it can't happen again."

"Do you agree with Brian, then?"

"I agree it's serious. About going on tonight, I think that's your decision."

Gene looked around the table. The others were nodding. "All right," he said; "we'll go on."

In the focus of the lights and the ten thousand faces, hearing the echoes of his words come back like the sound of handballs bouncing from a court, he said, "The Bible tells you that you must worship God, but I tell you that God doesn't care if you worship him or not. The Bible tells you that you must follow God's commandments, but I tell you that there are no commandments, except the ones built into your bodies, and you haven't got much choice about those—when you are hungry, you eat, and when you are sleepy you sleep. The Bible tells you that you will be rewarded in heaven if you are good, but I tell you that there is no heaven or hell except in the minds of human beings. This is our life, right here, right now, and it's the only one we've got. The Bible tells you that God is all-knowing, but I tell you that if he knew everything, he would be bored for all eternity. God made us, not because he knew what we would do, but to *find out* what we would do.

"Remember I didn't say that God doesn't care about us. He does care, because we give him joy and delight, but he won't step in to save us from starving, or getting sick, or falling out a window. He might like to, but that would spoil his great experiment—to see what will happen if he brings us into the world and then leaves us alone. That's what the world is all about, and that's why he takes delight in us, along with all his other creatures—because we do things he never expected us to do. What would be the point of an experiment if you knew how it was going to turn out? Or what would be the point of it if you stopped it in the middle and made it turn out the way you thought it would? How would you ever learn anything that way?

"God doesn't care if the human race survives or not. We are not his chosen people. If we become extinct, he's got millions of other species—species that we're killing off right now at the rate of about one a day. He's got the leopards and the deer and the elephants and the fish in the ocean and the spiders with their wonderful webs. Everything in God's world reflects his beauty, and he can get along without us. We depend on him, not the other—"

The flat crack of an explosion echoed from the rear of the hall. A little gray smoke was drifting above the distant balcony, and there was a confusion there—people standing, moving like ants; there were shouts and screams. Ushers and security people were converging on the spot. Just below the podium, the head of the security detail was speaking into his walkie-talkie. "What is it?" Gene said.

"A bomb, looks like. We don't know yet how many are hurt."

Gene said into the microphone, "Please remain in your seats." To the security man he said, "Get me up there."

Seven people were lying between the rows of seats, bloody and ragged. He healed five of them, one after the other; but two were dead.

"You were right," he said to Brian. "Lisa, you were trying to tell me the same thing. It was my damned pride. Those people would be alive if I'd listened to you. Cancel the rest of the tour. We're going home."

Chapter Twenty-seven

Driving down the wrong road and knowing it,
The fork years behind, how many have thought
To pull up on the shoulder and leave the car
Empty, strike out across the fields; and how many
Are still mazed among dock and thistle,
Seeking the road they should have taken?

—Gene Anderson

At the airport the next morning, as they approached the fence, a man in a gray suit came up to them, followed by three armed men in uniform.

"Mr. Anderson, you are under arrest for the crime of felony murder, as defined in section three oh-nine of the U.S. Criminal Code. I warn you that anything you say may be taken down and used in evidence against you." He put a hand on Gene's arm.

"I'm Mr. Anderson's attorney," said Brian. "Let me see your warrant."

The man in the gray suit took a paper from his breast pocket, unfolded it and held it out. Before Brian could take it, Gene plucked it out of his hand and examined it. "There must be some mistake," he said, and held the paper up. It was blank on both sides.

"Give me that," said the man in the gray suit. He took the

paper and looked at it in disbelief. He fumbled in his pocket again, then stared at Gene. "That was a properly executed warrant when I gave it to you," he said. "This kind of stunt won't get you anywhere, Mr. Anderson."

"I don't see any warrant," Brian said, "all I see is a blank sheet of paper. Come on, everybody."

They crossed the boarding area and climbed into the airplane. "Close that door quick," said Brian. He called to the pilot, "Have you got clearance? Let's go."

When they were airborne, he said, "Did you blank out that warrant?"

"Yes."

"Well, I wish you hadn't done that—now we don't know what was on it. Wait a minute." He took his phone out of his pocket and punched in a number. "Phil? Gene Anderson was just hit with a federal warrant for felony murder, but the warrant disappeared—Never mind that now, they couldn't serve it because it disappeared, but we don't know what the specific charge was. . . . Yes, all right, tell them anything you want. Okay." He put the phone back in his pocket. "He's going to try to find out and call me back. Meanwhile, let's see what our options are. Assuming that's a valid warrant, number one, Gene can surrender and stand trial. I don't think they can get a conviction, whatever it is, but we'll wait and see. If they do get a conviction, we'll appeal."

"How long would that take?"

"In the worst case, if it had to go to the Supreme Court, two, three years."

"And in the meantime, what, is he out on bail?"

Brian hesitated. "I can't promise that. The new Criminal Code gives federal judges the right—" His phone buzzed. "Excuse me, that's my call." He took the phone out of his pocket. "Yes?"

He listened for a moment. "Okay, Phil, thanks. I don't know, I'll call you back. We haven't got our feet under us yet. Okay? Okay, Phil."

He turned to face them. "Well, it's bad. They pulled a double whammy on us. They must have been hoping for something like this, or maybe they rigged it, I wouldn't put anything past them."

"What are you talking about?"

"The bomb victims. By holding that meeting in defiance of the Anti-Cult Act, you technically committed a felony. If anybody gets killed while you're committing a felony, you can be charged with murder."

"Can they make that stick?"

"I don't know. Now wait a minute, let's not get excited, let's talk about our options. Surrender is one. What else is there?"

"Gene could get out of the country."

"Yes, but think about the consequences. It would have to be to some country that doesn't have an extradition treaty with the U.S. That would effectively restrict his movements from then on—he'd be stuck in some place like Venezuela."

"How about this? Gene submits to arrest, they put him in jail, and he opens the doors and walks out. You could do it, couldn't you, Gene?"

"Yes."

"Then they come and arrest him again, and he walks out again. *That* would be a shot in the arm for the Movement, when they see no jail can hold him."

"That's beautiful, but it won't work. After the first time, they'd put a twenty-four-hour guard on him."

"Well—"

"No, Lisa, he's right," said Gene. "I could knock out the guards, I could unload their guns—that's the kind of thing you're thinking of, isn't it? That's all true, but then if they locked me up a third time, they would take extraordinary measures. Either I couldn't get out at all, or I could do it only by killing somebody."

"What's the answer, then?"

After a moment Gene said, "I don't know."

That night in Florida he dreamed of an enormous canvas marked off in squares and diagonals in preparation for transferring a cartoon to it. That was curious, because he had not thought of drawing or painting in over a year. Then the canvas somehow faded away, and only the charcoal lines remained; he was climbing them like a trellis, but he knew there was something waiting for him at the center, and that when he got there he would fall.

Early in the morning, before anyone was awake, he put

some food and clothes in the motor home. He left a note for Pongo in his cottage, and another, addressed to everyone, in the kitchen of the big house.

"Where do you suppose he's gone?" Margaret asked. "Where *can* he go?"

"As long as they don't know where to look for him, he can go anywhere he wants. He'll travel at night, use back roads."

"I think I know where he has gone," said Linck.

It would take Gene at least six days, more likely seven or eight, to drive across the continent. Linck made his preparations carefully. He packaged a revolver and a box of cartridges and airmailed them to Portland, Oregon—an illegal act, but he could not carry a weapon onto an airplane. He spent several days in the Pinellas Park offices, settling policy questions and making contingency plans. For the time being at least, until the legal problems were settled, the Movement would have to go underground. There was, after all, a good precedent for that. Linck bought a few necessary things and packed a suitcase. On the eighteenth, four days after Gene's departure, he boarded a flight for Portland, Oregon.

He was well aware that from one point of view he was about to commit a monstrous act of betrayal. He did not underestimate the duties of friendship or the claims of sentiment, but he believed in the existence of something more important.

It was Linck's conviction that Jesus of Nazareth had been a man like Gene Anderson, gifted with the same power; all but a few of his reported miracles could be explained in that way, and in addition there was a suggestive passage in the Gospel of Peter, where he was made to say on the cross, not "My God, my God," but "My power, my power, thou hast deserted me."

It was even possible, although Linck did not excuse himself on this ground, that Gene expected and willed this betrayal —as Jesus had given the sop to Judas, saying, "What you do, do quickly."

One of the great puzzles was the fact that within three centuries of the execution of its founder by one of the most degrading methods known to the Romans, the Christian religion had become the dominant force in Europe. That was absurd, and it was true, and this absurd truth, for many theologians, was the ultimate proof of the divinity of Jesus. Linck did not go so far, but he was convinced that if Jesus had not been arrested, tried, and executed, the movement he had founded would have remained an obscure sect.

After Caesar, Augustus. After Christ, Paul.

In Portland he picked up his parcel at the post office. The weather was cool and damp. He stayed overnight in a motel, and rented a car the next morning. The rental agent was very helpful. "I know the place you mean," he said. "It isn't on most maps, but I can tell you how to get there. Now see, here's Bend. You keep going on route twenty, and in about forty miles you'll hit a place called Brothers. Don't turn off there, take the next exit south, and that'll take you right down to it."

Linck drove with the map beside him, south on the interstate, then east on route 22, rising through forests of conifers still with snow on their branches, then down again.

In his suitcase was a block and tackle and two forty-foot lengths of half-inch manila rope. When Anderson was dead, he would find a tree with a suitable limb, draw up the block and tackle and secure it. Then, using the block and tackle, which had a ratio of five to two, he could easily hoist Anderson's body, by a rope around its neck, until it hung clear of the ground.

He took the wrong exit from Bend and wound up at a crossroads settlement called Fort Rock, where he stopped for gas. "Can you tell me how to get to the Lost Forest?"

"You lose one?" the attendant asked gravely. "Just a joke. Naw, what you do, you head right on out this way about five miles, then you'll see a road going south. It ain't a *good* road, but it'll get you there if it ain't full of water. Then you take the first left turn, and that'll bring you over to Christmas Valley. There's another turnoff north just past the lake, but don't go there, take the next one. That'll take you right up to Lost Forest." He hung up the nozzle. "Seven fifty."

"This certainly is the wettest desert I have ever seen," Linck said pleasantly. "Is it always like this?"

"This time of year, yeah. Dries out along about June. See, this is what they call high desert. Dry because it's high. You're about four thousand feet up right here. Get a lot of snow and rain in the winter, but it runs off, and the summers'll curl your hair.''

"Is there a motel near here?'' Linck asked. "Or up near the Lost Forest?''

"Nope. Was two at Christmas Valley, but they closed down. Nearest one'd be Burns, that's about a hundred miles.''

Linck followed the man's directions, but the road quickly became impassable; there were deep potholes full of water, some of them so big that the car could not go around them. He turned and drove back the way he had come; the gas station attendant waved at him as he passed.

He got onto the paved road again, followed it all the way to Bend, then turned southeast on route 20. The map showed an unimproved road that should take him directly to the Lost Forest, but when he tried it, it was worse than the other. He got back onto the paved road and drove to Burns, where he found a motel.

What he needed for the desert, the manager told him, was a van or camper. There was none to be had in Burns, but he found a man who was willing to rent him a Dodge pickup truck at an exorbitant price. The truck had a high wheelbase and big heavy-duty tires; it would, the owner assured him, go anywhere.

He drove back by a different route, south for twenty miles on a bad gravel road, then west on a road that was not even gravel but dirt, one car wide. Every quarter mile or so there was a pothole too big to cross, and then the tire-tracks ahead of him swung up into the brush and down again. The truck, rocking and groaning on its springs, took him forward at five miles an hour. Once he met a cow and a calf in the road; the calf stared at him dumbly, then, with a start of horror, turned and ran. The cow followed more placidly, swinging the bell under her neck. After fourteen miles of this, the scrub gave way to a forest of dark evergreens, widely spaced, growing in white sand. Linck stopped the truck and sat a moment, listening to the silence; then he drove on.

That night in his room he put himself into deep trance, lying on his back with his arms folded in the darkness:—When you see Gene Anderson you will forget why you came. You will forget what you intend to do. When he goes to sleep, you will remember everything. You will be very calm.

The next day, and the next, he drove the same route. The truck was coated with pale mud up over the bottoms of the doors. On the third day he saw the familiar chevron patterns in the road and followed them until he came to Gene's motor home parked under the trees. Footsteps led northward in the white sand.

Linck's hands were trembling. He put himself into light trance for a moment, gave himself a calming suggestion. He got his suitcase out of the truck and began to follow the footprints.

It was absolutely still under the trees. Whenever he stopped to listen, there was nothing; not a rustle of branches or the sound of a bird; nothing.

Around the edges of the forest grew stunted and deformed juniper trees, their ropy wood twisted into tormented shapes—skeletal trees, the color of ox skulls. In the forest itself the giants stood in proud isolation; they were pines with reddish bark broken into dry hexagonal plaques. Under one of them he found Gene Anderson, sitting on a gray pile of duff with his back against the tree.

"Hello, Piet. You knew, didn't you?"

"Yes. May I sit down?"

"Of course."

A wind was rising; Linck could hear it whispering in the branches overhead, and the sound made him uncomfortable. "Gene, I know I shouldn't be here. If you want to be alone—"

"It doesn't matter right now. Stay tonight, if you want. Are you hungry or thirsty?"

"No."

The wind was whipping the branches, and yet Linck felt that they two were surrounded by a core of stillness.

"I'm tired," Gene said. "I've been driving—" He settled himself against the tree-trunk; after a moment he closed his eyes.

The wind was still rising, but Gene did not seem to hear it. His chest rose and fell with a slow and regular rhythm. Linck stood up cautiously. He felt a moment of confusion; then he remembered. He picked up his suitcase, opened it, got the revolver out.

He sat down facing the giant and steadied his forearm across his knee. He felt calm and clear. Somewhere submerged in his mind there was pity and sorrow, but the time for that was not now.

He aimed the gun at Gene Anderson's forehead. Slowly he squeezed the trigger. There was a loud report, the gun bucked in his hand, and then all motion ceased. The wind was no longer stirring the branches, although they leaned aslant. Linck found that he could not move. He was not breathing; the blood was not moving in his veins. A little drift of smoke hung in the air as if painted there. Beyond it was a little dark pellet, with streams of disturbed air radiating from it; it, too, was fixed and motionless. Time itself had come to a stop. Then, to his unutterable horror, he saw that Gene Anderson's eyes were opening.

Like a man underwater, Gene Anderson stood up and stepped away from the tree. He felt the suspension of time as a weight in his flesh; he let it go, and heard the echo of the pistol shot. When he turned, he could see where the bullet had gone into the tree-trunk. The wind had died.

After a moment he stepped over the dead man and opened the suitcase Linck had brought. He found the block and tackle, and understood Linck's intention. He put his head in his hands and wept.

Presently he took one of the ropes from the suitcase and tied a noose around the neck of the man he had killed. He threw the other end of the rope over a branch fifteen feet overhead, drew the body up until it hung clear, and tied the rope to the trunk. Then he sat on the ground and closed his eyes, waiting for a voice.

After a time he realized that he was hearing it, and that he did not know when it had begun. It was the same as before, a vast echoing sky-sound, not in words, but in meaning. And then he knew.

He stood up again. All around him he could sense the other worlds, more clearly than ever. They were like sheaves of shadows, multiplying in every direction. He found one where there was something in the air that said, "Here." There was a welcoming feeling in that world, a feeling of belonging, of peace and acceptance. He gathered himself, reached in, and turned with a convulsive effort.

Then there was no one in the forest but the dead man hanging from the tree.

• • •

From *The Book of Gene*, Chicago, 2036:

Then his enemy rose up before him to kill him; but GENE touched him with the power that was in him, and he fell dead on the ground. Then GENE said, "O God, what shall I do?" And God answered, "Hang this one from a tree, and come to another place that I have prepared for you; and let not your disciples sorrow, for I will return you to them at the proper season and will gladden their hearts: and then you shall come in your glory." So it was done; so it was told; and so it shall be.